MORE FAST & FRESH

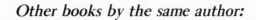

Other books by the same author:

Fast & Fresh: Delicious Meals to Make
    in an Hour . . . or Less

Julie Dannenbaum's
    Creative Cooking School

Menus for All Occasions

drawings by Ruth Bornschlegel

Julie Dannenbaum

MORE FAST & FRESH

1817

HARPER & ROW, PUBLISHERS, New York

Cambridge, Philadelphia, San Francisco, London,
Mexico City, São Paulo, Sydney

MORE FAST AND FRESH. Copyright © 1983 by Julie Dannenbaum. All rights reserved. Printed in the United States of America. No part of this book may be used or reproduced in any manner whatsoever without written permission except in the case of brief quotations embodied in critical articles and reviews. For information address Harper & Row, Publishers, Inc., 10 East 53rd Street, New York, N.Y. 10022. Published simultaneously in Canada by Fitzhenry & Whiteside Limited, Toronto.

FIRST EDITION

Designed by Ruth Bornschlegel

Library of Congress Cataloging in Publication Data

Dannenbaum, Julie.
  More fast and fresh.
  Includes index.
  1. Cookery. I. Title.
TX652.D323 1983   641.5   82-48114
ISBN 0-06-015084-X

83 84 85 86 87 10 9 8 7 6 5 4 3 2 1

DEDICATED TO MY CHILDREN

Thanks to Betty Barlow and Grace
Benson, who tested recipes. Thanks to
Rose Guarrera and Will Kratz, who
supplied me with recipes and
encouragement. Thanks, too, to my
husband, who ate all manner of weird
combinations while I was working on
this book. A special thanks to longtime
good friend Jim Quinn, who kept my
thoughts together in preparation of this
book. More thanks to Jay Acton, the
very best agent, and to Larry
Ashmead, the very best editor
anybody could have.

J.D.

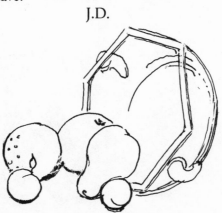

CONTENTS

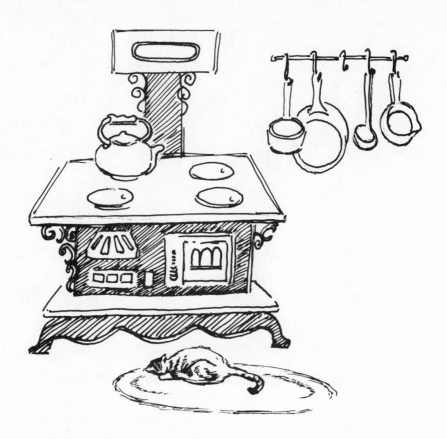

COOKING THEN AND NOW

For years I've kept a notebook of meals I've had in famous restaurants—meals that were especially good or especially disappointing. I frequently look back through it to the trips I took to Europe twenty-five to thirty years ago and I am amazed. Two restaurant meals a day, each loaded with cream sauces, hollandaise, béarnaise, buttery soups, rich desserts. I don't understand how I managed never to gain weight. And I wonder how I managed to survive!

No one eats like that anymore. Part of it is that all of us eat less as we grow older. But a more important part is that our children, people in their twenties and thirties today, have too much sense. I remember when we all used to laugh at the "kid's food"—everything cooked with raisins and honey and nuts. But there really has been a revolution in American cooking, one which trusts the food to taste good.

In a way, this revolution seems like a step backward: back to Grandma's cooking. I remember my grandmother's kitchen and my mother's kitchen. My grandmother's kitchen was the most important room in the house. I remember the big round table, big enough for four or five children, grown-ups, and any guests who might show up. The chairs were high-backed old

1

wooden ones, so that you could see a foot or so of chair over the heads of the other children at the table. My grandmother served all weekday meals in the kitchen, and on Sunday everybody moved to the dining room. We all loved that kitchen. Grandmother didn't have a bare wood table, of course, but one covered with oilcloth. I haven't seen oilcloth for years, but I still remember the smell; no matter how old it got, it still reminded you of new machine crank case oil or kerosene. And, of course, all the children would spend their time picking at the holes in it, peeling it down to the canvas backing underneath. It gave the grown-ups something to complain about—my aunt was forever telling us to sit up straight, eat properly, and quit picking at the oilcloth like monkeys picking fleas in the zoo. Things were meant to last in those days, though, and no matter how we picked at the oilcloth, the same old oilcloth stayed on the table. We grew up with it, we went away to college, we came back to visit Grandma, and there was the same oilcloth with the same holes in it.

I remember when my mother remodeled her kitchen. The table was chrome and plastic; the appliances were stark white; the kitchen cabinets were stark white. If you looked in the ladies' magazines of the time, the women in the kitchens sometimes dressed in stark white dusters, with their hair pulled back in severe little buns, looking something like scientists concocting a new formula. New formulas were all around then. Frozen food had just appeared—and the frozen spinach tasted

pretty good to anyone who had actually managed to eat that canned soggy spinach. There were new mixes. Everything was designed to take place in minutes; just add water and serve. All new, all improved. I could hear my mother talking on the phone to a friend and saying, "Have you tried that new meringue mix?" There actually was a meringue mix, also a cream puff mix, cake mixes, etc. God knows what was in them, or in the rest of that instant stuff. They certainly didn't have to tell us on the label. And if they did nobody would have read it. Our children had to teach us to read labels. The pages of the food sections and the magazines were full of new convenience ideas: how you could combine tuna fish with noodles and make a fabulous casserole topped with French-fried onion rings from a can. Instant cake mixes that were no quicker than making a cake from scratch. Instant mashed potatoes that tasted like papier-mâché run through a paper shredder.

There had to be a reaction to all that scientific convenience, and there was. Suddenly everybody had to learn the most complicated and difficult techniques of French haute cuisine. Every woman had her own batterie de cuisine, and nothing was too difficult or too time-consuming to be made for family dinner. There were recipes for ratatouille that took lots of pots and hours to prepare. Ingredients were boned and fussed over at great length, as if we didn't trust food to be good enough to eat without working our mysterious kitchen magic on it. The convenience kitchens were spare and white, like little laboratories, where you combined the latest in chemical ingredients to produce the most scientifically correct food the world has ever known.

The contrived food kitchens filled up with gadgets. What was a home without a flan ring? Or a nest of soufflé dishes or bowls ranging in size from four-quart to a thimble-sized unusable one in the middle? One set of pots was no longer enough. You had to have

three or four. Aluminum pots and pans were suddenly a no-no, since they discolor sauces. (The visiting chefs who teach at my school pull them off my wall and make perfect sauces in them.) My pots are in constant use, and that seems to make the difference. If you cook every day in your home, you can cook in just about anything. I dislike stainless steel because it develops hot spots. I'll take professional aluminum or tin-lined copper. But when it comes to pots—pots is pots.

Some of the complicated recipes tried to make things seem a little simpler. They'd print a little star at one point in the recipe and say, "Can be prepared ahead to this point, then frozen and reheated." Then all you had left was fifteen minutes of hysteria in the kitchen as you simultaneously reheated the dish, finished the béarnaise, and whipped a little cream for dessert—by hand, of course. There is nothing wrong with mastering traditional kitchen techniques. It will always improve your style of cooking. But for most family dinners and most entertaining it's more important that the cook be relaxed and worry-free, and it's hard to be that when you're worrying your way through a recipe designed around some crucial ambidextrous juggling performed at top speed with three saucepans and a wire whisk. There is a lot of good food without agony.

The young people today taught us that, too. The young people in my family not only eat less than I did at their age, they also eat better. They don't bother with frozen or canned food, they never buy mixes, and they read the labels on everything. They work, as do their friends, and food shopping and food preparation are shared chores. They plan out menus in advance, the only way to do it if you want to shop once a week. They visit the super-markets when the produce is the freshest. And they usually manage to find time over the weekend to go to a farmer's market for more fresh produce, local chickens, local cheeses, anything that is in season or in good supply. Food is important enough to the children in my family that they are willing to spend the time looking for the best available ingredients.

Kitchens have changed once again. When I first had my kitchen installed eleven years ago, my friends were horrified. Quarry tile floors, tile and natural wood, rough plaster on the walls, a professional stove, and a professional butcher block work table on stainless steel legs. Some people thought it looked too old-fashioned. Some of them thought I'd ruin my feet standing on that tile floor. I told them I'd put a small rug in front of the stove just the way my grandmother used to do. I never figured out what that rug was for; the family pets used to sleep on it. I always suspected that rug was there just to

make sure everybody knew what an important place the front of the stove was. The tile floor is comfortable and easy to clean. In a few years, all my friends had tile floors too. We all wanted a country kitchen look, like Grandma, to go with our new simple and sensible and healthful style of cooking, which was similar to the best of Grandma's.

This book, like the first *Fast and Fresh,* was designed for quick and easy cooking and for the working couple. It is not written only for them, as everyone can use good, fast, easy recipes, but it is designed for people who share the young people's appreciation of good food and their appreciation for the uses that can be made of time not spent in the kitchen.

The approach is simple—fast and fresh. Look at any recipe, and you will see it does not rely on a myriad of spices and herbs. The basic flavors of these recipes come from the food itself. This isn't plain cooking, but the kind of cooking that recognizes the elegance of simplicity. There are a few show-stoppers in the book; who doesn't like coming out of the kitchen with a platter that looks just as spectacular as it is going to taste? But you don't have to combine the skills of Oriental flower arrangement and origami with broccoli florets and flounder filets to have a great-looking and good-tasting food.

Whenever I go to a restaurant and get a plate of food on which every Brussels sprout seems turned with its best side to the light, and the potato slices are laid one on top of the other as if they were dominoes fallen in a long sinuous line, I think: How pretty. Then I wonder how long the chef had his hands in my food in order to get everything so perfect. A little raggedy humanness in food is an advantage; it's as if you tried to make your own clothes. You'd want to get good enough so that they looked beautiful, but not so good that everybody thought you bought them off a rack ready-made. Don't try to make your food look professionally gussied up by a finicky restaurant chef; first of all, you might not be able to do as well, and even if you could, all that work isn't worth the effort in home cooking.

What is worth the effort is making good food properly. And that is easy. There are no complicated techniques in this book. No chicken or rabbits to bone, no long and involved sauces, no stirring gingerly for an hour while everything else gets cold or burns. You can tell from the list of ingredients in the recipes that it isn't going to take all day to buy them. And you can tell from the short and simple list of directions that it's not going to take all day to cook. Relax. Trust the taste of fresh food. And trust your own pace. Nobody is going to mind if you take an hour and fifteen minutes instead of an hour to prepare a menu. This is fast cooking, but not breakneck cooking.

A few cautions. I urge you to substitute ingredients when necessary and when something in your area is especially fresh and good. But I also urge you to spend a little time looking for hard-to-come-by ingredients. It seems strange to me that sometimes students in

my classes are so disheartened when I mention a new product I've found in New York.

"Oh, New York," they sigh, as if New York were halfway across the continent from Philadelphia, instead of ninety miles away—and as if they didn't go to New York once a month or so for the theater and opera and art galleries. New York, a wonderful source of imported foods from almost every corner of the world, may actually be half a continent from your home. But surely you have a major city near you, where you can find ethnic and Oriental ingredients. If not, there are mail order catalogs in which you can find anything short of bear paws. And no matter where you live there is a farmer's market, a street fruit and vegetable stand, or a store that specializes in fresh produce. And someplace where you can find cheeses that do not come presliced,

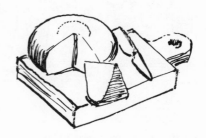

and tasting predigested, in neat little plastic envelopes. American farmer Swiss is not Gruyère, but it works a lot better as a substitute for Gruyère than the processed milkfat solids sold in supermarkets under that name. Not all supermarkets are equally bad—many suburban markets have a fresh vegetable department that a farmer's market could envy. But one of the pleasures of life is discovering a new source of good ingredients. Shopping for food is at least as much fun as shopping for clothes, and a lot cheaper.

I also urge you to find some way to get fresh herbs for your home. If you have any kind of garden, you can easily grow basil, rosemary, thyme, and oregano. I can do it, and I have a black thumb for every kind of houseplant and

garden flower. Remember herbs are only weeds that taste good. Even if you do not have any garden space at all, there are window boxes and tabletop greenhouses where herbs will grow fairly well. If all else fails, try the specialty shops in your area or even the local supermarket. I always find fresh dill year round, and in season basil and chives. Nothing will improve your cooking as

much as using fresh herbs, whatever herbs you can find, and throw away all those little boxes of things that all taste and look like lawnmower sweepings. If you must use dried herbs, at least dry them yourself—that way they retain some of their taste.

Most of us like to think that the family stove is perfect. We tend to think those little oven knobs are as accurate as room thermostats. Sometimes that's true in a very new oven. But gas and electric pressures vary from time to time; and dials, knobs and thermostats get out of whack. Buy yourself an oven thermometer, and you'll go a long way toward making your cooking consistent.

But, of course, no cooking can be perfectly consistent. I can prepare a poached fish dish one week and write down exactly the ingredients and the procedure. I make it again, and when I taste as I go along, I realize it is going to be different. The fish is always a little more or less fresh and firm (it has had different parents), the butter is different, the wine a little sour or sugary, the gas or electric pressure is stronger, the cream is older or younger, or richer or thinner, and sometimes I am different. In my own kitchen, at my own stove, I can easily adjust for all those changes. I can't do the same in your kitchen. Each time you make a dish you essentially conduct an experiment with changing ingredients, and with your own changing taste. Don't say "I can't understand it—I used exactly the same amount of butter and it doesn't taste as rich." Use the right amount of butter to make it taste the way you want. A recipe is not the

Constitution or the Bible; it is meant to be changed at will.

Finally, have fun. There are people for whom cooking is one of life's dreariest chores. They expect everything they make to be a long and complicated failure, and somehow they manage to live down to their expectations. But cooking is a chance to be creative and exciting—every day of our lives. You don't have to spend hours in the kitchen for the pleasure of taking good ingredients and combining them in delicious ways. Among the most sincere and heartfelt compliments most of us will ever receive is one from the guest who says, "This tastes great! May I have the recipe?"

I remember the beautiful country where I grew up in central Pennsylvania: an old red brick house with acres and acres of land, streams, orchards—a wonderful place to raise a family. My grandmother lived nearby and had the same kind of property. In the middle of her backyard stood an old pump, where pure spring water came up icy cold in winter and summer. These were depression days. The roads in the early thirties were filled with tramps, men out of work, wandering across the country. The grown-ups always thought these men had a series of signs to let each other know where to get a good handout. My grandmother's house was famous for miles around, as she always had something on hand to feed these men who were hungry. Men would come through alone and sometimes in twos or threes, asking for food.

"Go get yourself a drink of cold water from the well," my grandmother would tell them, "and I'll fix you something." She'd make up sandwiches, or bowls of soup, slices of pie, or just leftovers; those men would eat anything. I remember as little children my brothers and I would go watch them sitting on my grandmother's back porch, those strange and dusty men, eating steadily and hungrily whatever was brought to them, taking long drinks of that cold water. Maybe that's when I decided that making food was one of the most important things you could do in life. And I still think so. Try it and see.

Recipes in this chapter:

ASPARAGUS TIP CONSOMMÉ
SPINACH CONSOMMÉ
ZUCCHINI AND POTATO
CRAB AND CORN CHOWDER
SUMMER VEGETABLE WITH BASIL
CURRY
JULIENNE OF VEGETABLE
JERUSALEM ARTICHOKE
CREAM OF CAULIFLOWER
EGG DROP
PUMPKIN
SWEET POTATO BISQUE
MULLIGATAWNY
BUTTERMILK, WATERCRESS, AND
    CUCUMBER
GREEN PEA
THICK AND HEARTY POTATO AND
    CARROT
SHREVEPORT CLUB SHRIMP AND
    CRABMEAT
CARROT AND MUSHROOM
BACON, LETTUCE, AND TOMATO
"ONE-OF-EACH"
AVOCADO WITH GOLDEN CAVIAR
WILD RICE
CHICKEN BROTH WITH POACHED
    EGGS
COLD BLUEBERRY
COLD CHERRY

SOUPS

I love soup—from the clearest and most delicate consommé down to thick rich chowders where the spoon stands straight up in the middle of the bowl. And I think everybody who loves to cook loves soup. Because soup is the bonus dish we get out of fresh scraps, trimmings, and bones—all the things we save that people who hate to cook call "that mess in the kitchen." Soup is a wonderful dinner, a hearty lunch, or even a delicious breakfast. On a cold dark day, full of snow or winter rain, a big warming soup for breakfast will take you a lot further than oatmeal or one of those sugary cold cereals. And on fewer calories, too.

Back in Grandmother's day there was always a big kettle of soup on the back of the old wood stove, kept at a constant simmer. All the bones and peels and parings of everything went into that soup pot. Nothing was thrown away in Grandmother's kitchen. You can still make soup that old-fashioned way— I do. Just strain off the stock after simmering, let cool, put in the refrigerator, and remember to reboil it every two to three days. Add some fresh bones and scraps to intensify its flavor, simmer, strain, and put it back into a clean container.

9

Not everyone has the time to boil and reboil stocks, but with kitchen gadgets we have around now, everyone can make delicious soups in less than an hour. Like all soups, these quick soups keep for weeks in the freezer and make great emergency meals. Every year I teach a course at the Gritti Palace Hotel in Venice, and every year I seem to fly back home on a slower and later flight. All I can think of when I get off that plane at some ungodly U.S. time is that at least there is soup in the freezer at home. "Soup is a great comfort," my mother used to say; and she was right. It even takes the edge off jet lag.

A deceptively simple soup, and refreshing at the same time. These broth-type soups may be garnished with chopped cooked bacon, croutons, grated Parmesan cheese, chopped parsley or chives, then lemon slices, or a dollop of sour cream or whipped cream. A few grinds from the pepper mill enliven all soups. If calories are no problem add a spoonful of one of the butters (pages 169–70).

Asparagus Tip Consommé

6–8 cups well-flavored chicken
    stock
2 cups thin asparagus tips

Salt and fresh pepper to taste
2 tablespoons chopped chervil
    (or less)

Bring stock to boil in saucepan. Add asparagus, salt, pepper, and chervil and return to a boil. Turn heat to a simmer. Cook 5 minutes; asparagus should still be crunchy. Serve.

Serves 4–6.

VARIATION:

You can add up to 1 cup grated carrot and/or finely chopped celery instead of the asparagus tips if desired.

Spinach Consommé

6 ounces spinach, with stems	Salt and fresh pepper to taste
6–8 cups strong chicken stock	1 lemon, thinly sliced
Freshly grated nutmeg to taste	

Remove spinach stems by pulling them back from the leaves. Wash spinach leaves in warm water to loosen dirt or sand. Rinse in cold water, and dry well with paper towel or cloth. Gather spinach together and cut into chiffonade or thin strips, using chef's knife with spinach placed on cutting board (should be 2 cups spinach, well packed, after removing stems).

Heat chicken stock. When really hot, add spinach. Cook while stirring 5 minutes. Grate nutmeg on top and season with salt and pepper. Float thin lemon slices on each serving. *Serves 4–6.*

VARIATION:

Substitute 1 cup sliced mushrooms for the spinach. In this case, omit the nutmeg.

Zucchini and Potato Soup

4 tablespoons butter	2–3 cups chicken stock
1 medium onion, chopped	2 pounds zucchini, diced
1 garlic clove, chopped	1½–2 cups cream
2 medium potatoes, peeled and diced	Salt and fresh pepper to taste
1 tablespoon chopped fresh marjoram	

Melt butter in saucepan. Add onion and garlic and cook 3–4 minutes. Add potatoes, marjoram, and enough chicken stock to cover potatoes. Cover, bring to a boil, reduce to a simmer, and cook 5–10 minutes, or until potatoes are soft. Add zucchini and cook 10 minutes more. When zucchini is added to soup, add water, if necessary, to cover. Add cream, salt, and pepper.

Purée and serve hot or cold. Thin, if necessary, with cream. *Serves 4–6.*

VARIATION:

Yellow squash may be used in place of the zucchini.

For a richer chowder, substitute chicken stock for the water. This chowder can stand on its own as a main course, in which case add more crab.

Crab and Corn Chowder

4 tablespoons butter or bacon fat	2 cups milk or more
2 medium onions, finely chopped	1 cup cream
1 small green pepper, finely chopped	½ pound crabmeat
2 large potatoes, peeled and diced	Salt and red pepper to taste
3 cups corn, cut off cob	2 tablespoons finely chopped parsley

Melt butter or bacon fat in pan. When hot, add onions and green pepper. Sauté 5 minutes. Add potatoes and cover vegetables with water. Cook 10 minutes. Add corn and continue to cook until potatoes are tender. Add 2 cups milk and the cream. Stir and bring to a boil. Add crabmeat and just heat through. If too thick, thin with milk. Season with salt and pepper. Stir in parsley. *Serves 6–8.*

The basil sauce here is similar to a pesto but without pine nuts. Try this sauce on potatoes, vegetables, and especially sliced tomatoes.

Summer Vegetable Soup with Basil

¼ cup olive oil	2 cups shelled lima beans
2–3 zucchini, chopped	4 cups chicken stock
4 carrots, peeled and chopped	2–4 cups water
2 medium onions, chopped	Salt and fresh pepper to taste
3 cups green beans	½ teaspoon chopped thyme
4 leeks, chopped (white part)	2 cups julienned spinach
3 celery ribs, chopped	Basil sauce (see below)
3 potatoes, peeled and diced	
3 tomatoes, peeled, seeded, and chopped	

Put oil in soup kettle. When hot, add the vegetables except spinach and stir well. Add the chicken stock and water to cover vegetables. Add salt, pepper, and thyme. Bring to a boil. Half-cover with a lid. Simmer 30–40 minutes or until vegetables are barely tender. Stir in spinach. It will cook in 1–2 minutes. Taste and rectify seasoning. Serve in soup bowls and spoon the basil sauce in each serving to taste.   *Serves 6–8.*

Basil Sauce

1 cup basil leaves	6–8 cloves garlic, chopped
¾ cup Parmesan cheese, freshly grated	1–1½ cups olive oil

Place the basil, cheese, garlic, and half the oil in blender. Blend 1 minute. Slowly add rest of oil to mixture and blend well.   *Makes about 2 cups.*

Curry Soup

1 medium onion, finely chopped	2 tomatoes, peeled and chopped
2 tablespoons butter	Juice of 1 lemon
2 tablespoons flour	2 tablespoons freshly grated coconut
1 tablespoon curry powder	
4 cups chicken stock	1 cup light cream
1 large apple, peeled, cored, and chopped	Salt and fresh pepper to taste

In medium saucepan, cook onion in butter until tender. Add flour and curry. Cook 2 minutes. Gradually add chicken stock. Cook, stirring, until slightly thickened. Add remaining ingredients except cream. Bring to a boil, then reduce heat. Cover and cook over medium heat 20 minutes. Purée a small amount at a time in electric blender, food processor, or food mill. Chill in a bowl placed in a bowl of ice cubes, stirring frequently. Just before serving, add cream, salt, and pepper.

Serves 4–6.

This soup can be prepared rapidly if all vegetables are julienned in the food processor or done on a Mouli-julienne. A fresh, elegant flavor.

Julienne of Vegetable Soup

3 carrots, peeled and julienned
2 potatoes, peeled and julienned
1 turnip, peeled and julienned
2 onions, peeled and finely chopped
1 tomato, peeled, seeded, and diced

½ pound green beans, slivered
2 celery ribs, julienned
1 garlic clove, chopped
  Chicken stock to cover (about 8 cups)
  Salt and fresh pepper to taste
¼ cup chopped parsley

Put everything except parsley into a kettle. Bring to a boil, then reduce to a simmer. Put on lid and cook until vegetables are tender, about 20 minutes. Sprinkle parsley over.

Serves 8.

Mystify your family and guests with this soup. No one will be able to identify the Jerusalem artichoke. If the artichokes are terribly knobby and difficult to peel, simply scrub them to death.

Jerusalem Artichoke Soup

4 tablespoons butter
1 large onion, chopped
4 celery ribs, chopped
2 pounds Jerusalem artichokes, peeled and coarsely chopped
2 tablespoons flour
4 cups chicken stock

2 cups milk
  Salt and fresh pepper to taste
  Few grains of freshly grated nutmeg
1 cup heavy cream
2 tablespoons chopped parsley

Melt the butter in a saucepan and sauté onion 1 minute. Add celery and artichokes and stir for 1–2 minutes. Rub in flour with a wooden spatula. Pour on chicken stock and milk and bring to a boil. Season with salt, pepper, and nutmeg. Put on lid and simmer, covered, for 20–30 minutes or until vegetables are tender. Purée in food mill or food processor. Return to pan and add cream. If too thick, thin with chicken stock or cream to desired consistency. Reheat. Garnish with parsley.

Serves 6–8.

Cream of Cauliflower Soup

4 cups cauliflower, cut into
   small pieces
5–6 cups chicken stock
4 tablespoons butter
4 tablespoons flour

3 cups milk, light cream, or
   heavy cream
Salt and fresh pepper to taste
Few grinds of fresh nutmeg
2 tablespoons chopped parsley

Put cauliflower in pan. Cover with stock. Bring to a boil. Cover and turn to simmer. Simmer 20 minutes or until cauliflower is tender. Purée in food mill, blender, or food processor. Return to pan.

Melt the butter in a saucepan. When the foam subsides, add flour. Turn heat to medium and stir with wooden spatula, getting into corners of pan. Let mixture bubble up without browning. Cook for 3 minutes or until flour taste is gone. Add milk or cream and switch to a whisk, whisking until sauce comes to a boil. Boil gently 5 minutes. Add salt, pepper, and nutmeg. Combine sauce with puréed cauliflower. Thin to desired consistency with cream or stock. Garnish with parsley. *Serves 6–8.*

VARIATION:

Any of these vegetables can be substituted for the cauliflower: spinach, broccoli, carrots, peas, lettuce, onion, mushrooms, leeks, potatoes, turnips.

Egg Drop Soup

6 cups chicken stock
4 scallions, thinly sliced
2 eggs

1 tablespoon water
Salt and fresh pepper to taste

Combine stock and scallions in a saucepan. Bring to a boil. Combine eggs and water; mix well. Gradually pour in a thin steady stream into boiling stock, stirring constantly. Heat a few minutes to cook egg. Season if desired. *Serves 4–6.*

VARIATION:

To make Greek lemon soup, omit water and add 1 tablespoon lemon juice after egg has been added.

I usually serve this soup at Thanksgiving dinner and let everybody try to figure out what it is. Garnish with slivers of chestnuts.

Pumpkin Soup

3 pounds pumpkin, cut into cubes and peeled
3 cups chicken stock or more to cover pumpkin
1 medium onion, chopped
2 celery ribs, chopped

Salt and fresh pepper to taste
Few grains of freshly grated nutmeg
2–3 tablespoons butter, softened
1 cup heavy cream
2–3 tablespoons rum, or to taste

Put all ingredients except butter, cream, and rum into saucepan. Bring to a boil and cover. Simmer until pumpkin is tender, about 15 minutes. Purée in food processor, blender, or food mill. Return to saucepan. Beat in the butter with a whisk. Add heavy cream and rum to taste. If too thick, thin with chicken stock or cream. Reheat.

Serves 4–6.

Another hard-to-guess soup—people think it may be squash.

Sweet Potato Bisque

1½ pounds sweet potatoes
2 celery ribs, chopped
1 large tart apple
2 tablespoons butter
¼ cup chopped shallots

2½ cups light cream
Salt and fresh pepper to taste
2 tablespoons sherry or Madeira
1 tablespoon finely chopped parsley

Peel and cube the sweet potatoes. Put into a saucepan, add the celery, and cook, covered, in a small amount of water 10–15 minutes. Meanwhile, peel, core, and chop the apple. Melt the butter and, when hot, add the shallots and sauté 1 minute. Add the apple and cook, while stirring, for 5 minutes. Drain potatoes and combine in pan with the apple mixture. Purée through blender, food mill, or food processor until smooth. Return to pan and add cream, salt, and pepper. Add the sherry or Madeira and bring to a boil. Stir the parsley through the bisque for color. Serve hot.

Serves 4–6.

Mulligatawny is usually made with chicken or at least garnished with chicken. To shorten the cooking time, I eliminated the chicken.

Mulligatawny

4 tablespoons butter
2 apples, cored, peeled, and chopped
1 medium onion, chopped
1 garlic clove, chopped
1 small green pepper, chopped
2 medium carrots, chopped
2 tablespoons flour
1–2 tablespoons curry powder
8 cups chicken stock

½ cup freshly grated coconut
1–2 teaspoons sugar
Salt and fresh pepper to taste
2–3 tablespoons chopped parsley
4 tomatoes, peeled, seeded, and chopped
Cooked rice (see page 104)
Thin lime slices
2 tablespoons finely chopped fresh coriander

Melt the butter in a large saucepan. Sauté apples, onion, garlic, green pepper, and carrots for 3–4 minutes. Sprinkle on the flour and curry. Rub them into the vegetables thoroughly with a wooden spatula, and cook for 2–3 minutes. Add the stock and bring to a boil. Turn to a simmer and add the coconut, sugar, salt, pepper, parsley, and tomatoes. Cook 20 minutes or so until vegetables are tender. Rectify seasoning. Place a good spoonful of rice in each soup bowl. Ladle soup over. Garnish each serving with a thin slice of lime and a bit of fresh coriander.

Serves 8–10.

Nothing could be quicker than this delightful soup. If the soup is too thick after puréeing, simply thin with a bit of buttermilk or stock.

Buttermilk, Watercress, and Cucumber Soup

2 cucumbers, peeled, seeded, and cut into chunks
1 cup watercress leaves
1 cup chicken stock

3 cups buttermilk
2 tablespoons chopped fresh dill
Salt and fresh pepper to taste

Place all ingredients in blender jar or food processor in batches. Purée until smooth. Taste for seasoning. Serve in glass bowls, well chilled. *Serves 4–6.*

If there is any left over, it's delicious cold.

Green Pea Soup

4 tablespoons butter
1 onion, chopped
4 cups fresh peas
1 small head Boston lettuce
2–3 tablespoons chopped mint
2–3 tablespoons flour

4 cups chicken stock
2 cups light cream
Salt and fresh pepper to taste
2 egg yolks
½ cup heavy cream
2 tablespoons chopped parsley

Melt butter in saucepan. Add onion and cook 2–3 minutes. Add peas, lettuce, and mint. Cook 3 minutes. Sprinkle on flour and cook 2–3 minutes. Pour on stock and cream. Bring to boil. Cook until vegetables are tender. Purée in blender, food processor, or food mill. Reheat. Season with salt and pepper. Beat egg yolks and heavy cream together in a little bowl and add to soup. Whisk until soup barely thickens. Garnish with chopped parsley.   *Serves 4–6.*

This soup is fantastic cold.

Thick and Hearty Potato and Carrot Soup

3 lbs. potatoes, peeled and cubed
4 carrots, peeled and cubed
2 large onions, peeled and cut into chunks

2½ cups milk, or more
1 cup light cream
Salt and fresh pepper to taste
¼ cup minced parsley

Place potatoes, carrots, and onions in a large saucepan in boiling water. Cover. Cook for 20 minutes or until tender. Drain. Mash vegetables or purée in food processor. Stir in milk and cream. Season to taste. Heat soup just to boiling. Sprinkle with chopped parsley. If a thinner soup is desired, add additional milk. This soup contains no butter. If a richer soup is desired, place 1 tablespoon butter on each serving.   *Makes about 2 quarts or 4–6 servings as main dish.*

The delightful and talented French chef in charge of food at the Shreveport Club in Louisiana created this soup for a luncheon in my honor while I was visiting that charming city conducting several cooking demonstrations. The soup is simplicity itself, but keep in mind that the crab and shrimp in that area are outstanding, since Shreveport is directly on the Gulf. I wouldn't use pasteurized crabmeat and canned shrimp in this recipe.

Shreveport Club Shrimp and Crabmeat Soup

4 tablespoons butter
2 onions, finely chopped
2 leeks, finely chopped
1½ pounds medium shrimp, shells removed

4–6 cups chicken stock to cover
  Salt and fresh pepper to taste
1 pound crabmeat
½ teaspoon saffron
  Green onion tops, slivered

Melt the butter in a saucepan. Sauté the onions and leeks until limp, 5 minutes. Add shrimp and sauté without browning for 5 minutes. Do not overcook. Add the chicken stock, salt, and pepper. Add the crabmeat and saffron. You may need to add additional stock. Simmer 10 minutes. Add the green onion tops and serve.

Serves 6–8.

Carrot and Mushroom Soup

¼ cup butter
1½ pounds mushrooms, sliced
2 cups thinly sliced carrots
½ cup chopped onion
  Chicken stock to cover vegetables (3–4 cups)

¼ cup Madeira or sherry
  Salt and fresh pepper to taste
1–2 tablespoons finely chopped fresh dill

In large saucepan, melt the butter. When hot, add mushrooms, carrots, and onion. Cook 5 minutes. Add stock; bring to boil. Reduce heat, cover, and simmer 15 to 20 minutes until carrots are tender. Add Madeira or sherry, salt, pepper, and dill. Reheat and serve.

Serves 6–8.

Instead of a bacon, lettuce, and tomato sandwich, have soup instead.

Bacon, Lettuce, and Tomato Soup

6 slices of bacon, diced
1 medium onion, chopped
½ cup chopped celery
8 tomatoes, peeled, seeded, and chopped
Salt and fresh pepper to taste

1 tablespoon freshly chopped basil
4 cups chicken stock
2 teaspoons potato starch
1 cup shredded romaine lettuce

Cook diced bacon in medium-size kettle until brown; remove from kettle. Add chopped onion and celery to bacon fat and cook over medium heat until translucent. *Do not brown.* Add chopped tomatoes, cooked bacon, salt, pepper, basil, and chicken stock. Simmer without lid, for 30–35 minutes, or until all is well cooked. Purée mixture through food mill, processor, or blender. Return soup to kettle. Add potato starch blended with a little cold water. Cook over medium heat until slightly thickened. Taste for flavor. Just before serving, add shredded lettuce. *Serves 6.*

"One-of-Each" Soup

1 large potato, peeled and roughly chopped
1 large onion, peeled and roughly chopped
1 large apple, cored and roughly chopped
1 large banana, peeled and roughly chopped

1 celery heart with leaves, roughly chopped
2 cups chicken stock
1 cup light cream
1 tablespoon butter, melted
½ teaspoon curry powder
Salt and fresh pepper to taste
Chopped chives

Place potato, onion, apple, banana, and celery in a saucepan and add chicken stock. Simmer them until soft. Purée in food mill, processor, or blender. Stir cream, melted butter, curry, salt, and pepper into smooth purée. Do not cook any more. Serve hot or cold. Sprinkle with chopped chives before serving. *Serves 4–6.*

Avocado Soup with Golden Caviar

4 tablespoons butter
¾ cup chopped green onions
2 ripe avocados, peeled, seeded, and chopped
3–4 cups chicken stock
Juice of 1 lemon or lime

Salt and fresh pepper to taste
1 cup heavy cream, barely whipped
Golden caviar (a few grains for each serving).

Melt the butter in a saucepan. Sauté the green onions 3 to 4 minutes. Add the avocados and stir around. Add the stock and lemon or lime juice; bring to a boil. Cook 5 minutes. Purée in blender, food processor, or food mill. Season with salt and pepper. Fold in the whipped cream. Reheat slowly. Garnish with the caviar.

Serves 4-6.

VARIATIONS:

This soup is excellent served cold. To chill rapidly, set bowl of soup over another bowl filled with ice. Stir until soup chills.

If golden caviar seems an affectation to you, omit it or use a bit of red caviar.

This is an adaptation of a wild rice soup I enjoyed in Minneapolis. Food editor Eleanor Oestman of the paper in that city happily sent me a recipe. This is quite different from hers but equally good.

Wild Rice Soup

1 medium onion, chopped
¼ pound mushrooms, chopped
2 tablespoons butter
½ cup uncooked wild rice
5 cups chicken stock

Salt and white pepper to taste
2 tablespoons flour
¼ cup water
½ cup light cream
2–4 tablespoons sherry

Cook onion and mushrooms in butter in a large kettle until tender. Add rice, chicken stock, salt, and pepper. Bring to boil, then reduce heat. Cover and cook over medium heat 35 minutes or until rice is tender. Combine flour and water until smooth. Gradually add to soup, stirring constantly, until mixture thickens slightly. Add cream and sherry; heat.

Serves 4-6.

Chicken Broth with Poached Eggs

6–8 cups strong chicken broth
4–6 eggs
1 cup heavy cream

2 tablespoons chopped chervil
Salt and fresh pepper to taste
¼ cup grated Parmesan cheese

Place broth in a saucepan and bring to simmer. Poach eggs while broth is simmering. Place an egg in each serving bowl or cup. Add cream to broth. Bring to a boil. Gently spoon the broth and cream over the eggs. Sprinkle each serving with chervil, salt and pepper, and Parmesan cheese.   *Serves 4–6.*

I personally am not fond of cold fruit soups. It seems to me they should be served for dessert. However, when hot weather arrives and fresh fruit is plentiful, these soups are certainly refreshing.

Cold Blueberry Soup

4 cups blueberries (save 4–6 large
  berries for garnish)
1 tablespoon cornstarch
½ cup sugar

Ground cardamom to taste
3 cloves
Juice of ½ lemon
½ cup sour cream

Place blueberries in a pan with water to cover. Bring to a boil on high heat, lower heat, and simmer berries until very soft, 5–10 minutes. Put berries and liquid through food mill, using the finest disk, or do in blender or processor. Pour berry juice through finest sieve, allowing it to strain through without pressing (there are many very tiny seeds in blueberries, so the clearer this soup is, the nicer result when it is served). Return strained juice to pan, add cornstarch mixed with a little water, sugar, spices, and lemon juice, and cook for 5 minutes. Remove. Cool. Chill very well in refrigerator. Serve in glass bowls. Garnish with sour cream and a blueberry on top.   *Serves 4–6.*

Note: Cornstarch gives body to soup. Omit if you desire.

Cold Cherry Soup

4 cups sour cherries, pitted
2 cups water
1½ cups red wine
½ cup sugar
3 cloves
1 stick cinnamon, crumbled

A little freshly grated nutmeg
1 tablespoon cornstarch
1 lemon
½ cup sour cream
Thin lemon slices

Chop cherries in food processor or blender until just chopped. Place in bowl and refrigerate. Into a saucepan put water, wine, sugar, cloves, cinnamon, and nutmeg. Cook while stirring for 5 minutes, then strain.

Mix together cornstarch and the juice of ½ lemon to make a paste. Whisk it into the strained mixture. Bring to a boil to thicken slightly. Cool by stirring over a bowl of ice. Add the chopped cherries. Mix well.

To serve cherry soup, place sour cream in chilled bowl and slowly whisk cherry soup into sour cream. Serve in chilled glass serving bowls with slices of lemon.

Serves 4–6.

Note: Cornstarch gives body to soup. Omit if you desire.

Recipes in this chapter:

MUSHROOMS WITH CREAM
SAUTÉED MUSHROOMS
KOHLRABI DAUPHINOIS
BAKED ZUCCHINI AND TOMATOES
BAKED ONIONS
BROILED TOMATOES
OKRA AND TOMATOES
CARROTS AND ZUCCHINI
FRITTERS AND VARIATIONS
GREEN BEANS AND JULIENNE CELERY
SHREDDED RED CABBAGE
PEAS FRENCH STYLE
CABBAGE TIMBALES
FRESH ASPARAGUS LOAF
SAUTÉED BELGIAN ENDIVE
ASPARAGUS WITH WALNUT BUTTER
GREEN TOMATO SAUTÉ
SUCCOTASH
BRAISED SLICED CELERY
COOKED HERBED CUCUMBERS
ACORN SQUASH WITH GLAZED APPLES
STUFFED ONIONS
PURÉED BUTTERNUT SQUASH
ACORN SQUASH WITH SESAME SEEDS
SPINACH WITH BROWN BUTTER
SOUR CREAM SPINACH
BOILED ARTICHOKES
LEMONY TURNIP STICKS
EASY SUMMER SQUASH
BAKED CAULIFLOWER
BROILED TOMATOES AND YOGURT
PARSNIPS WITH PARSLEY
BABY EGGPLANT
BABY LIMA BEANS IN CHERVIL CREAM
SAUTÉED SAUERKRAUT
PENCIL-THIN ASPARAGUS WITH
    WALNUT OIL
QUICK RATATOUILLE
STEAMED GREEN BEANS WITH LEMON
    AND OLIVE OIL
CARROTS STEAMED IN FOIL
VEGETABLE SKILLET
CARROTS WITH PISTACHIO NUTS
SUMMER SQUASH SAUTÉ

MEATS

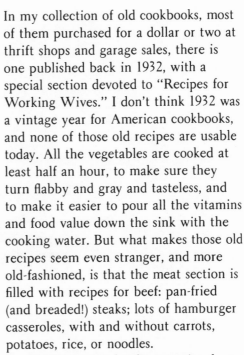

In my collection of old cookbooks, most of them purchased for a dollar or two at thrift shops and garage sales, there is one published back in 1932, with a special section devoted to "Recipes for Working Wives." I don't think 1932 was a vintage year for American cookbooks, and none of those old recipes are usable today. All the vegetables are cooked at least half an hour, to make sure they turn flabby and gray and tasteless, and to make it easier to pour all the vitamins and food value down the sink with the cooking water. But what makes those old recipes seem even stranger, and more old-fashioned, is that the meat section is filled with recipes for beef: pan-fried (and breaded!) steaks; lots of hamburger casseroles, with and without carrots, potatoes, rice, or noodles.

Beef seems to be disappearing from the American diet. Even on restaurant menus you see nothing more than a steak, in lonely splendor, priced at least five dollars higher than any other entrée; sometimes a filet, too, at three dollars more than the steak. The steak is always sirloin or New York strip. I can't remember when I last saw a porterhouse—the famous old T-bone steak that was the American restaurant standard. Apparently even the people willing to pay beef prices refuse to pay them for bones. Even if you are willing to pay for the best possible beef, you don't always get the best possible beef. Lowered federal standards for prime have all but driven real prime beef from the market.

Although I've included a few recipes for beef, I've concentrated in this section on recipes for other meats. Both veal and liver are cooked quickly, and they offer more consistent value for your money. Chicken and turkey breast can be substituted for veal in any recipe in this or any other cookbook and is a delicious and versatile low-cost convenience meat.

Getting consistently good meat can be a problem. The best way to solve it is to find a butcher you can trust and buy all your meat from him. Actually, that's the second-best way. The best way is my way: my gal Friday, Rose Guarrera, who contributed three of the veal recipes in this book. Rose is married to Vito Guarrera, who owns the best butcher shop in Philadelphia—and every time I order meat, she acts as if her job, and her husband's business, were on the line. Every piece of meat I get has been inspected for the slightest blemish or hint of toughness by an Italian-American housewife—the world's fussiest food shopper. So I thought I should take the time at the beginning of this section to say: Thanks, Rose.

These loaves are excellent cold with horseradish or hot with fresh tomato sauce.

Mini Meat Loaves

1 pound ground beef	1 small green pepper, chopped
½ pound ground pork	1 tablespoon chopped basil
½ pound ground veal	Salt and fresh pepper to taste
1 small onion, chopped	2 eggs, beaten
1 clove garlic, chopped	¼ cup red wine or water
1 small carrot, grated	Six 1½-inch cubes sharp Cheddar
1 medium potato, grated	cheese

Place all ingredients except cheese in a large bowl. Mix together lightly but thoroughly. Divide and shape mixture into 6 small loaves. Place loaves on a baking pan or in individual loaf molds. Press a piece of cheese into the top of each loaf. Bake at 375° F. for 30 minutes. Serve warm or cold.

Serves 6.

How many times I have come home late from work and desired the taste of a good old-fashioned stew, but time was against me. I usually prepare those kinds of dishes on weekends.

However, after some experimenting, I came up with this solution. I must be honest and say that it doesn't have that flavor of being cooked over a long period of time, but it does satisfy. It is important to have a good quality of meat so stew cooks rapidly. Do not cut meat in larger chunks, as it takes too long to cook.

Basic One-Hour Stew

2 cloves garlic, chopped
2 shallots, chopped
2 medium onions, chopped
1 large tomato, peeled, seeded, and chopped
5 tablespoons butter
2 tablespoons vegetable oil
2½ pounds beef round or sirloin, cut into small, 3/4-inch cubes, or cut into strips, size of index finger (see note below)
1/4 cup brandy

1 teaspoon chopped fresh thyme
1 bay leaf
1 tablespoon roughly chopped parsley
Salt and fresh pepper to taste
2 cups chicken stock
1 cup dry red wine
1½ cups sliced carrots
1½ cups sliced mushrooms
2 teaspoons potato starch (optional)

Chop garlic, shallots, onions, and tomato in food processor. Heat 4 tablespoons butter with oil in a casserole and sauté beef pieces a few at a time on both sides. Pour off fat. Return meat to pan.

Flame with brandy (see instructions p. 28). Add garlic, shallots, tomato, onions, thyme, bay leaf, parsley, salt, and pepper. Stir well to mix. Add the stock and wine. Bring to a boil. Turn to a simmer. Cover with heavy lid. Cook for 45 minutes. While meat is cooking, place carrots in boiling water; cook 5–10 minutes until tender-crisp. Drain and add to stew. Melt 1 tablespoon butter in a pan. When hot, sauté mushrooms for 2–3 minutes. Add to stew. The entire cooking time for the stew is 45 minutes. If sauce is too thin, dissolve potato flour in 1 tablespoon cold water. Whisk into stew.

VARIATIONS:

1. Substitute lamb or veal for the beef and use either red or white wine. Use lamb and veal from the leg or shoulder.

2. A cut-up chicken may be used. Cook until leg juices run clear.

3. If time allows, add 1 cup peas, shelled and boiled for 3–5 minutes.

(continued)

To Flame Meat for Stews

For a gas stove: Always pour off fat from pan before flaming. Return meat to pan, add brandy and tilt pan into gas flame to ignite. (Don't forget to tilt your head back and away from the flame!) Shake pan until flame dies out.

For an electric stove: Heat brandy in a small pipkin or little pan over electric burner until just finger warm. Strike a match and ignite. Pour flaming brandy over meat in pan. Shake pan till flame dies down.

Brush these bacon slices with honey or brown sugar for a flavor change.

Broiled Canadian Bacon Slices

1–1½ pounds Canadian bacon, sliced ¼ inch thick

Lay bacon slices on broiler rack 3 inches from unit. Broil 3 minutes on one side, turn, and broil 3 minutes on other side.   *Serves 4–6.*

For the best flavor use a ham with a rich, smoky flavor. I favor country hams.

Ham Fritters

2 cups flour
1 tablespoon curry powder
2 cups boiling water

4 large eggs
1½ cups ground country-style
   smoked ham

Combine flour and curry in a saucepan. Add boiling water all at once; stir until mixture leaves sides of pan. Beat in eggs one at a time, beating well after each addition. Add ham. In deep fryer, heat fat to 375° F. Drop ham mixture by tablespoonfuls into hot fat. If desired, drop by teaspoonfuls and use as snacks. Fry 4–5 minutes or until golden brown.   *Makes 36 fritters.*

Ground Lamb Kabobs

Kabobs

1 pound lamb, ground
½ cup grated carrots
1 egg
1 medium onion, finely chopped
¼ cup Parmesan cheese
Salt and fresh pepper to taste

Marinade

½ cup olive oil or salad oil
Juice of 1 lemon
1 clove garlic, finely chopped
Salt and fresh pepper to taste

Mix all ingredients of kabob mixture in a bowl until well blended. Scoop out a rounded tablespoon of the meat mixture and make balls, pressing the meat firmly together with your fingers. Spear lamb balls in the center with wooden kabob sticks—3 on a stick. Place in a shallow dish. Combine marinade ingredients and pour over kabobs. Place baking dish 4–5 inches from top of meat to heat, turning kabobs until brown on all sides. Brush with the marinade as you turn the kabobs.

Serves 6.

Spicy Shoulder of Lamb

6 medium onions, finely chopped
5 tablespoons butter
1½ pounds lamb, shoulder cut, in ¾-inch cubes
1½ tablespoons finely chopped fresh coriander
¾ tablespoon turmeric
½ tablespoon cumin
1 teaspoon grated fresh ginger

Red chilies to taste
Salt and fresh pepper to taste
½ cup yogurt
¼ cup white seedless raisins
1 small tart apple, chopped
3 tomatoes, peeled, seeded, and chopped
½ cup red wine
Rice Pilaf (see page 105)

In a deep 10-inch pan that has a lid, cook onions in butter until well browned. This takes 8–10 minutes, as a lot of moisture is given off by the onions. Add lamb, coriander, turmeric, cumin, and ginger. Cook over medium heat, stirring constantly, 10–12 minutes. Add chili, salt, pepper, yogurt, raisins, apple, and tomatoes. Stir well with wooden spoon and cook without a lid until all moisture has been absorbed, which takes 25–30 minutes (there is a lot of moisture). Add wine, cover, cook until meat is tender, 20–30 minutes. Serve with rice pilaf.

Serves 8.

Don't be put off by this strange combination. It works!

Lamb in Rhubarb Sauce with Coriander

2½ cups sliced fresh rhubarb
¾ cup sugar
¾ cup water
¼ cup butter
1 large onion, chopped
1½ pounds shoulder of lamb, cut in ¾-inch cubes
Salt and pepper to taste

½ teaspoon cinnamon
Freshly grated nutmeg
1 cup chopped parsley
1 tablespoon cornstarch
Rice Pilaf (see page 105)
Chopped fresh coriander

Place rhubarb in a bowl, add sugar and water, and set aside. In a 10-inch skillet with a lid, melt butter, add onion, cook 3 minutes, then remove. Sauté lamb on all sides until golden brown, replace onion, and add seasonings, parsley, and rhubarb. Continue simmering, covered, 20–30 minutes or until meat is tender. Combine cornstarch with a tablespoon of water and stir into mixture until slightly thickened. Serve over rice pilaf. Sprinkle with fresh coriander, to taste.   *Serves 4–6.*

Scrapple has long been a Philadelphia favorite. It is a mixture of ground pork scraps and cornmeal, usually sold in bricks, loaves, or thick slices. It is usually fried or sautéed for breakfast. I like broiling it, as it then does not cook in its own fat. Scrapple is very popular in the Pennsylvania Dutch country and often served with apple butter.

Philadelphia Scrapple

1 pound scrapple

Cut scrapple in six pieces and place on rack of broiler pan. Place pan on oven rack so top of scrapple is 4–5 inches from broiler heat. Brown on first side, then turn and brown on second side. Surface will be brown and slightly crisp. Apple rings that have been dipped in melted butter and brown sugar may be cooked at the same time on the broiler pan as a nice complement to scrapple.

Serves 4–6.

Curry-Glazed Pork Butt

1½ – pound boneless pork butt
¼ cup packed brown sugar
1 teaspoon curry powder

1 tablespoon orange juice
2 tablespoons orange rind

Place pork butt in large pan with water to cover. Bring to boil, reduce heat, cover, and simmer 45 minutes. Remove from pan. Make 4 or 5 slashes about 1 inch apart almost three-quarters through meat. Place in baking pan. Make a curry glaze by mixing together the brown sugar, curry powder, orange juice, and orange rind. Spread it over the pork. Bake at 350° F. for 15 minutes.   *Serves 4-6.*

This is good finger food, especially to carry on a picnic.

Ham Salad Rolled in Lettuce Leaves

2 cups ground ham (preferably smoked country-style to get good flavor)
3 tablespoons finely chopped onion
1 tablespoon capers, chopped

3–4 tablespoons mayonnaise, preferably homemade
2 teaspoons Dijon mustard
6 lettuce leaves, blanched if desired

Combine all ingredients except lettuce leaves; mix well. Place about ⅓ cup ham salad mixture on each lettuce leaf; roll up. Chill.   *Serves 6.*

Savory Pork Steaks

6 pork steaks (about ½ inch thick)	½ teaspoon ground cinnamon
¼ cup flour	Dash of ground cloves
2 tablespoons butter	2 tablespoons vinegar
¼ cup water	Salt and fresh pepper to taste
¼ cup packed brown sugar	2 large cooking apples, thinly sliced

Coat pork well with flour. In a 10-inch skillet, brown steaks in butter. Add water; cover and cook over medium heat 15 minutes. Combine brown sugar, spices, and vinegar. Pour over meat; salt and pepper; top with apples. Cover and simmer 15 minutes more.

Serves 4–6.

These are sometimes called beef roll-ups or rouladen. Don't forget to remove the picks or string before serving.

Beef Birds

Birds

1 pound round steak, cut very thin in ovals about 4 by 8 inches, then each cut in half
1 tablespoon vegetable oil
1 tablespoon butter
2 tablespoons brandy
1½ cups chicken stock
½ cup water

Stuffing

1 tablespoon butter
¼ pound sweet Italian sausage, casing removed
1 small rib celery, chopped fine
1 medium onion, chopped fine
1 small apple, chopped fine
1 tablespoon finely chopped parsley
1½ cups fresh bread crumbs
Salt and fresh pepper to taste

Preheat oven to 350° F. For the stuffing, melt butter and sauté pieces of sausage, broken fine, with the celery, onion, apple, and parsley, stirring constantly. Place lid on to cook for 2–3 minutes on medium-high heat. This will give some moisture to mixture. Add this mixture to the bread crumbs and season with salt and pepper. Stir around lightly with fork.

To prepare the birds, lay all pieces of beef out on board. Pound once or twice with a wet cleaver. Add a rounded tablespoon of filling on top of each piece. Roll birds over and stick with a couple of toothpicks or tie. Heat oil and butter in large sauté pan and brown birds on all sides over medium-high heat. Place in baking dish. Deglaze sauté pan with brandy, stirring around to loosen the brown bits. Pour into casserole. Add chicken stock and water, cover, and cook in oven at 350° F. for 45 minutes or until birds are fork-tender. Test meat at end of 30 minutes.

Remove birds to serving dish. Reduce juices to half. Pour over birds and serve. *Serves 6.*

Ham Balls with Mustard Sauce

Ham Balls

1 pound precooked well-flavored ham, ground
1 egg, beaten
1 medium onion, finely chopped
2 teaspoons Dijon mustard
½ cup dry bread crumbs
2 tablespoons chopped parsley
1 teaspoon Worcestershire

Salt and fresh pepper to taste
6 tablespoons milk
4 tablespoons vegetable oil

Mustard Sauce

½ cup white vinegar
¾ cup light brown sugar
1 tablespoon horseradish mustard
2 teaspoons potato starch

Have the butcher grind precooked ham or use processor to grind or finely chop pieces of ham or leftover ham from a previous menu. Add egg, onion, mustard, bread crumbs, parsley, Worcestershire, salt, and pepper and combine thoroughly. Add milk, a little at a time, until the ham mixture feels that it will hold together when making the ham balls. Use a rounded tablespoon of meat mixture and roll balls firmly with the fingers.

In a 10-inch sauté pan over medium heat, heat 2 tablespoons of vegetable oil and brown half the balls carefully, moving them around with a wooden paddle. Don't crowd the balls. Remove ham balls from pan, scrape and clean the pan thoroughly, then start a second frying with remaining 2 tablespoons of oil and sauté remaining balls. Cook vinegar, brown sugar, and horseradish mustard together, allowing vinegar fumes to cook off. Mix the potato starch with a little cold water and stir it into the sauce while it simmers 3–5 minutes. Serve the warm sauce with the ham balls. *Serves 6.*

Veal can be substituted for pork in this recipe.

Medallions of Pork

3 tablespoons butter
6 medallions of pork (rib chops, boned and tied) 1½ inches thick
Juice of ½ lemon

½ cup chicken stock
½ teaspoon chopped fresh thyme
½ cup heavy cream
Salt and fresh pepper to taste

Melt butter in a skillet. Sauté the medallions until brown, about 3 minutes on each side. Remove from pan. Add the lemon juice, chicken stock, and thyme and boil 3 minutes. Add the cream and bring to a boil. Turn burner to medium. When the mixture coats a spoon (3 to 5 minutes), put back medallions. Season with salt and pepper. Cover. Simmer for 20 minutes until tender. Remove lid. If there is too much sauce, reduce. Remove strings from meat and pour sauce over medallions.

Serves 4–6.

This recipe—plus Parmesan Veal and Veal Scallops with Asparagus—is an adaptation of those prepared by my gal Friday, Rose Guarrera.

Veal Scaloppine Marsala

8–12 veal scallops
Salt and fresh pepper to taste
½ cup flour

6 tablespoons butter
½ cup chicken stock
1 cup dry Marsala

Pound veal slices as thin as possible between sheets of wax paper. Season with salt and pepper. Pat with flour. Shake off excess. Brown in 4 tablespoons butter in large frying pan over high heat until golden brown. Transfer to a hot serving platter and keep warm. Add stock and Marsala to pan and reduce over high heat to half. Remove from heat and stir in 2 tablespoons of butter. Pour sauce over veal and serve.

Serves 4–6.

Parmesan Veal

1½ cups fresh bread crumbs
½ cup freshly grated Parmesan
 cheese
2 tablespoons chopped parsley
 Salt and fresh pepper to
 taste

8–12 veal scallops (3 by 5 inches),
 cut very thin
2 eggs, slightly beaten
½ cup oil

Mix together bread crumbs, Parmesan cheese, parsley, salt, and pepper. Dip veal in egg and cover thoroughly with bread crumb mixture. Heat oil in a large frying pan over medium-high heat. Cook veal slices for about 2 minutes on each side until golden brown.

Serves 4–6.

Veal Scallops with Asparagus

16–24 thin or 8–12 large asparagus
 spears
8–12 veal scallops (3 by 5 inches)
 Salt and fresh pepper to
 taste
½ cup flour

3 tablespoons butter
3 tablespoons oil
⅓ cup dry white wine
⅓ cup chicken stock
8–12 thin slices of fontina cheese

Cook asparagus in boiling water until tender-crisp, 5–7 minutes for thin and 7–12 minutes for thick. Refresh in cold water. Pat dry. If using large spears, cut in half lengthwise. Set aside.

Pound veal scallops as thin as possible between sheets of wax paper. Season with salt and pepper. Pat with flour, shaking off excess. Brown over high heat in hot butter and oil for 1 minute on each side. Transfer veal to a large shallow baking pan that can accommodate it in a single layer.

Pour out fat from fry pan, add wine, stock, and any juices that have dripped into baking pan, and reduce to half. Top each slice of veal with asparagus, dividing it evenly, and 1 slice of cheese. Spoon a little sauce over each scallop. Seal baking pan with foil, making sure it is airtight. Bake in upper part of 425° F. preheated oven for 10 minutes.

Serves 4–6.

This lamb is superb as is but even better if there is time to marinate it for at least an hour. Lamb haters devour this with relish.

Butterflied Leg of Lamb

½ cup olive oil
Juice of 2 lemons
2 cloves garlic, chopped
Salt and fresh pepper

1 tablespoon chopped rosemary
6- pound leg of lamb, boned and butterflied

Mix olive oil, lemon juice, garlic, salt, pepper, and rosemary in a bowl. Lay meat flat on a rack over a baking pan. Brush with the oil mixture. Place meat 4 inches from broiler. Broil 10 minutes, baste, and broil 10 minutes longer. Turn over, brush with oil mixture, and broil until done, basting every 10 minutes. It takes 25–35 minutes to broil. The meat is uneven and will give rare, medium, and well-done servings. Carve on the diagonal into very thin slices. *Serves 6.*

Pork Medallions and Apple Rings

1 pork tenderloin, cut into medallions ½ inch thick
¼ cup flour
Salt and fresh pepper to taste
3 tablespoons butter
Juice of ½ lemon

2 tablespoons finely chopped parsley
1 large apple, cored and cut across into thin rings
2 tablespoons sugar

Pound medallions with flat side of a wet cleaver to make them thin. Pat the medallions on both sides with flour, salt, and pepper. Melt 2 tablespoons butter in a large skillet and, when hot, sauté medallions to lightly brown on each side. Make certain that they are cooked all the way through, about 5–10 minutes. Sprinkle them with lemon juice and parsley. For the apple rings, melt 1 tablespoon butter in another pan. When hot, add apples, carefully! Sprinkle half the sugar over, turn apples, and sprinkle with remaining sugar. Cover with lid. Cook 2–3 minutes. Apples should be tender, crisp, and caramelized. *Serves 4–6.*

Stuffed Pork Chops with Watercress

6 loin pork chops, 1 inch thick
4 tablespoons butter
1 medium onion, finely chopped
¾ cup soft bread crumbs
½ teaspoon chopped fresh thyme
½ cup finely chopped watercress
   leaves

Salt and fresh pepper to taste
1 egg, beaten
½ cup dry sherry
½ cup chicken stock

Slit each chop to make a pocket. Melt the butter in a skillet. Sauté onion 2–3 minutes, add the crumbs, and stir to mix. Add thyme and mix in. Remove to a bowl. Add watercress, salt, pepper, and egg. Mix well with spatula or hand. Stuff mixture into pork chops and close slits with toothpicks. Place chops in baking pan. Add sherry to pan, cover, and bake at 350° F. for 30 minutes. Remove cover, turn chops over, and continue to cook until done, another 10 minutes. Remove chops. Remove fat from baking pan, add the chicken stock, and boil for 2–3 minutes. Pour over chops. *Serves 6.*

Note: You may use whole wheat or rye crumbs.

VARIATION:

You may substitute veal chops for pork, in which case reduce cooking time to 30 minutes total.

Parmesan Bacon

1 tablespoon olive oil
1 tablespoon butter
12 slices of Canadian bacon, ¼
   inch thick

2 eggs beaten with 1 tablespoon
   milk
1 cup dry bread crumbs
2 tablespoons freshly grated Parmesan cheese

In large 10-inch sauté pan, heat oil and butter. Dip bacon in egg mixture, then drop in bread crumbs mixed with Parmesan cheese. Firmly pat each side. When fats are foaming, add bacon, cooking on medium heat to brown—2–3 minutes on each side. Use a pancake turner so as not to break up coating. Bacon should be golden crisp. *Serves 4–6.*

Pork Patties with Sage and Orange

1½ pounds ground pork	1 tablespoon grated orange rind
2 eggs, beaten	1 tablespoon oil (optional)
Salt and fresh pepper to taste	2 tablespoons butter
½ teaspoon chopped fresh sage (or more)	1 medium onion, chopped
	1 cup red wine

Put ground pork into bowl. Add eggs, salt, pepper, sage, and orange rind. Form into 6 patties. Sauté in dry, heavy pan (fat will come out of patties) and cook 3 minutes on each side. If pork is extra lean, add 1 tablespoon oil. Remove patties from pan and add butter. Sauté onion until limp, 2–3 minutes. Add wine and bring to a boil. Boil 3 minutes. Add the patties, cover, and simmer 10 minutes. Remove cover, raise heat, and cook 3 minutes longer. Serve with the juices and onion in pan.

Serves 4–6.

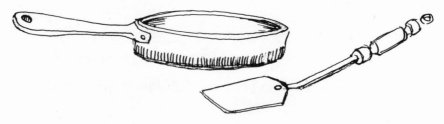

This is a meal in itself.

Baked Sausage with Zucchini

4 tablespoons butter	Salt and fresh pepper to taste
2 pounds zucchini, sliced	½ cup fine dry bread crumbs
½ cup finely chopped onion	2 eggs, beaten
1 pound bulk sausage	½ cup freshly grated Parmesan cheese
1 teaspoon chopped fresh thyme	

Heat butter in skillet. When hot and foamy, add zucchini. Toss for 2–3 minutes. Remove zucchini and add onion. Cook 2–3 minutes. Add sausage, thyme, salt, and pepper. Stir to break up meat. Put back zucchini. Mix well. Add bread crumbs, eggs, and ¼ cup cheese. Mix. Pour into 1½-quart shallow casserole or baking dish. Sprinkle with remaining cheese. Bake at 350° F. for 15–20 minutes.

Serves 4–6.

Veal Paprika

1 large onion, thinly sliced	2 tablespoons paprika
4 tablespoons butter	¼ cup dry white wine
2 pounds leg veal cut in thin strips	1½ cups chicken stock
	1 cup sour cream
¼ cup flour	Cooked noodles

In a 10-inch skillet, cook onion in 1 tablespoon butter until tender but not browned. Remove from pan. Coat veal well with flour. Add some of remaining butter to skillet and brown veal, a small amount at a time, until all butter is used and all meat browned. Remove meat as each portion is browned. Add paprika and cook 1–2 minutes stirring well. Add wine to skillet; cook until reduced to syrup. Add chicken stock, onions, and veal. Bring to boil, reduce heat and cook, covered, over low heat about 25 minutes. Uncover; reduce liquid by cooking 10 minutes more. Just before serving, add sour cream. Serve over noodles. *Serves 4–6.*

VARIATION:

Substitute chicken strips for veal.

Lamb with Eggplant

1 large onion, thinly sliced	chopped
4 tablespoons butter	2 cloves garlic, chopped
1½ pounds ground lamb	Salt and fresh pepper to taste
1 medium eggplant, peeled and cut in ½-inch cubes	½ cup dry white wine
	1 teaspoon potato flour (optional)
3 large tomatoes, peeled and	

In a 10-inch heavy skillet, sauté onion in 3 tablespoons butter; push to one side. Add remaining 1 tablespoon butter and the lamb. Cook until pink color disappears, stirring to break up meat. Add remaining ingredients except potato flour. Cover, then cook over medium heat, stirring occasionally, 15 to 20 minutes or until eggplant is done. Combine potato flour and 1 tablespoon water; add to skillet. (The liquid in pan depends upon how much juice there is in the tomatoes and eggplant. If there is none, do not thicken.) Heat, stirring, until liquid thickens slightly. *Serves 4–6.*

Chicken Livers and Mushrooms on Skewers

8 pieces of bacon, partially
  cooked, cut into thirds
24 chicken livers

24 mushrooms, stems removed
  Salt and fresh pepper
¼ cup (½ stick) butter, melted

Wrap the bacon pieces around the livers. Thread the livers alternately with the mushrooms on each of 6 skewers. Salt and pepper to taste. Roll the skewers in the melted butter. Place on rack over baking pan and broil 2 inches from unit for 5–10 minutes or until nice and brown. Turn once or twice to broil evenly. For outdoor grill, cook 4 inches from hot coals, turning and basting frequently, for 5–10 minutes. Salt and pepper to taste. Some people think salt in bacon is enough.

Serves 4–6.

VARIATIONS:

1. Thread parboiled peeled baby onions on each skewer.

2. Thread pieces of parboiled green pepper on each.

3. Thread slices of apple between each liver.

Sirloin Steak on Skewers

1½ pounds sirloin steak, cut in
  1-inch cubes
1 clove garlic, peeled and
  mashed

¼ cup (½ stick) butter, melted
24 mushrooms, stems removed
  Salt and fresh pepper to taste

Rub meat cubes with garlic. Add remaining garlic to melted butter in a small pan. Thread meat and mushrooms alternately on 6 skewers. Salt and pepper them. Roll them in the butter or brush the butter on them. Place on rack 3 inches from broiler unit. Turn to brown all sides, 5–10 minutes. Pour any remaining butter over skewers and serve.

Serves 6.

VARIATION:

For lamb on skewers, substitute 1½ pounds lamb cubes cut from shoulder.

Baked Whole Calf's Liver

1 whole calf's liver, 1½–2
  pounds
4 tablespoons olive oil
¼ cup lemon juice
¼ cup orange juice

Few sprigs of fresh thyme
Salt and fresh pepper
3 slices of bacon
1 medium onion, sliced

Place liver in a roasting pan. Brush or rub well with oil, lemon and orange juice, and thyme. Salt and pepper to taste. Lay the bacon on top, and slice the onion over the bacon. Bake in a 375° F. oven for 30 minutes. If too pink for your taste at this stage, continue to cook for another 15–20 minutes. Baste every 10 minutes with pan juices. Serve in very thin slices. *Serves 4–6.*

Chicken Livers with Pears

4 tablespoons butter
1½ pounds chicken livers, cleaned
  and dried well
1 large pear, peeled, cored, and
  sliced
1 medium onion, finely
  chopped

Salt and fresh pepper
2–3 tablespoons pear vinegar or
  other vinegar (such as cider
  vinegar)
2 tablespoons finely chopped
  parsley

Melt butter in a skillet. When hot, add the livers. Do not move them around. Cook 3 minutes. Turn over and cook 3 minutes longer or until no longer red. They should be just pink. Remove to a platter and keep warm. Add the pear and onion and cook until barely tender, 3–5 minutes. Add the livers to the onion-pear mixture and season to taste. Stir to mix well. Add the vinegar, bring to a boil, sprinkle the parsley on top, and serve. *Serves 4–6.*

Orange Ham Slice

4 tablespoons butter	1 tablespoon Dijon mustard
2 center slices ham, ½ inch thick	1 tablespoon brown sugar
4 oranges: 3 sectioned and 1	¼ cup vinegar
juiced (½ cup juice)	Salt and fresh pepper

Melt butter in a large skillet. When hot, sauté ham on both sides until brown. Remove and keep warm on a platter. Add orange sections to fat in the pan and heat for 2 minutes. Remove to platter with ham. Mix together the orange juice, mustard, brown sugar, and vinegar. Add to pan and cook until reduced to half. Season to taste. Arrange oranges on top of ham, and pour the few tablespoons of sauce over. *Serves 4–6.*

Note: Please use a ham slice of good smoky flavor.

Slivers of Liver with Orange

Flour	Salt and fresh pepper to taste
1½–2 pounds calf's liver, cut into	Juice and rind of ½ orange
finger-size strips	2 tablespoons chopped chives
4 tablespoons butter	¼ cup chicken stock

Flour the liver strips. Melt the butter. Sauté the liver for 3–5 minutes. Season with salt and pepper. Remove liver strips to serving dish. Add the orange juice and rind, chives, and chicken stock. Reduce to half while scraping any brown bits. Pour over liver. *Serves 4–6.*

Lamb Chops with Parsley and Garlic

4 tablespoons butter	½ cup chopped parsley
6 loin lamb chops, 1 inch thick	2 cloves garlic, chopped
Salt and fresh pepper	Juice of ½ lemon

Melt 3 tablespoons butter in pan. When hot, add chops and brown on both sides (3–4 minutes each side). Salt and pepper to taste. Remove chops. Add remaining tablespoon of butter to pan. Add parsley, garlic, and lemon juice and stir around. Pour over chops. *Serves 4–6.*

Stuffed Veal Chops

¼ cup diced prosciutto ham (or other ham)
¼ pound mushrooms, sliced
¼ cup diced Swiss cheese
   Salt and fresh pepper to taste
1 tablespoon chopped tarragon

6 veal chops, 1 inch thick
4 tablespoons butter
4 tablespoons chopped shallots
¾ cup heavy cream
2 tablespoons port wine

Mix the ham, mushrooms, cheese, salt, pepper, and tarragon in a bowl. Make a slit in each chop for a pocket. Stuff mixture into chops. Pinch open edges together. Melt butter in a large skillet. When hot, brown the chops, about 3 minutes on each side. Season with salt and pepper. Remove chops and keep warm. Add the shallots to the pan and cook a minute or two. Add the cream and port and stir. Put back the chops, cover, and cook 10–15 minutes on medium heat. Remove cover. Turn chops and cook 10 minutes longer or until they are tender. *Serves 4–6.*

Lamb Patties with Mint

1½ pounds ground lamb
  1 teaspoon chopped garlic
  1 egg, slightly beaten
    Salt and fresh pepper to taste

4 tablespoons fresh bread crumbs
2 tablespoons chopped mint
2 tablespoons butter

Put all ingredients except butter into a bowl. Mix thoroughly but lightly. Form into 6 patties. Melt butter in skillet. Sauté the patties 3–5 minutes on each side.
Serves 4–6.

Minute Steaks

4–6 minute steaks (I use N.Y. strip steak ½ inch thick)
1 clove garlic, mashed

2 tablespoons oil
Salt and fresh pepper to taste
Watercress for garnish

Rub each steak with garlic. Brush each steak on both sides with oil. Salt and pepper steaks. Cook 2 minutes on each side in very hot pan. (I use a black iron frying pan, well seasoned and no fat for frying steaks.) Serve immediately with watercress.   *Serves 4–6.*

Note: You can substitute steaks 1 inch thick. Cook exactly the same, but count 3–4 minutes on each side for rare, longer for medium. Rather than ruin a good steak by cooking it well done, I would eat pot roast instead.

Oriental Pork Chops

6 thin loin pork chops (about 1½ pounds)
2 tablespoons butter
1 large onion, thinly sliced
½ pound mushrooms, sliced
1 green pepper, cut into thin strips
6 thin slices of lemon

Fresh pepper to taste
¼ cup soy sauce
¼ cup sherry
Juice of ½ lemon
1 teaspoon chopped or grated fresh ginger
2 cloves garlic, chopped

In 12-inch heavy skillet, brown chops on both sides in 1 tablespoon butter; remove from skillet. Add remaining 1 tablespoon butter; sauté onion, mushrooms, and green pepper. Remove from skillet. Return chops to skillet; top with onion, mushrooms, peppers, and sliced lemon. Combine remaining ingredients; pour over chops. Cover and cook over medium heat 20–30 minutes or until chops are tender.   *Serves 4–6.*

Chili Liver Strips

1½ pounds beef or calf's liver
¼ cup butter
1 large onion, sliced

Salt and fresh pepper to taste
½ teaspoon chili powder (or more)

Cut liver into 4-inch pieces and then into ¼-inch strips. Melt butter in large skillet until hot. Add onion slices and sauté until soft and golden, about 3–4 minutes. Add liver. Sprinkle with salt, pepper, and chili powder. Cook over medium heat, stirring, until liver is cooked through but still pink, about 5 minutes. *Serves 4–6.*

Twenty Meatballs

1 pound ground beef	2 tablespoons sour cream
1 clove garlic, chopped	1 tablespoon roughly chopped
¼ cup grated Parmesan cheese	parsley
½ cup finely grated bread crumbs	Pinch of fresh oregano
1 egg	Salt and fresh pepper to taste
1 small onion, finely chopped	2 cups Tomato Sauce (page 177)

Put all ingredients except sauce into a mixing bowl. Combine and mix well. Wet hands with cold water. Form mixture into walnut-size balls. Drop them into the tomato sauce. Cook, covered, 25–30 minutes.

Serves 4–6 (or more if you make them smaller).

Note: You can also sauté the balls in olive oil until nicely browned.

Picadillo

1 medium onion, chopped	2 large tomatoes, peeled, seed-
1 small green pepper, seeded	ed, and chopped
and chopped	1 tablespoon capers
1 small clove garlic, chopped	½ cup dry red wine
2 tablespoons oil	¼ cup chopped green olives
1½ pounds ground beef	Salt and fresh pepper
¼ cup raisins	Hot cooked rice (page 104)

Sauté onion, green pepper, and garlic in hot oil in a large skillet. Stir in ground beef. Cook until beef loses its color, stirring to break up meat. Drain off fat. Stir in tomatoes, raisins, capers, wine, and olives. Reduce heat. Simmer for about 30 minutes. Season to taste. Serve over hot cooked rice. *Serves 4–6.*

Baked Lamb Chops in Zingy Sauce

6 lamb shoulder chops (about
  2½ pounds)
  Salt and fresh pepper to taste
¼ cup cooking oil
¼ cup chopped shallots
2 tomatoes, peeled, seeded, and
  chopped

2 tablespoons red wine vinegar
1 tablespoon chopped basil
2 teaspoons freshly grated ginger
¼ cup dry vermouth

Season chops with salt and pepper. Place oil in a large skillet. Brown chops in hot oil, 2–3 minutes on each side. Remove and place in 13-by-9-by-2-inch baking pan. Meanwhile, combine remaining ingredients in the same skillet. Stir around with a wooden spatula for 2 minutes. Pour over chops. Bake at 375° F. for 30–40 minutes or until chops are tender, basting meat with sauce occasionally.   *Serves 4–6.*

Note: Thicken sauce, if desired, with 1 teaspoon potato flour dissolved in 1 tablespoon cold water. Whisk into juices. Or instead of using starch to thicken the sauce, remove the chops, keep warm, raise heat, and reduce any excess liquid.

Curried Mustard Pork Chops

6 pork chops, ¾–1 inch thick
2 tablespoons Dijon mustard
¾ cup bread crumbs

2 teaspoons curry powder
2 tablespoons butter, melted
  Salt and fresh pepper to taste

Brush chops with mustard. In a shallow dish, combine bread crumbs, curry powder, and butter. Coat pork chops with crumb mixture. Arrange chops on a well-greased shallow baking pan. Season with salt and pepper. Bake at 400° F. for about 30 to 40 minutes or until chops are tender.   *Serves 4–6.*

VARIATION:

Substitute chicken pieces for the pork. Adjust cooking time: bake at 350° F. for 45 minutes.

Chili Pork Patties

1½ pounds lean ground pork
¼ cup chopped shallots
½ teaspoon chili powder
1 teaspoon dry mustard

2 tablespoons oil
½ cup dry white wine
Salt and fresh pepper to taste

Combine pork, shallots, chili powder, and mustard. Shape into 6 patties. Heat oil in large skillet. Add patties to hot oil. Brown slowly on both sides on low heat, about 10 minutes. Drain. Add white wine, cover, and simmer 15 minutes (make certain that the pork is thoroughly cooked). Remove patties. Reduce wine, season with salt and pepper, and pour over patties.   *Serves 6.*

Fast Beef Stroganoff

½ cup flour, or as needed
2½–3 pounds filet of beef, cut into finger-size strips
4 tablespoons butter, or as needed
1 medium onion, finely chopped

¾ pound mushrooms, sliced
1 tablespoon flour
1½ cups sour cream
Salt and fresh pepper to taste

Lightly flour each piece of meat. Melt butter in a large skillet. Quickly sauté the meat for 1–2 minutes. Remove meat and set aside. Add onion and mushrooms to pan (you may need more butter). Cook until onion is soft and mushrooms are cooked, about 5 minutes. Sprinkle over 1 tablespoon flour and rub in with a wooden spatula until flour disappears. Add the sour cream and bring to a boil, stirring. Put back beef strips. Season with salt and pepper. Reheat meat and serve.

Serves 4–6.

Note: Stroganoff usually looks like dog food when it is served on a buffet table. That's because the sour cream separated. To eliminate this the flour is added to the pan and rubbed in.

Recipes in this chapter:

CHICKEN IN RED OR WHITE WINE
WALNUT CHICKEN
CHICKEN THIGHS WITH ROSEMARY
CHICKEN THIGHS WITH VERMOUTH
BROILED DUCK
GINGER-GLAZED CHICKEN
ROAST SQUAB WITH MUSTARD
EASY BROILED CHICKEN
CHICKEN WITH APPLE CREAM
ROAST TARRAGON CHICKEN
FRIED DUCK
CHICKEN IN SAFFRON CREAM
CHICKEN WITH MUSHROOMS
GINGERED CHICKEN WITH YOGURT
DELICIOUS DRUMSTICKS
CRISPY CHICKEN WINGS
CHICKEN BREASTS WITH BASIL
   BUTTER
MINT JULEP CHICKEN
TEPID CHICKEN SALAD WITH SAFFRON
QUICK CHICKEN SUPREMES
CORNISH HENS WITH LIME

POULTRY

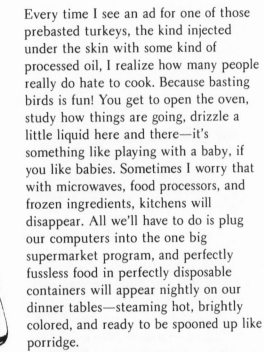

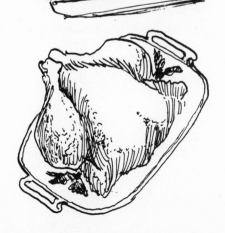

Every time I see an ad for one of those prebasted turkeys, the kind injected under the skin with some kind of processed oil, I realize how many people really do hate to cook. Because basting birds is fun! You get to open the oven, study how things are going, drizzle a little liquid here and there—it's something like playing with a baby, if you like babies. Sometimes I worry that with microwaves, food processors, and frozen ingredients, kitchens will disappear. All we'll have to do is plug our computers into the one big supermarket program, and perfectly fussless food in perfectly disposable containers will appear nightly on our dinner tables—steaming hot, brightly colored, and ready to be spooned up like porridge.

But then I remember the students in my classes who seem eager to make everything from scratch—from classic sauces to chili sauce and chocolate syrup. There seem to be more and more of them every year—and more and more of those prebasted birds, too. That seems to mean that we're dividing up into two camps: the cooks and the anticooks, with absolutely nothing in common. Even our children are going to

49

be divided. Imagine a marriage between a man raised on homemade blueberry muffins and a woman who grew up on Pop Tarts. It's worse than Romeo and Juliet. No matter how polite the families tried to be, the kids would hate each other every time they sat down to a meal.

So stay away from the prebasted birds. Otherwise you'll be sentencing your children to a lifetime of TV dinners.

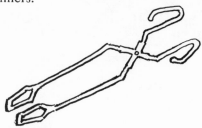

Chicken in Red or White Wine

6 tablespoons butter
4 pounds chicken pieces
 (breasts, legs, or thighs)
2 cloves garlic, chopped
2 onions, sliced
1 tablespoon flour
3 tomatoes, peeled, seeded, and
 chopped

1 cup red or white wine
½ cup sour cream
 Salt and fresh pepper to taste
1½ cups sliced mushrooms
 Juice of ½ lemon
2 tablespoons chopped parsley

Melt 4 tablespoons butter in a large skillet. When hot and foamy, add the chicken (in batches if necessary) and sauté until brown on all sides—about 8–10 minutes. Remove chicken from pan and put into a casserole. Add garlic and onions to fat remaining in pan and cook 2–3 minutes while stirring. Add the flour and rub it in with a wooden spatula. Add the tomatoes and wine. Mix well. Let cook, uncovered, 5 minutes, while stirring. Whisk in the sour cream. Season with salt and pepper. Pour mixture over chicken in the casserole. Melt the remaining 2 tablespoons butter in a small skillet. Add mushrooms and sauté for 2–3 minutes. Sprinkle with lemon juice. Scatter on top of chicken. Cover casserole. Place in 350°F. oven and cook 20–30 minutes, or until juices of chicken run clear. Garnish with parsley.

Serves 4–6.

VARIATION:

For a different texture, purée the sauce in blender or food processor, pour over the chicken, add the mushrooms, cover, and bake.

Walnut Chicken

2 cups walnut halves
1½ cups peanut or vegetable oil
1 tablespoon cornstarch
2 tablespoons water
2 teaspoons soy sauce

3 whole raw chicken breasts,
cut into 3/4-inch cubes
½ cup chicken stock
Salt (optional)

Fry walnuts in hot oil, but don't brown. Drain and reserve oil. Combine cornstarch, water, and soy sauce. Place 3 tablespoons of the hot oil in a skillet. Sauté chicken cubes until browned. Add stock. Cover. Cook over high heat 5 minutes. Stir in cornstarch mixture and stir until thickened. Taste and add salt if needed. Add walnuts. *Serves 4–6.*

Chicken Thighs with Rosemary

8 chicken thighs
2 cloves garlic, chopped
Salt and fresh pepper to taste
8 tablespoons butter

8 sprigs fresh rosemary, crushed (1
tablespoon or more)
8 thin slices onion
8 mushrooms, stems removed

Take 8 pieces of aluminum foil. Lay a chicken thigh on each. Sprinkle garlic over each. Season with salt and pepper. Dot each thigh with 1 tablespoon butter. Sprinkle on the rosemary. Lay a thin onion slice on each and top with a mushroom. Fold packages tightly and lay them on a baking sheet. Place in a 375° F. oven for 35–40 minutes to bake. Serve the chicken in its own juices. *Serves 4–6.*

Chicken Thighs with Vermouth

8 chicken thighs
2 tablespoons butter
1 medium onion, sliced
½ pound mushrooms, sliced

½ cup vermouth or sherry
Juice of ½ lemon
Salt and fresh pepper to taste
2 tablespoons chopped parsley

In skillet, brown chicken in butter; remove and set aside. Add onion and mushrooms; cook until lightly brown and tender. Add vermouth or sherry and lemon juice; cook over high heat to reduce liquid. Return chicken to skillet. Cover; cook over low heat 30 minutes or until done. Season with salt and pepper if desired. Garnish with parsley. *Serves 4–6.*

You can grill these ducks over charcoal for an outdoor dinner.

Broiled Duck

2 ducks (3½–4 pounds each), at room temperature
2 large cloves garlic, peeled and mashed

Juice of 2 lemons
Salt and fresh pepper to taste

Wash and dry ducks thoroughly. Remove any visible interior fat. Remove tail and backbone by cutting on either side of backbone from neck to vent. Cut on other side from breast to vent. Cut each duck into 4 pieces. Rub pieces on each side with garlic. Place ducks, bone side up, on broiler rack over roasting pan to catch the grease. Squeeze lemon juice on ducks. Sprinkle with salt and pepper. Place 4–6 inches from broiler unit and broil 15 minutes. Remove pan from oven, pour off fat, and turn pieces skin side up. Squeeze lemon juice over duck, sprinkle with salt and pepper, and return to oven. Continue to broil for 20–25 minutes. If duck is getting too brown or charred, move to a lower position in oven. *Serves 4–6.*

Ginger-Glazed Chicken

2–2½ pounds frying chickens, cut up
½ cup ginger marmalade
2 tablespoons ginger-flavored brandy

2 tablespoons oil
Juice of 1 or 2 limes

Arrange chicken pieces in a large, shallow baking pan. Combine marmalade, brandy, oil, and lime juice in a small bowl. Brush on chicken pieces. Bake at 375° F. for 30–40 minutes or until tender and glazed, basting frequently.   *Serves 4–6.*

VARIATION:

Substitute quarters of duck, whole game hens, or squabs for the chicken and adjust cooking times accordingly.

Roast Squab with Mustard

6 squabs	¾ cup dry red wine
6 tablespoons butter	¾ cup heavy cream
Salt and pepper to taste	2 tablespoons chopped parsley
2 tablespoons mustard	

Rub each squab with butter. Place breast side up on rack in roasting pan. Salt and pepper birds to taste. Place in 425° F. oven and roast 25–30 minutes or to desired doneness. Remove from oven and keep warm. Remove rack from pan. Add to pan mustard, wine, cream, and parsley. Bring to a boil. Reduce a few minutes, to thicken. Place squabs on serving platter. Pour sauce over birds.   *Serves 6.*

Note: You can also roast the birds by simply rubbing them with soft butter, salt, and pepper. Just before serving, place on each hot bird a spoonful of flavored butter (see page 169).

Easy Broiled Chicken

2 2½–3-pound chickens	Coarse salt and fresh pepper to
Juice of 1 lemon	taste
8 tablespoons butter, softened	Watercress

Cut chicken into serving pieces. Rub pieces with lemon juice, then with butter. Sprinkle with salt and pepper. Place skin side down on broiler pan and place 3–4 inches from broiler unit. Broil 15 minutes. Turn pieces skin side up. Broil 10–15 minutes longer. Baste with juices frequently. Serve with watercress.   *Serves 4–6.*

VARIATION:

Mix 1 clove garlic, chopped, with the butter if a garlic flavor is desired.

Chicken with Apple Cream

2 frying chickens (2½ pounds each), quartered
¼ cup butter
¼ cup Calvados
1 cup dry white wine

1 pound mushrooms, sliced
1 large cooking apple, peeled, cored, and cubed
1 cup heavy cream
Salt and fresh pepper to taste

Partially bone chicken breasts and remove backbone from leg quarters. In a 12–14-inch skillet, brown chicken in butter. Heat Calvados, ignite, and pour over chicken in a large skillet or use 2 skillets. When flame dies down, add wine. Cover; cook over medium heat until chicken is tender (about 20 minutes). Remove chicken to platter and keep warm. Add mushrooms and apple to skillet. Cook over high heat until most of liquid evaporates. Add cream; heat. Season with salt and pepper. Serve chicken with sauce.   *Serves 4–6.*

Roast Tarragon Chicken

1 chicken (3½ pounds), visible fat removed
1 lemon
3 tablespoons butter, softened

2 tablespoons chopped fresh tarragon
Salt and fresh pepper to taste
¼ cup dry white wine

Rub chicken all over with the lemon juice. Put the lemon pieces in the cavity along with 1 tablespoon each of butter and tarragon. Gently separate the chicken skin from the breast meat, using your fingers to loosen the skin without tearing.

Distribute the remaining 1 tablespoon of tarragon mixed with 1 tablespoon of butter between the breast and skin. Rub outer skin with remaining 1 tablespoon of butter. Salt and pepper bird, if desired.

Place chicken in a snug casserole, just to fit, and put ¼ cup wine in bottom. Roast at 375°, uncovered, for 45 minutes or until juices run clear. Remove chicken to carving board and pour juices into a pan. Spoon off fat and boil the juices vigorously to reduce; there should be about 2-3 tablespoons rich juices.

To carve, remove legs and cut across at joints to separate drumsticks and thighs. Remove breast with wing on one side and cut crosswise into 2 pieces. Repeat with other side. You will have 8 pieces of chicken plus the carcass for the cook. Drizzle a bit of juices over the pieces before serving.   *Serves 4-6.*

Note: Turn chicken from side to side every 15 minutes, if desired.

VARIATION:

Rosemary and/or thyme are good substitutes for tarragon, which is sometimes hard to find.

Most of us never think of frying duck because it is so full of fat to begin with. Here the fat comes out of the duck, the skin becomes crispy, and the meat remains moist.

Fried Duck

Oil or shortening	2 ducks (3½–4 pounds), cut into
1 cup flour	pieces
Salt and fresh pepper to taste	Watercress

Place oil or shortening in heavy skillet to depth of ¼ inch. Put the flour, salt, and pepper in a brown paper bag. Shake the pieces of duck, a few at a time, in the flour. When fat in pan is very hot, carefully add the duck. (For 2 ducks, it will probably be necessary to use 2 pans.) Brown on one side for 15 minutes. Turn over and brown other side 15 minutes. Pour off half the fat from skillet. Add ¼ cup water to skillet. Cover, reduce heat, and cook until duck is tender, about 20 minutes, turning twice. Uncover duck last 5–10 minutes to crisp it. Serve with crisp watercress.   *Serves 4-6.*

Chicken in Saffron Cream

6 tablespoons butter
2–2½ pounds frying chickens, cut up
Salt and fresh pepper to taste
1 large tomato, peeled, seeded, and finely chopped

½–1 teaspoon saffron
1½ cups heavy cream
2 tablespoons finely chopped parsley

Melt the butter in a skillet. When hot and foaming, brown the pieces of chicken, 5 minutes on each side. Season with salt and pepper. Pour off the fat. Add the tomato. Add the saffron to the cream and pour over the chicken. Cover and simmer 20 minutes. Stir frequently. Sprinkle with parsley. *Serves 4–6.*

VARIATIONS:

1. Substitute 1 tablespoon chopped fresh tarragon for the saffron.

2. Substitute 1 tablespoon fresh thyme for the saffron.

Chicken with Mushrooms

4 tablespoons butter
4 chicken breasts, split, skinned, and boned
½ pound large mushrooms, sliced
1 tablespoon flour

¾ cup chicken stock
½ cup light cream
1 teaspoon chopped fresh tarragon leaves
Salt and fresh pepper to taste

In large skillet, melt the butter. When hot, add the chicken and brown quickly on both sides; remove. Add mushrooms and cook 3 minutes; remove. Add flour to drippings. Stir in stock, cream, and tarragon. Cook, stirring, until mixture thickens. Return chicken and mushrooms to pan. Cover; simmer 10 minutes or until chicken is done. Season with salt and pepper. *Serves 4–6.*

Gingered Chicken with Yogurt

1 cup plain yogurt
1 teaspoon chopped or grated
   fresh ginger
   Salt and fresh pepper to taste
1 small onion, chopped

1 medium clove garlic, chopped
4 chicken breasts, split, skinned,
   and boned
1 cup fine dry bread crumbs
½ cup melted butter

Preheat oven to 350° F. In a flat dish combine yogurt, ginger, salt, pepper, onion, and garlic. Add chicken and coat well. Dip chicken in crumbs to coat. Place in 3-quart baking dish. Drizzle with butter. Bake 10–15 minutes or until chicken is done.   *Serves 4–6.*

Delicious Drumsticks

4 tablespoons butter
8 chicken drumsticks
2 cloves garlic, chopped
1 large onion, chopped
4 tomatoes, peeled, seeded, and
   chopped
1 tablespoon flour
½ cup sherry or Madeira
1 cup chicken stock

  Salt and fresh pepper to taste
4 tablespoons freshly grated Parmesan cheese
½ cup almonds, browned and
   slivered
½ cup sour cream
2 tablespoons chopped parsley

Melt the butter in a skillet. When hot and foamy, add the drumsticks and brown well on all sides. Turn them frequently. This should take about 8 minutes. Remove chicken and set aside. Add garlic and onion to pan and sauté 2–3 minutes. Add tomatoes and stir well. Add the flour and rub it in with a wooden spatula. Add the wine and stock. Bring to a boil. Cook 2–3 minutes. Return chicken to pan and season with salt and pepper. Cover and simmer 15–20 minutes. When drumsticks are tender, remove them from the pan. Add cheese and almonds to the sauce. Whisk in sour cream. Reheat, and return chicken to sauce. Sprinkle with chopped parsley.   *Serves 4–6.*

VARIATION:

For a somewhat different texture, purée the sauce in a blender or food processor, return to pan, and add chicken, parsley, and almonds.

For my taste, the wings are the best part of the chicken. The wing tips may be removed, but it's not necessary.

Crispy Chicken Wings

2 eggs, beaten	12–16 chicken wings
1 cup flour	1 cup fine bread crumbs
Salt and pepper to taste	Fat for frying
¾ cup milk	Lemon wedges

Beat together eggs, flour, salt, pepper, and milk. Dip chicken wings in batter and roll in crumbs. Heat fat 2 inches deep in pan to point of smoking. Fry wings, 2 at a time, 5–7 minutes. Serve with lemon wedges. *Serves 4–6.*

Both the basil butter and béarnaise are adaptations for the chicken served at the restaurant next to my school. The chef, Billy Weaver, has had great success with these chicken dishes. For other butters that combine well with chicken, see page 169.

Chicken Breasts with Basil Butter

4 tablespoons butter	Salt and fresh pepper to taste
3 whole chicken breasts, split, skinned, and boned	Basil Butter (see below)

Melt the butter in a skillet. When hot, add the chicken breasts, a couple at a time, and sauté 3–5 minutes on each side, or until no longer pink. Season with salt and pepper. Serve with a spoonful of basil butter on top of each breast. *Serves 4–6.*

Basil Butter

8 tablespoons butter, softened	2 tablespoons chopped basil leaves
1 clove garlic, chopped	Few drops of lemon juice

Combine all ingredients in a bowl and beat with wooden spatula until smooth.

Place on wax paper or foil and form into a roll. Refrigerate until serving time.

Makes ½ cup.

VARIATIONS:

Chicken Breasts Béarnaise Cook chicken breasts as above. Serve with a spoonful of Béarnaise Sauce (see page 176).

Chicken Breasts Piccata Cook chicken breasts as above. Squeeze juice of 1 lemon in butter in pan and pour over chicken. Serve with a thin lemon slice on each breast.

Chicken Breasts with Ham and Cheese Cook chicken breasts as above. Place a thin slice of prosciutto ham on each breast and top each with thin slice of fontina cheese. Place directly under broiler until cheese melts.

Mint Julep Chicken

6 tablespoons butter
4 whole chicken breasts, skinned and boned
¼ cup chopped shallots
½ pound mushrooms, sliced
Juice of ½ lemon

Salt and fresh pepper to taste
¼ cup bourbon
1 cup heavy cream
2 tablespoons finely chopped mint

Melt 4 tablespoons butter in pan. When hot, sauté chicken breasts 1 minute on each side. Remove chicken and keep warm. Add shallots and cook 3 minutes. Add 2 tablespoons butter and sauté mushrooms with lemon juice, salt, and pepper for 3 minutes. Add bourbon and heavy cream and bring to a boil. Put chicken back, cover, and cook 10 minutes. If sauce is too thin, remove chicken and reduce sauce, stirring, until it coats a spoon. Garnish with chopped mint. *Serves 4-6.*

Tepid Chicken Salad with Saffron

3 whole chicken breasts, boned and split
2 cups chicken stock
2 ribs of celery, julienned
1 medium cucumber, peeled, seeded, and julienned
1 tablespoon very finely chopped onion

Juice of ½ lemon
½ teaspoon chopped fresh thyme
2 tablespoons finely chopped parsley
½ teaspoon saffron dissolved in a bit of chicken stock
Salt and fresh pepper to taste
¼ cup heavy cream

Poach chicken breasts in stock 10 minutes or until fork tender. Drain. Cut chicken in julienne and place in a bowl with celery, cucumber, onion, lemon juice, thyme, parsley, and dissolved saffron. Season, toss lightly, then add cream to just coat salad mixture.

Serves 4–6.

Quick Chicken Supremes

1½ cups fresh bread crumbs
4 tablespoons finely chopped parsley
4 cloves garlic, finely chopped
Grated rind of 1 lemon

Salt and fresh pepper to taste
4 tablespoons butter, melted
4 whole chicken breasts, skinned and boned
4 tablespoons Dijon mustard

Preheat oven to 375° F. Mix bread crumbs, parsley, garlic, grated lemon rind, salt, and pepper. Toss lightly with fingers. Add 2 tablespoons melted butter and continue to toss. Hold a chicken breast in palm of hand while spreading a teaspoonful of mustard on top of its smooth side. Drop it on the crumb coating. Spread mustard on facing side and turn breast over. Pat coating firmly but carefully. Lay in shallow baking dish or pan. Follow same procedure for remaining pieces. Drizzle the remaining 2 tablespoons of melted butter over the chicken. Bake at 375° F. 15–20 minutes, or until done.

Serves 4–6.

Cornish Hens with Lime

4–6 Cornish hens (about 1 pound each)
Salt and fresh pepper to taste
2–3 tablespoons butter, melted

½ cup honey or more
4 tablespoons soy sauce
Juice of 2 limes

Preheat oven to 350° F. Season hens with salt and pepper; brush with butter. Place on rack in roasting pan. Combine remaining ingredients for basting sauce. Roast hens 20 minutes; remove from oven. Brush with basting sauce. Return to oven. Continue to roast 30 minutes or longer, basting several times.   *Serves 4–6.*

Recipes in this chapter:

SOFT-SHELL CRABS WITH CAPERS
STEAMED FLOUNDER FILETS
BROILED SHRIMP
SHRIMP IN BEER I
SHRIMP IN BEER II
MARINATED SHRIMP
SPEEDY BAKED CRABMEAT
FLOUNDER SICILIAN STYLE
JAMBALAYA
POACHED SALMON STEAKS
FRESH CRAB CAKES
SWORDFISH AND CUCUMBER KABOBS
BROILED BONELESS SHAD
BAKED OYSTERS IN CREAM
CLAMS CASINO
SAUTÉED SCALLOPS
CRÊPES BOMBAY
CREOLE SHRIMP
HELEN'S BAKED SHRIMP
BAKED FLOUNDER FILETS WITH
    HERBS
BAKED FISH STEAKS WITH ANCHOVY
    BUTTER
FISH IN PARCHMENT
OVEN-BAKED SCALLOPS WITH SPINACH
BUTTERFISH WITH MUSTARD
FISH BAKED WITH SOUR CREAM
FRIED CATFISH
ALMOND FISH FILETS
BROILED SHRIMP AND SCALLOPS
SHRIMP TEMPURA

SEAFOOD

Where I grew up in central Pennsylvania in a family who loved to fish, I had plenty of fresh trout and catfish. These fresh-water fish were delicious. But I'll never forget coming to Philadelphia and for the first time seeing a whole fish in a market. It was a big silver and black striped bass, and I'd never seen a fish that fat and funny-looking. I bought it, cooked it that night in lemon and butter, and couldn't believe that anything could taste so wonderful. I've been in love with the taste of fresh seafood ever since.

Now, even if you are land-locked a thousand miles from the coast, fresh seafood is available in quantity. Just be sure you know from whom you are buying it. Fresh fish poaches beautifully. Fish that is not fresh or is frozen will not poach properly. It will fall apart into pieces. This happened to me when I decided to have a party to pay back friends. I decided to poach trout, curl it up with a string through the tail and eye, cover it with aspic, and knock everybody's socks off. I needed twenty-eight trout. I poached them two at a time and every other one disintegrated. I realized some had been over the hill and frozen and some not. I marched over to my brand-new fish seller and told him he was about to become my brand-new ex-fish seller. He couldn't understand how anyone could sell him bad fish—or so he said—but he did scour the market and came up with enough really fresh fish for my party. And we never had any more trouble. Your fish dealer is even more important than your butcher. If you get a tough piece of meat you can always stew it until it is tender. All you get from bad frozen fish is watery shreds.

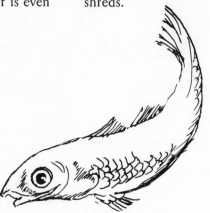

In New Orleans, soft-shell crabs are called buster crabs. I always thought they were somehow named after the old movie actor Buster Crabbe. But it turns out that they are called busters because they bust out of their shells when they shed. And they have been called busters for over a century—much longer than the movie star has been alive. So, by coincidence or by design, Buster Crabbe is a movie star named after a crustacean.

Soft-Shell Crabs with Capers

8–12 medium soft-shell crabs
½ cup flour
    Salt and fresh pepper to taste
8 tablespoons butter

2–4 tablespoons capers, or more, washed and drained
Juice of ½–1 lemon
Lemon wedges

Lay crabs on back shell and pull shell from point on back about halfway to remove spongy matter and lungs. Repeat on other side. Remove apron. Rinse and pat dry. (Since this is a *fast* book, it would be easier to have fishmonger clean the crabs.) Flour the crabs and pat off excess. Season with salt and pepper. Heat butter in pan until foamy. Add the crabs and sauté on both sides until brown, 2–3 minutes on each side. Remove crabs and add capers and lemon juice to pan. Stir 1 minute and pour over the crabs. Serve with lemon wedges. *Serves 4–6.*

VARIATION:

Sauté ½ cup slivered almonds in butter left in pan and sprinkle over crabs.

This recipe is an adaptation of one taught by my assistant Will Kratz. Will has studied with me for years and now teaches classes.

Steamed Flounder Filets

4–5 carrots, peeled and julienned	Salt and fresh pepper to taste
6 leeks, trimmed and julienned	8 whole thin filets of flounder
3 tablespoons butter, melted	Fish stock (see page 178)

Lightly butter a shallow baking dish and place in it the carrots, leeks, butter, salt, and pepper. Cover with a piece of foil. Place in a 350° oven and cook for 20–25 minutes, stirring frequently. (If preferred, the vegetables may be sautéed on top of stove.)

Lay filets on a work surface with the skin side down. Place a spoonful of vegetables in the center of each filet and fold over lengthwise. Fold the ends under to keep the vegetables inside. Place remaining vegetables in a layer on bottom of a steamer basket. Lay filled filets on top of vegetables. Pour fish stock (reserving ½ cup for sauce) in bottom of steamer. Place the steamer basket containing fish and vegetables in the steamer. Cover and steam 8–10 minutes, until just done.

Serve with the following sauce:

1 tablespoon butter	8 tablespoons butter, softened
1 shallot, finely chopped	Salt and fresh pepper to taste
½ cup fish stock	Juice of ½ lemon
½ cup dry white wine	2 tablespoons finely chopped
2 tablespoons heavy cream	parsley

Heat butter in small saucepan and add shallots. Cook 1 minute, add fish stock, and reduce until 3 tablespoons remain. Add wine and reduce by half. Add cream. Heat. Beat in butter, 1 tablespoon at a time. Add salt and pepper, lemon juice, and parsley. Reheat any remaining vegetables. Transfer to serving dish. Lay steamed filets on top. Top with a small amount of sauce. Serve remaining sauce on side.

Serves 4–6.

Broiled Shrimp

2 pounds shrimp, peeled
3 cloves garlic, chopped
½ cup olive oil

Juice of 2 lemons
Salt and fresh pepper to taste
2 tablespoons chopped parsley

Lay shrimp in 1½-quart baking dish. Combine garlic, oil, and lemon juice. Pour over shrimp. Salt and pepper, if desired. Place 4 inches from broiler unit. Broil 2 minutes on each side. Sprinkle parsley over. Serve with rice (see page 104).

Serves 4–6.

Shrimp in Beer I

2½–3 pounds shrimp, unpeeled   Beer to cover

Place shrimp in pan. Cover with beer. Bring to boil. Cook 5 minutes. Turn off and let shrimp stay in beer 5 more minutes. Serve warm. Each guest should peel his own. Dip in Cucumber Sauce (see page 174) or melted butter with lemon or eat plain.

Serves 4–6.

Shrimp in Beer II

6 peppercorns
Salt to taste
Juice of 1 lemon
1 bay leaf, crumbled
Leaves from 3 ribs celery
1 tablespoon parsley sprigs,
stems removed

2 tablespoons horseradish
Cayenne pepper to taste
Two 12-ounce cans beer
1½–2 pounds shrimp

Combine all ingredients except shrimp in a saucepan. Bring to a boil. Add shrimp. Return to boil and cook 3 minutes. Turn off heat. Let stand 10–15 minutes. Serve from liquid or strain, as desired.

Serves 4–6.

Marinated Shrimp

Prepare Shrimp in Beer II (see above)
1 cup vinaigrette (page 176)
Lettuce leaves

Lemon wedges
2 tablespoons chopped parsley, dill, or chives

Peel shrimp. Place in bowl. Add vinaigrette and toss well. Serve on lettuce with a lemon wedge. Sprinkle tops with parsley, dill, or chives. *Serves 4–6.*

For crabmeat lovers this method of cooking is the best. Nothing in the recipe adulterates the sweet flavor of the crab.

Speedy Baked Crabmeat

2 pounds crabmeat, membranes removed
½ cup butter, melted
Salt and fresh pepper to taste

Juice of 1 lemon
1 tablespoon chopped parsley
4 tablespoons brandy

Place crabmeat in shallow baking dish. Pour melted butter over. Season with salt and pepper. Squeeze lemon juice over crab. Sprinkle with parsley and brandy. Bake at 375° F. for 10 minutes, until hot. *Serves 4–6.*

Flounder Sicilian Style

3 sweet red peppers
3 medium zucchini, sliced
8 tablespoons butter
Salt and fresh pepper to taste
4 tomatoes, peeled, seeded, and chopped

1 tablespoon chopped fresh basil
4–6 filets of flounder
½ cup flour
1 tablespoon chopped parsley

Roast peppers under broiler or place on long fork and hold over flame. Keep turning until charred, about 10 minutes. Peel, seed, and cut into strips. Sauté zucchini in 2 tablespoons hot butter until tender-crisp, about 3–4 minutes. Salt and pepper to taste. Sauté chopped tomatoes in 3 tablespoons hot butter for 10 minutes. Add basil, salt, and pepper. Pat the filets with flour on both sides. Sauté in remaining hot butter for 3 minutes on each side over medium-high heat. Arrange vegetables on a heated platter and top with filets. Sprinkle with parsley.

Serves 4–6.

Jambalaya

1 pound cubed cooked ham	½ cup chopped parsley
1 large onion, sliced	½ teaspoon crushed thyme
1 large clove garlic, chopped	leaves
3 tablespoons butter	1 large bay leaf
½ pound thinly sliced peperoni	4 cups chicken stock
4 large tomatoes, peeled and	2 cups rice
chopped	1½ pounds shrimp, cooked and
1 large green pepper, diced	cleaned
½ cup chopped celery leaves	Salt and fresh pepper to taste

In large heavy kettle, brown ham and cook onion with garlic in butter until onion is transparent. Add peperoni, tomatoes, green pepper, celery leaves, parsley, thyme and bay. Bring to boil; reduce heat. Cover; simmer 10 minutes. Add chicken stock; bring to boil. Add rice, reduce heat, cover, and cook 20 minutes or until rice is tender. Add shrimp, salt, and pepper; heat.

Serves 6–8.

If there is no time to make court bouillon, poach the salmon steaks in a mixture of 8 cups of water and 1 cup of vinegar.

Poached Salmon Steaks

6 salmon steaks, 1 inch thick   Court Bouillon (see page 179)

Arrange salmon steaks in a pan. Pour court bouillon over to cover. Bring to a boil. Reduce heat to simmer. Cover and simmer 7 minutes. Serve with Béarnaise (page 176) or a Flavored Butter (page 169).

Serves 6.

Fresh Crab Cakes

1½ pounds fresh crabmeat,
   membranes removed
1 tablespoon finely chopped
   parsley
¼ cup chopped chives
1 tablespoon Dijon mustard
  Juice of ½ lemon

2 eggs, beaten
1–1½ cups fresh bread crumbs,
   lightly packed
¼ cup heavy cream
  Salt and red pepper to taste
4 tablespoons butter

Put crabmeat in a bowl. Add the parsley, chives, mustard, lemon juice, and eggs. Blend well. Add the bread crumbs and mix, adding the heavy cream, salt, and red pepper. If mixture is too dry to form cakes, add a little more cream. Form into about 8 cakes. Melt butter in skillet. When hot and foamy, sauté crab cakes 1–2 minutes on each side or until heated through. Serve with Tartar Sauce (see page 179). *Serves 4–6.*

Note: You can also put all these ingredients into a shallow baking dish and bake in the oven for 10–15 minutes at 375° F.

Any other firm fish can be used in this recipe. Try salmon, halibut, monkfish, lobster, shrimp, or scallops.

Swordfish and Cucumber Kabobs

2½ pounds swordfish, cut in 1-
   inch cubes
2 cucumbers, peeled, seeds removed, cut in 1-inch pieces

Salt and fresh pepper to taste
½ cup olive oil
  Juice of ½ lemon
1 bay leaf, crushed

Thread fish and cucumbers alternately on each of 6 skewers. Season with salt and pepper. Mix together the oil, lemon juice, and bay leaf. Brush each serving with the mixture. Broil kabobs 4 inches from heating unit (or over charcoal) for 5–10 minutes, turning skewers and basting frequently. *Serves 6.*

Broiled Boneless Shad

Shad is and always has been my favorite fish. I remember when my mother baked it in milk for hours to dissolve the bones. Now I buy it boned and broil it for maximum flavor.

1½–2 pounds boneless shad
Salt and fresh pepper to
taste
Juice of 1 large lemon

2 tablespoons butter, in small
pieces
2 lemons, cut into wedges

Generously butter an ovenproof dish and lay shad in dish skin side down. Salt and pepper the shad to taste and sprinkle lemon juice over. Dot with pieces of butter and place in a preheated broiler 4 inches from source of heat. Broil for approximately 5 minutes. Serve with lemon wedges.

Serves 4–6.

I have my fishmonger open the oysters for this recipe.

Baked Oysters in Cream

24 oysters on the half shell
1¼ cups heavy cream
¾ cup freshly grated Parmesan
cheese

Fresh pepper (optional)
½ cup butter, melted

Place oysters on heated rack or salt, or lay them on a baking sheet. Pour the cream over them. Sprinkle the cheese evenly over them, and sprinkle on fresh pepper if desired. Drizzle the butter over the cheese. Place in oven and broil 5 minutes, 2 inches from unit, or bake at 400° F. for 7–10 minutes.

Serves 4–6.

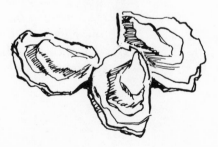

I have my fishmonger open the clams. Be certain not to overcook clams, as they will become rubbery.

Clams Casino

8 slices bacon	4 tablespoons fresh bread crumbs
24 cherrystone clams on the half shell	1 tablespoon finely chopped parsley
Salt and pepper (optional)	¼ cup butter, melted
½ large green pepper, very finely chopped	Lemon wedges

Partially cook the bacon—it should still be limp. Cut into 3 pieces each. Arrange clams on heated rack, or lay them on a baking sheet. Salt and pepper if desired. Mix together the green pepper, bread crumbs, parsley, and butter. It should resemble a paste. If too thick, add the bacon fat. Place a bit of this mixture on each clam. Place piece of bacon on each. Broil 5 minutes 2 inches from unit or bake at 400° F. for 7–10 minutes. Do not overcook or clams will be tough. Serve with lemon wedges.   *Serves 4–6.*

Sautéed Scallops

1½ pounds bay scallops	Salt and fresh pepper to taste
½ cup flour	2 tablespoons chopped parsley
6 tablespoons butter	Lemon wedges

Roll the scallops in flour. Pat off excess. Melt butter in skillet. When hot and foaming, add scallops, salt, pepper, and parsley. Toss over high heat 5 minutes. Serve with lemon wedges.   *Serves 4–6.*

Note: If using sea scallops, sauté longer—about 7 minutes.

VARIATION:

Sometimes I add fresh ginger to taste and toss it with the scallops. This combination was served to me by Richard Nelson in Portland, Oregon.

This dish will take you right down to the wire of one hour with not much time to spare!

Crêpes Bombay

Batter for Crêpes (see page 174)
3 tablespoons butter
3 tablespoons flour
2 teaspoons curry powder
1 cup chicken stock
Salt and fresh pepper to taste
½ cup sour cream
1 pound crabmeat
Melted butter
Chutney

Make crêpe batter.

Meanwhile, to make filling: In saucepan, melt butter; blend in flour and curry and cook for 2 minutes. Gradually add chicken stock. Cook, stirring constantly, until mixture comes to a boil and thickens. Season with salt and pepper; blend in sour cream until smooth. Gently fold in crabmeat, being careful not to break into flakes. Keep warm over very low heat.

To make crêpes: Heat 6-inch omelet pan over high heat; add a small amount of butter. Pour in about 2 tablespoons crêpe batter, tilting pan to coat bottom evenly. Brown quickly on each side; stack on wire racks. Repeat until all batter is used.

To assemble: Preheat oven to 375° F. Place about ⅓ cup crab filling on center of each crêpe. Roll and place seam side down in individual baking dishes (or 1 large dish). Repeat until all crêpes are filled. Brush with melted butter. Bake on shelf near top of oven about 15 minutes or until hot and bubbly. Serve with chutney. Makes 9 crêpes. *Serves 4–6.*

Creole Shrimp

1 large onion, chopped
1 small green pepper, chopped
2 celery ribs, chopped
1 large clove garlic, chopped
Few sprigs of fresh thyme
3 tablespoons butter
2 tablespoons flour
1 cup chicken stock
6 large ripe tomatoes, peeled and chopped
1 teaspoon chili powder
Salt to taste
2 dashes hot pepper sauce
2 pounds raw shrimp
Salt
Cooked rice

In 10-inch skillet, cook onion, green pepper, celery, garlic, and thyme in butter until vegetables are tender. Blend in flour, then gradually add chicken broth, stirring constantly. Add remaining ingredients except shrimp and rice; simmer 20 minutes. Meanwhile, shell and devein shrimp. Add shrimp to skillet and cook 5–10 minutes or until shrimp are done. Salt to taste. Serve over rice. *Serves 4–6.*

Helen's Baked Shrimp

12 raw jumbo shrimp
1 cup butter, melted
1 cup fine dry bread crumbs
1 tablespoon finely chopped parsley
1 tablespoon finely chopped fresh dill
¼ cup dry white wine
Salt and fresh pepper to taste

Remove little legs from shrimp. With sharp knife, split shrimp in half through top shell, being careful not to cut through membrane on lower side. Remove intestinal vein. Preheat oven to 350° F. To make stuffing, combine ½ cup melted butter with remaining ingredients; mix well. Stuff each shrimp with about 2 tablespoons mixture. Place in individual baking dishes; drizzle with remaining butter. Bake in 350° F. oven for 15–20 minutes. *Serves 4–6.*

Baked Flounder Filets with Herbs

1½–2 pounds filets of flounder, fluke, or other white fish
8 tablespoons butter
Juice of 1 lemon
Salt and fresh pepper to taste
1 small onion, chopped
4 tablespoons chopped parsley
2 tablespoons chopped chives

Put the butter into a small pan. Melt, add lemon juice, salt, pepper, and onion, and cook 2 minutes. Add the parsley and chives and cook 1 minute. Take a baking dish and pour half the butter mixture in. Lay fish filets on the butter and pour rest of the mixture on top of fish. Bake at 350° F. for 10–15 minutes, depending on thickness of fish. Serve from baking dish. *Serves 4–6.*

Baked Fish Steaks with Anchovy Butter

6 tablespoons butter
Juice of 1 lemon
2 tablespoons anchovy paste
2 tablespoons finely chopped
chives, parsley, or dill

2–3 pounds fish steaks (tuna, halibut, swordfish), 1 inch thick
Salt and fresh pepper to taste

In a small pan, melt the butter with lemon juice, anchovy paste, and chives, parsley, or dill. Lay steaks on baking pan. Brush tops with half the butter mixture. Bake at 400° F. for 10 minutes, basting once. Fish should just flake. Cook a few minutes longer if better-done fish is preferred. Pour remainder of butter over fish.

Serves 4–6.

These filets were demonstrated in my classes at the Greenbrier by my two favorite young chefs, Liz and Bob Briggs.

Fish in Parchment

Vegetable oil
6 thin fish filets: salmon, flounder, or trout
¾ cup peeled, seeded, and diced tomato
½ cup sliced mushrooms
4 tablespoons finely chopped shallots

4 tablespoons butter, melted
Juice of 1 lemon
4 tablespoons white wine
Salt and fresh pepper to taste
2 tablespoons chopped fresh parsley, chives, or dill

Cut 6 hearts from 6 pieces of parchment measuring 6 inches wide by 10 inches long. Lay parchment hearts out flat and brush oil on them. Lay each filet on the right side. Divide all remaining ingredients among the 6 hearts. Fold the edges together by pleating so no steam can escape. Brush outside of hearts with oil. Put on baking sheets into 350° F. oven for 7–10 minutes. Serve 1 to each guest and slit the packages at the table. They should be beautifully puffed.   *Serves 6.*

VARIATIONS:

1. Use a Flavored Butter (see page 169).

2. Use Fennel Butter (see page 170).

3. Use aluminum foil if parchment is not available.

4. Bake a few at a time if oven is not large enough.

Oven-Baked Scallops with Spinach

9 tablespoons butter	Juice of ½ lemon
2 tablespoons finely chopped shallots	1 cup spinach leaves, stems removed, chopped
1½–2 pounds bay scallops, or sea scallops cut in rounds	2 tablespoons flour
¾ cup vermouth	1 egg yolk
½ cup water	½ cup heavy cream or more
1 pound mushrooms, sliced Salt and fresh pepper to taste	½ cup bread crumbs
	¼ cup freshly grated Parmesan cheese
	2 tablespoons butter, melted

Melt 4 tablespoons butter in saucepan. Sauté the shallots for 1 minute. Add the scallops. Stir around. Add vermouth and ½ cup water. Simmer 5 minutes or until scallops have an opaque look. Remove scallops. Reduce juices to ¾ cup.

Meanwhile, melt 3 tablespoons butter in skillet and add mushrooms, salt, pepper, and lemon juice. Add spinach. Toss mushrooms and spinach for 2–3 minutes. Add juices, if any, to reduction. Next, melt 2 tablespoons butter, stir in flour, and cook 1 minute. Add the scallop juice reduction; whisk until thick. With a fork, beat the egg yolk and heavy cream together. Warm with a bit of the sauce and whisk this mixture into the sauce. If too thick, thin with more cream, just to napping consistency. Combine scallops and mushrooms and spinach mixture with cream mixture. Place in an oval gratin dish. Sprinkle top with bread crumbs and cheese and drizzle melted butter over. Bake at 350° F. until bubbly, about 15 minutes. Place under broiler to brown, if desired.   *Serves 4–6.*

Butterfish with Mustard

8–12 butterfish (2 per serving),
  cleaned
½ cup white wine
¼ cup Fish Stock (see page
  178)
Salt and fresh pepper to
taste

½ cup heavy cream
1 tablespoon sweet mustard
1 tablespoon strong mustard
2 tablespoons butter, softened

Lay butterfish in baking dish. Sprinkle the wine, fish stock, salt, and pepper over them. Place in a 400° F. oven. Bake 5–7 minutes. Drain juices into saucepan while keeping the fish warm. Add cream and mustards. Cook on medium high flame for 3–4 minutes. Whisk in the butter. Serve sauce over fish.   *Serves 4–6.*

Notice that there is no butter on this fish. The sour cream keeps it moist.

Fish Baked with Sour Cream

1 large onion, sliced thin
1 lemon, sliced thin
¾ cup dry white wine
6 filets of fish, 1 inch thick (halibut, swordfish, or any thick
  fish)

Salt and fresh pepper to taste
1 cup sour cream

Cover the bottom of a shallow baking dish with slices of onion. Lay the lemon slices over the onion. Add wine and stir. Put into 400° F. oven and cook 10–15 minutes to soften. Arrange fish filets on top of onion and lemon. Sprinkle with salt and pepper. Place in 400° F. oven and bake 10–15 minutes covered. Uncover. Spread the sour cream over the fish and place dish 2 inches from broiler unit. Glaze the top until cream is lightly brown. Serve from baking dish.   *Serves 4–6.*

Catfish is one of the best-tasting fish I know. I still remember when the Forpaugh Circus came to town. The owner, who was a family cousin, always came to our house for dinner. My mother served catfish more than once, as it was cousin Billy's favorite. The circus was later sold to Ringling Brothers, but we still ate catfish.

Fried Catfish

Shortening or bacon fat
4–6 medium-size catfish, skinned, heads and tails removed

1½ cups yellow and white corn-meal, mixed (equal parts)
Salt and fresh pepper to taste

Put fat in a heavy skillet to a depth of ¼ inch. Dip each fish into cornmeal mixture. When fat is hot and to the point of smoking, drop in the fish and fry until brown, crisp, and done—about 8 minutes on one side and 5 on the other. Season with salt and lots of pepper. *Serves 4-6.*

Almond Fish Filets

6 fish filets (any white fish in season: flounder, fluke, sole, monk, or trout)
Juice of ½ lemon
1 egg
2 tablespoons milk

½ cup flour
¾ cup ground almonds
2 tablespoons butter
1 tablespoon vegetable oil
Salt and fresh pepper to taste
½ lemon, sliced thin

Wash filets and pat dry with paper towels. Sprinkle lemon juice over fish and pat dry again. Mix the egg and milk. Dip each filet in the mixture, then coat in a mixture of flour and ground almonds. Heat butter and oil in a 10-inch sauté pan until foaming. Add filets and brown on each side on medium-high heat or until filets are golden brown. Sprinkle with salt and pepper and serve with thin slices of lemon. *Serves 4-6.*

Broiled Shrimp and Scallops

½ cup vegetable oil
½ cup Tomato Sauce (see page 177)
¼ cup soy sauce
Juice of 1 lime
Salt and fresh pepper to taste

1 tablespoon finely chopped onion
1 clove garlic, chopped
1 pound large shrimp, peeled and deveined
1 pound scallops

Combine all ingredients except shrimp and scallops; mix well. Place shrimp and scallops in shallow dish; cover with marinade. Refrigerate until ready to broil. Stir occasionally to coat well. Place seafood on rack of broiler pan. Broil 4 inches from heat about 3 minutes. Turn; brush with remaining marinade; broil 3 minutes more until done.

Serves 4–6.

Tempura vegetables can be served with the shrimp. Use fresh asparagus tips (cook 3 minutes), green beans (3 minutes), wax beans (3 minutes), parsley (1 minute), mushrooms (2 minutes), cauliflower florets (5 minutes), carrot sticks (5 minutes). If you prefer, vegetables (but not parsley and mushrooms) can be parboiled, but all should be golden brown with a slightly crunchy texture.

Shrimp Tempura

Batter

1 egg (beaten)
1 cup ice water
1 cup flour (or more)

2 tablespoons vegetable oil
½ teaspoon salt
½ teaspoon sugar
½ teaspoon baking powder

Make batter by beating the egg and water together in a bowl. With a fork, stir in remaining ingredients. No matter if a few lumps remain. Batter should have consistency to cling to food to be fried.

Shrimp

Fat for frying

2 pounds raw medium shrimp, shelled

Place fat in pan to a depth of 2 inches and heat to 375°F. Dip shrimp in tempura batter, letting excess drip off. Put a few shrimp at a time in hot fat. Cook 2–3 minutes or until golden. Serve while hot and crisp. Keep skimming batter off top of fat. Serve with equal parts of grated turnips and white radishes and dipping sauce. *Serves 4–6.*

VARIATION:

Instead of shrimp, fry smelts or pieces of fish filets cut into finger strips.

Dipping Sauce

1 cup chicken stock
1 tablespoon sugar
6 tablespoons soy sauce

1 clove garlic, chopped
1 tablespoon grated fresh horse-radish
1 teaspoon grated fresh ginger

Mix all ingredients together and beat for 1 minute.

Recipes in this chapter:

VEGETABLES

It's hard to find a recipe for fresh succotash made from scratch. Most cookbooks don't bother with it, and the few that do add a helpful hint like "Succotash is also good made with canned or frozen vegetables." That must be because cookbook writers, like most Americans, don't know anything about fresh succotash, made in the height of the season when baby limas and new corn are both available. Fresh succotash is easy to make, delicious, and a genuine American culinary invention, three good reasons why you should try it. A fourth is that sooner or later the French will discover it, the way they discovered canned corn a few years ago, and put corn in everything, even in salads. When your friends come back from Paris with the latest food fad, you'll be a whole step ahead of them if you start making succotash now!

Many of these recipes are ideal as entrées. There are still some people who think that if they don't eat meat every day their teeth or hair will fall out, but it is not really necessary, or even desirable, to eat meat every day. Corn fritters or vegetable tempura, baked acorn squash or mixed vegetable skillet—all work equally well as main courses or side dishes.

And now, a few words in praise of

roots. We all owe a debt of gratitude to our children, who discovered how wonderful good fresh vegetables can taste. But the funny thing about these kids is that they've rediscovered the pretty vegetables. I look through shelves of vegetarian cookbooks for the kind that come out in flower-decked paperbacks, all hand lettered and with illustrations showing willowy couples in willowier caftans, and the vegetables turn out to be carrots, daikon, or leafy greens all covered with granola or sprouts. I like sprouts in salads, though if you eat too many of them you come away feeling as if you have hair caught in your teeth. But I rarely see anything about root vegetables. Beets, turnips, rutabagas, parsnips and Jerusalem artichokes are the dark secrets of the American kitchen.

The young people probably dislike root vegetables because not all of them can be cut into slivers and served on a bed of romaine lettuce with a honey walnut dip. But I think my generation dislikes root vegetables because they associate them with the Depression. Mashed rutabagas with old-fashioned uncolored margarine convinced a whole generation that root vegetables on the plate were a confession of poverty in the house.

Whenever I give a turnip recipe to my classes, I hear a soft sigh of despair: "Ohhhhh, turnips . . .

"How many hate turnips?" I ask. Almost all the hands go up.

"How many have tasted turnips in the past five or ten years?" I ask.

And almost all the hands go down.

So try some of these recipes for turnips and parsnips and other roots. Get brave and try Kohlrabi Dauphinois (on opposite page). Many people have never tasted many of the root vegetables, or have forgotten the taste long ago. They're shocked to discover what they have been missing. You can help to convince them that it's time to bring root vegetables up out of the root cellar.

Mushrooms with Cream

4 tablespoons butter	¼ cup sherry
2 tablespoons chopped shallots	1 cup heavy cream
1½ pounds mushrooms, cleaned and sliced	1 tablespoon chopped parsley
	Salt and fresh pepper to taste

Melt butter in a skillet. Sauté shallots for 2–3 minutes. Add mushrooms and cook 3 minutes. Add the sherry and cook until almost evaporated. Add cream and cook, stirring, until it coats a spoon. Add parsley, salt, and pepper.   *Serves 4–6.*

Note: To speed up cooking time, add 1 tablespoon flour after sherry has reduced.

Sautéed Mushrooms

4 tablespoons butter
1–1½ pounds mushrooms,
cleaned, stems removed
Salt and fresh pepper to
taste

Juice of ½ lemon
2 tablespoons finely chopped
parsley

Melt the butter in a skillet until hot. When foamy, add the mushrooms, salt, pepper, and lemon juice. Toss over high heat for 3 minutes. Sprinkle parsley over.
Serves 4–6.

VARIATION:

To vary the flavor of mushrooms, add different herbs. Try tarragon or thyme rather than parsley.

I discovered this method of cooking kohlrabi from a restaurateur student of mine. At first it tastes like turnips or cabbage. It is an intriguing way of fooling your guests. Other vegetables may also be prepared this way, such as turnips, rutabagas, thin slices of onion, leeks, carrots, and potatoes.

Kohlrabi Dauphinois

4–6 medium-size kohlrabi
1 clove garlic, mashed
6 tablespoons butter
Salt and fresh pepper to taste

1 cup shredded Gruyère cheese
¾ cup freshly grated Parmesan
cheese
1½ cups heavy cream or more

Remove leaves and trim kohlrabi. Peel, if desired, and slice as thin as possible in the food processor, on a mandoline, or by hand. Rub a baking dish with the garlic and grease with 2 tablespoons butter. Arrange half the slices in the dish. Salt and pepper them. Scatter the Gruyère cheese over them. Arrange the remainder of the kohlrabi in the dish. Sprinkle with the Parmesan cheese. Dot with slivers of 4 tablespoons butter. Pour the heavy cream carefully into the dish. Shake it to let it settle. Add enough heavy cream to come halfway up the side of the baking dish. Place in a 350° F. oven and bake 45 minutes or until the kohlrabi is tender when pierced with the tip of a knife.
Serves 4–6.

This is exceptionally tasty served at room temperature.

Baked Zucchini and Tomatoes

4–6 medium zucchini, sliced on
    the diagonal, ½-inch slices
4–6 tomatoes, sliced vertically
  2 medium-size red onions, sliced
  2 cloves garlic, chopped
  2 tablespoons chopped parsley

Salt and fresh pepper to taste
2 bay leaves, crumbled
1 tablespoon chopped fresh
  thyme
½ cup olive oil

Grease a baking dish with oil. Alternate the slices of zucchini, tomato, and onion. Pack the vegetables into the dish tightly. Sprinkle with garlic and parsley. Season with salt and pepper. Sprinkle with the bay leaf and thyme. Drizzle the olive oil over the top. Place in a 350° F. oven for 30 minutes or longer, until tender-crisp.

Serves 4–6.

Baked Onions

3 large yellow onions
  Salt and fresh pepper to taste
2 tablespoons butter

½ cup shredded Cheddar cheese
½ cup buttered fresh fine dry
  bread crumbs

Preheat oven to 350° F. Peel onions and cut in half crosswise; season with salt and pepper. Place in shallow 1-quart casserole; add enough water to reach ¼ inch up the sides of the casserole. Cover and bake 45 minutes. Combine cheese and crumbs; sprinkle over onions. Bake uncovered 15 minutes more. *Serves 4–6.*

Broiled Tomatoes

3 large tomatoes
  Salt and fresh pepper to taste
1 egg, beaten

1 cup fresh fine dry bread crumbs
2 tablespoons butter
2 tablespoons brown sugar

Cut thin slices from bottom and top of tomatoes; cut in half crosswise. Sprinkle with salt and pepper. Dip in egg, then bread crumbs. Place on broiler rack with bottom or top side up. Dot each with butter; broil 4 inches from source of heat; turn and repeat on other side. Sprinkle with brown sugar; brown quickly (few seconds) under broiler.   *Serves 4–6.*

Note: If you do not care for sugar on tomatoes, eliminate it.

Okra and Tomatoes

¾ pound okra, sliced	2 tablespoons water
Curry powder to taste	1 clove garlic, chopped
1 medium onion, chopped	1 bay leaf, crumbled
3 tablespoons butter	1 teaspoon chopped thyme
3 medium tomatoes, peeled and chopped	Salt and fresh pepper to taste

In 10-inch skillet, cook okra, curry, and onion in butter about 10 minutes. Add remaining ingredients. Reduce heat to low and simmer about 25 minutes or until vegetables are done.   *Serves 4–6.*

This is a very colorful combination.

Carrots and Zucchini

1 medium onion, chopped	1 pound carrots, thinly sliced
1 tablespoon chopped marjoram	1 pound zucchini, thinly sliced
4 tablespoons butter	Salt and fresh pepper to taste

In 10-inch skillet, cook onion with marjoram in butter until tender. Add carrots and cook 5 minutes, stirring occasionally. Push carrots to one side, add zucchini, and cook 5 minutes more or until vegetables are crisp-tender. Mix or toss cooked vegetables together. Season with salt and pepper.   *Serves 4–6.*

Fritters and Variations

2 eggs	1 teaspoon salt
½ cup milk	1 tablespoon melted shortening
1 cup all-purpose flour	Vegetable oil for deep frying
1 teaspoon baking powder	

Beat eggs on medium speed of electric mixer for at least 1 minute. Add milk. Mix together flour, baking powder, and salt and add to milk mixture. Add shortening. Beat on medium speed until well blended. You can mix in bowl with a whisk if an electric mixer is not available; or use a processor or blender. Stir in desired fruit or vegetable (see variations below). Heat vegetable oil to 375° F. Allow about 3 minutes for frying time of fruits or vegetables. Makes about 1 dozen.   *Serves 4–6.*

VARIATIONS:

Corn Fritters Add 2 cups fresh uncooked corn to standard fritter batter. Drop by spoonfuls into preheated shortening. Serve with maple syrup.

Fruit Fritters Add 1 tablespoon sugar to fritter batter. Mix 1 cup of any fresh fruit—pears, peaches, or slices of oranges—into batter and fry as above. If using apple or banana slices, dip in lemon juice first to prevent discoloration. Drain fritters on brown paper. Sprinkle with confectioners' sugar.

Vegetable Fritters Any cooked or blanched vegetable, such as cauliflower, asparagus, eggplant, may be cut up and added to standard fritter batter. Use about 1 cup. A good way to use leftovers.

Note: For a thinner batter, increase the milk to create a consistency that will just cling to food to be fried.

Green Beans and Julienne Celery

1½ pounds young green beans	2 tablespoons butter
2 large ribs of celery, about 10 inches long	Juice of ½ lemon
	Salt and fresh pepper to taste

Cut off ends of beans. Cut ribs of celery in 2-inch lengths and julienne. Bring a large pot of water to a boil and drop beans in to cook for about 7–8 minutes. Remove and refresh in cold water. Add julienne celery and cook for 5–7 minutes.

Taste for tender-crunch vegetables. Drain vegetables. Mix together. Add butter and squeeze on lemon juice. Season with salt and pepper. Reheat.   *Serves 4–6.*

Shredded Red Cabbage

2½-pound head red cabbage
2 tablespoons butter
½ cup chicken stock
1 cup red wine

¼ cup sugar
Grated rind of 1 orange
Salt and fresh pepper to taste

Remove any bruised outer leaves of cabbage. Cut cabbage in quarters and shred it into a bowl. Melt butter in large saucepan on high heat. Add cabbage and chicken stock. Cover with lid. Cook on high heat until steamed almost tender— 15–20 minutes. Add wine, sugar, orange rind, salt, and pepper. Continue cooking on low heat 10–20 minutes.   *Serves 6.*

Note: To keep cabbage from turning color, add a few drops of vinegar or juice of half a lemon to it after shredding.

It is definitely worth the effort it takes to shell the peas and peel the onions for this dish.

Peas French Style

8 baby white onions, peeled
2 pounds peas, shelled
2 tablespoons butter
Pinch of sugar

1 small head Boston lettuce, shredded
1 tablespoon flour
Salt and fresh pepper to taste

Bring 1½ cups water to a boil. Add the onions and parboil them for 5 minutes. Add the peas, 1 tablespoon of butter, and a pinch of sugar. Cover with the lettuce and cook, covered, over low heat until the peas are tender, about 15 minutes. While the peas are cooking, make a beurre manié by blending together 1 tablespoon of butter and the flour. When the peas are tender, add the beurre manié in small bits and stir until the liquid has thickened. Season with salt and pepper.

Serves 4–6.

These timbales dress up a dinner. Serve them plain, or with melted butter and lemon juice, or reduce 1½ cups heavy cream to 1 cup and add 2 tablespoons chopped fresh dill to serve as a sauce.

Cabbage Timbales

5 tablespoons butter, melted
½ pound cabbage, shredded
¼ cup chopped onion
½ teaspoon caraway seed
Salt and fresh pepper to taste

4 eggs, beaten
1½ cups light cream
2 tablespoons finely chopped
parsley

Preheat oven to 350° F. Generously grease eight ½-cup timbale molds with 2 tablespoons melted butter. Cook cabbage with onion and caraway in covered skillet until barely tender, 15–20 minutes. Stir frequently. Purée in food processor with 3 tablespoons melted butter until smooth. Combine with remaining ingredients. Spoon into prepared molds; set molds in a pan of hot water. Bake 25 minutes or until knife inserted near center comes out clean; unmold.   *Serves 8.*

This loaf is not very high, as it would take too long to cook. If there is time, bake in a smaller loaf pan. Or bake in individual timbale molds or custard cups.

Fresh Asparagus Loaf

1 tablespoon butter for greasing
baking dish
1 pound fresh asparagus
2 tablespoons finely chopped
onion
2 tablespoons chopped parsley

¼ cup butter
1 cup fine fresh bread crumbs
Salt and fresh pepper to taste
3 eggs, beaten
2 cups light cream
½ cup Cheddar cheese, grated

Preheat oven to 375° F. Generously butter a 9-by-5-by-3-inch loaf pan. Clean asparagus and cut into 1-inch pieces (there should be about 2 cups). Cook; drain well. Meanwhile, in skillet, cook onion and parsley in butter; add crumbs, salt, and pepper. In bowl, combine eggs, cream, asparagus, and crumb mixture. Pour into prepared pan. Bake 25 minutes or until set. Let stand 5 minutes before un-molding. Unmold and sprinkle with cheese.   *Serves 4–6.*

Belgian endive is one of those vegetables one either loves or loathes. I like it cooked or uncooked.

Sautéed Belgian Endive

8 Belgian endive	1 cup heavy cream
8 tablespoons butter	2 tablespoons chopped fresh
½ cup chopped shallots	chervil
Juice of ½ lemon	1 lemon, thinly sliced, slices
Salt and fresh pepper to taste	halved

Trim endive. Remove tough cores. Cut across into small pieces. Melt butter in skillet. When hot, add shallots. Sauté 3–4 minutes. Add endive. Squeeze lemon juice over. Season with salt and pepper. Cook, covered, 20 minutes, stirring occasionally. Remove lid and add cream. Continue to cook 10–15 minutes longer. Stir in chervil. Serve with halves of thin lemon slices around edge of serving dish.

Serves 4–6.

The word "asparagus" evokes springtime, and when it is in season I eat it every day. You can also serve it with hollandaise (page 182), vinaigrette (page 176), or polonaise sauce (page 179).

Asparagus with Walnut Butter

24 stalks medium-size asparagus, trimmed and peeled, if desired	½ cup butter
2 tablespoons butter	2 tablespoons black walnuts, chopped
Salt and fresh pepper to taste	

Bring water to boil in a skillet to barely cover asparagus. Add asparagus and cook, uncovered, 7–10 minutes, or until tender-crisp. Drain and plunge into ice water to stop the cooking and refresh the color. To reheat, melt 2 tablespoons butter in skillet. Add drained asparagus and roll in the hot butter. Add salt and pepper. Melt ½ cup butter and add walnuts. Pour over asparagus. *Serves 4–6.*

Green Tomato Sauté

6 green tomatoes
¾ cup bread crumbs
½ cup brown sugar

8 tablespoons butter
Salt and fresh pepper to taste

Cut tomatoes in half. Trim bottoms and tops. Mix together the bread crumbs and brown sugar. Coat the tomato slices on both sides with the bread crumb–sugar mixture. Melt the butter in a large heavy skillet. When hot, add tomatoes and cook *slowly* for 3 minutes on each side. Season with salt and pepper. Tomatoes should be cooked through, crisp on outside. *Serves 6.*

VARIATION:

Add ½ cup heavy cream to juices remaining in pan, raise heat, boil, and scrape for 3 minutes. Pour over tomatoes.

In the summer when the corn and limas are at their peak, this combination is the best. They are the two vegetables I miss when in Europe in the summer.

Succotash

2½ pounds fresh lima beans, shelled
½ cup milk

Salt and fresh pepper to taste
4–5 ears corn on cob, scraped
2 tablespoons butter

Drop lima beans in boiling water to cover. Cook until tender, 10–15 minutes, depending on size. Drain. Return to pan. Add milk, salt, pepper, and corn. Simmer 5 minutes. Add butter and stir well. *Serves 4–6.*

Braised Sliced Celery

2 tablespoons butter
2 tablespoons chopped shallots
4–5 cups sliced celery
1 green pepper, diced

1 cup chicken stock
Salt and fresh pepper to taste
¾ cup Parmesan cheese

Melt butter in skillet. When hot, add shallots. Cook 1–2 minutes. Add celery and green pepper and sauté 2–3 minutes. Add the chicken stock; bring to a boil. Cover. Cook 10 minutes. Remove cover, add salt and pepper, and reduce the liquid in the pan. Add the Parmesan cheese. Stir well.   *Serves 4–6.*

Cooked Herbed Cucumbers

8 cucumbers
4 tablespoons butter
Salt and fresh pepper to taste

2 tablespoons chopped fresh dill, mint, or parsley

Peel and cut cucumbers lengthwise. Remove seeds with tip of spoon. Cut into 2-inch pieces crosswise. Parboil them for 4–5 minutes. Drain them, refresh in cold water, and dry thoroughly. Melt the butter in a fry pan. Add cucumbers and toss them until heated through. Season with salt, pepper, and chopped herb.
Serves 4–6.

Acorn Squash with Glazed Apples

3 small acorn squash (about ½ pound each)
¼ cup sugar

2 tablespoons butter
2 medium apples, peeled, cored, and chopped

Preheat oven to 400° F. Cut squash in half lengthwise; scoop out seeds and stringy pulp. Place cut side down in baking pan; add just enough water to barely cover bottom of pan. Bake 30–40 minutes. Meanwhile, to make glazed apples, in a 6-inch skillet melt sugar over medium heat (do not stir until completely melted). Add butter and apples; continue cooking and stirring until apples are glazed but still hold their shape. To serve, spoon glazed apples and syrup into each squash cavity.

Serves 4–6.

Stuffed Onions

4–6 medium-size sweet Spanish onions
1 pound fresh broccoli
4 tablespoons butter

4 tablespoons freshly grated Parmesan cheese
4 tablespoons light cream
Salt and fresh pepper to taste

Preheat oven to 400° F. Cut about ½ inch off top of onion and thin slice off bottom; peel. Scoop out center of onion, leaving about ½-inch shell (about 2 layers of onion). Cook, covered, in boiling salted water 10–15 minutes or until tender; drain. Wash broccoli well. Trim so flowerets have about 1 inch of stem attached. Cook in boiling salted water until *just* tender (7 minutes). Drain and chop. Meanwhile, chop scooped-out onion. In skillet, cook onion in butter until tender. Add broccoli, Parmesan, and cream; mix well. Season with salt and pepper. Stuff into cooked onion shells, mounding slightly. (Bake extra stuffing, if any, in custard cup.) Place in baking pan with water to just film bottom of pan. Bake 25–30 minutes.

Serves 4–6.

Puréed Butternut Squash

3 pounds butternut squash
1 tablespoon brown sugar
Freshly grated nutmeg to taste

Salt and fresh pepper to taste
1 tablespoon finely chopped parsley

Preheat oven to 375° F. Line baking pan with foil; oil lightly. Cut squash in half lengthwise; place cut side down in baking pan. Bake 30–45 minutes (depending upon size of squash) or until you can easily pierce the flesh with a knife or skewer.

Remove seeds. Scoop out pulp; place in blender or food processor with brown sugar, nutmeg, salt, and pepper. Purée until smooth. Serve garnished with chopped parsley. *Serves 4–6.*

Acorn Squash with Sesame Seeds

3 small acorn squash (about ½
   pound each)
¼ cup melted butter

Salt and fresh pepper to taste
Sesame seeds

Preheat oven to 400° F. Cut squash in half lengthwise; scoop out seeds and stringy pulp. Place cut side down in baking pan; add just enough water to barely cover bottom of pan. Bake 30 minutes; turn cut side up. Meanwhile toast sesame seeds: Place seeds in a shallow pan. Bake until golden, about 10 minutes. Brush squash with melted butter; season with salt and pepper to taste. Sprinkle with sesame seeds. Bake 10 minutes more or until squash is done. *Serves 4–6.*

You can do beet greens, collard greens, mustard greens, kale, Swiss chard, turnip greens, radish greens, and dandelion greens by this same method. Spinach wilts in a couple of minutes. Other greens will vary timewise. Serve with lemon juice and olive oil to taste, if preferred.

Spinach with Brown Butter

2 pounds spinach, well washed
   and tough stems removed
½ cup butter

Freshly grated nutmeg
Salt and fresh pepper to taste

Place spinach in pan with water that clings to it. Stir over medium heat with a wooden spoon until it wilts. Melt the butter in a pan and cook until brown but not burned. Add to spinach with nutmeg, salt, and pepper. Stir well and serve.

Serves 4–6.

Sour Cream Spinach

2 tablespoons butter
¼ cup finely chopped onion
2 pounds fresh spinach, well
washed and tough stems removed

½ cup sour cream
Juice of ½ lemon
Salt and fresh pepper to taste

In large kettle, heat butter on high heat until melted. Add chopped onion, and sauté until cooked but not brown, about 2 minutes. Add spinach to pan, allowing the water that clings to the leaves to remain. Cook spinach on high heat with lid until it steams. Remove lid, and continue to cook on high heat while stirring to reduce some of the liquid. Transfer to smaller pan. Add sour cream and lemon juice. Stir with wooden spatula to combine with the spinach. Add salt and pepper. Keep warm over hot water until ready to serve. *Serves 4–6.*

Boiled Artichokes

4–6 artichokes, 1 inch cut off top,
leaves trimmed with scissors,
and stem removed

1 tablespoon salt

Put artichokes in kettle and cover with 4–6 quarts water. Add salt to water. Bring to a boil and cook for 30–45 minutes, depending on size. If a leaf can be pulled off easily, the artichokes are done. Drain upside down and serve one to a person. Serve these with almond mayonnaise (page 181), vinaigrette (page 176), or hollandaise (page 182). *Serves 4–6.*

Lemony Turnip Sticks

1½ pounds turnips
3 tablespoons butter
Juice of ½ lemon

2 tablespoons chopped parsley
Salt and fresh pepper to taste

Peel turnips. Cut into slices ¼ inch thick. Cut into ¼ inch sticks. Drop in boiling salted water and cook 15 minutes or until tender. Drain. Toss with butter, lemon juice, parsley, salt, and pepper. *Serves 4–6.*

This is good cold the next day. Zucchini may be used instead of summer squash.

Easy Summer Squash

4 medium onions, thinly sliced
6–8 small yellow summer squash,
   thinly sliced (2–2½ pounds)
   Salt and fresh pepper to taste

2–3 tablespoons butter
   Chopped fresh marjoram to
   taste
½ cup heavy cream

Grease an 8- to 9-inch baking dish with a little of the butter. Arrange onions and squash alternately in dish. Sprinkle with salt, pepper, and marjoram between layers and on top. Drizzle heavy cream over top. Place in 375° F. oven for 20 minutes until tender.

Serves 4–6.

Baked Cauliflower

1 cauliflower, trimmed and cut
   into florets (2-2½ pounds)
2–3 tablespoons freshly grated Parmesan cheese

2–3 tablespoons bread crumbs
   Salt and fresh pepper to taste
2–3 tablespoons butter, melted

Steam the florets for 7 minutes, until barely tender. Lay in baking dish, mounding the florets to resemble a whole head of cauliflower. Sprinkle the crumbs and cheese over the cauliflower, sprinkle with salt and pepper, and drizzle the melted butter over. Bake at 350° F. for 5–10 minutes.

Serves 4–6

VARIATION:

This recipe is also good with broccoli instead of cauliflower.

Broiled Tomatoes and Yogurt

3–4 large tomatoes
  1 cup plain yogurt
  2 tablespoons chopped parsley
  2 tablespoons chopped dill

1 cup fresh bread crumbs
  Salt and fresh pepper to taste
1 clove garlic, chopped

Cut tomatoes in half crosswise. Lay them in a baking dish. Mix remaining ingredients and divide among the tomato halves. Spread evenly. Broil 4 inches from unit for 5 minutes.   *Serves 4–6*

Parsnips with Parsley

1½ pounds parsnips, peeled
  1 cup water
    Salt and fresh pepper to taste

1 teaspoon sugar
4 tablespoons butter
2 tablespoons chopped parsley

Shred the parsnips in the food processor or with a hand grater. Put parsnips in a saucepan. Add the water and sugar and bring to a boil. Cover. Cook until tender, about 10–12 minutes. Drain and add butter, salt and pepper; stir until melted. Place in serving dish. Garnish with chopped parsley.   *Serves 4–6.*

Serve this hot as a vegetable or serve at room temperature for a first course. It might seem to be an inordinate amount of oil, but it's necessary, as eggplant actually devours oil.

Baby Eggplant

8 baby eggplants (size of your fist)
¾ cup good olive oil
    Salt and fresh pepper to taste

1–2 tablespoons chopped mint
  2 cloves garlic, chopped
    Few sprigs of fresh thyme

Trim the eggplants. Make 4–5 slits, on an angle, top to bottom, and fan them out flat. Film the bottom of a baking dish with ¼ cup of the olive oil. Lay the eggplant in the dish. Sprinkle over ¼ cup of the oil. Salt and pepper the eggplant. Sprinkle over the garlic, mint, and thyme. Place in 350° F. oven 15 minutes. Remove eggplant and sprinkle over the rest of the oil. Return to oven and bake until barely tender.

Serves 8.

I still have the old slaw cutter that my mother used to make sauerkraut. Most of us don't have the time to make our own sauerkraut today, and it is possible to buy delicious sauerkraut in delicatessens and in farmers' markets. I buy mine from a farmer who sells it directly from a barrel. There are excellent brands available in plastic bags.

Sautéed Sauerkraut

1–2 pounds sauerkraut
4 tablespoons duck fat, vegetable oil, bacon fat, or butter
1 medium onion, peeled and chopped
1 clove garlic, chopped
1 small apple, peeled, cored and chopped
Fresh pepper

Heat fat and add onion, garlic, and apple. Cook 2 minutes and add the sauerkraut (do not drain or wash). Grind some pepper over kraut and stir to mix well. Turn to medium heat and cover. Cook 30–35 minutes. Sauerkraut will be crunchy.

Serves 4–6.

VARIATION:

Sauté ¼ pound finely diced bacon until crisp and add just before serving.

Baby Lima Beans in Chervil Cream

3 pounds baby lima beans, shelled
Salt and fresh pepper to taste

1 cup heavy cream
2 tablespoons finely chopped chervil

Put the shelled beans in a saucepan. Cover with water. Bring to a boil. Cook at a simmer for 10–15 minutes until beans are tender. Don't overcook, as they will split. Drain. Salt and pepper them to taste. Heat the cream and chervil together for 2 minutes while stirring. Pour over beans and serve.   *Serves 4–6.*

Pencil-Thin Asparagus with Walnut Oil

1½ pounds pencil-thin asparagus
Walnut oil

Salt and fresh pepper to taste

Trim any tough ends from the asparagus. Lay them in a large skillet. Cover with boiling water. Bring to a boil and cook 2–3 minutes. Turn off heat. Test one piece to make certain it is tender. Pour off hot water and serve asparagus while very hot. Drizzle with walnut oil, and sprinkle with salt and pepper.   *Serves 4–6.*

Quick Ratatouille

½ cup olive oil
6 medium tomatoes, peeled, seeded, and chopped
1 small eggplant, cubed
2 medium onions, peeled and sliced
3 medium zucchini, sliced

2 garlic cloves, chopped
A few fresh basil leaves, chopped
2 or 3 sprigs of fresh thyme
A little summer savory, if available
Salt and fresh pepper to taste

Place olive oil in large saucepan and heat. Add all ingredients and stir to thoroughly mix. Bring to a boil, turn to simmer, cover, and cook, stirring occasionally, for 30 minutes. Remove cover. If too much liquid remains, remove with a bulb baster, place in a small pan, and reduce to half over medium heat. Return liquid to vegetable mixture. Complete cooking time should be about 45 minutes.

Serves 4–6 generously.

Note: Good hot or tepid. Also good baked in a pastry shell. Leftovers keep well for 3–4 days.

Steamed Green Beans with Lemon and Olive Oil

1½–2 pounds green beans, topped
    and tailed
    Lemon quarters

Olive oil
Salt and fresh pepper to
    taste

Place water in large saucepan (2–3 inches deep in 2-quart saucepan) and insert collapsible steamer in place. Put beans in steamer. Put on lid and bring to a boil. Steam 5–7 minutes, until tender-crisp. Serve with lemon wedges and olive oil in a cruet. Salt and fresh pepper can be available, if desired. *Serves 4–6.*

VARIATION:

Yellow wax beans may be substituted for the green beans. Add 1 tablespoon chopped fresh dill to the yellow beans and toss.

Carrots Steamed in Foil

12–16 thin carrots, peeled and
    trimmed
1 tablespoon butter

1 tablespoon chopped pars-
    ley, dill, or mint
Salt and fresh pepper to taste

Lay carrots on a piece of aluminum foil and put butter on top. Sprinkle over the parsley, dill, or mint. Season with salt and pepper. Fold foil into a tight package. Put package on rack in oven preheated to 375° F. Bake 15 minutes. Open package and pierce a carrot with tip of knife. The carrots should be tender-crisp.

Serves 4–6.

VARIATION:

Try doing other vegetables in foil; I do parsnips, turnips, baby white onions, and small potatoes.

Serve this as a vegetable dinner.

Vegetable Skillet

4 tablespoons cooking oil or
enough to film bottom of pan
3 cups chopped cabbage
1 cup chopped celery
1 cup chopped green pepper

½ cup chopped onion
2 cups chopped seeded tomatoes
1 tablespoon chopped fresh basil
Salt and fresh pepper to taste
1 cup shredded Cheddar cheese

Heat oil in a large skillet. Add cabbage, celery, green pepper, onion, tomatoes, basil, salt, and pepper. Mix well. Cover. Cook over medium heat for about 15 minutes or longer until cabbage is tender but crisp. Remove from heat. Sprinkle with cheese. Toss 2 minutes to melt cheese.   *Serves 4–6.*

This recipe comes from a friend in Egypt.

Carrots with Pistachio Nuts

1½–2 pounds carrots, peeled and
thinly sliced
1½ cups water
Juice of ½ lemon
3 tablespoons butter

¼ cup shelled pistachio nuts
3 tablespoons Grand Marnier
Salt and fresh pepper to
taste

Combine carrots with water and lemon juice in a large skillet. Bring to a boil. Cover. Cook 10–15 minutes or until tender. Drain. Meanwhile, melt butter in a small skillet. Add pistachio nuts. Sauté for 3 minutes. Pour over cooked carrots along with Grand Marnier. Sauté, tossing gently for 5 minutes, or until carrots are glazed. Season with salt and pepper.   *Serves 4–6.*

Summer Squash Sauté

1½ pound small summer squash
    or zucchini
  2 eggs plus 1 tablespoon water,
    beaten
  ¾ cup yellow cornmeal

1 tablespoon chopped fresh
    basil
½ cup oil
    Salt and fresh pepper to taste
    Lemon wedges

Cut squash into 1-inch slices. Pour egg mixture into a shallow dish. Pour cornmeal and basil into another dish. Dip squash slices into egg mixture and then in cornmeal, coating well. Heat ¼ cup oil in a large skillet. Fry zucchini in hot oil, adding more oil if necessary, until golden brown. Drain on paper towels and season with salt and pepper. Serve with lemon wedges.   *Serves 4–6.*

Recipes in this chapter:

PLAIN RICE

BROWN RICE

RICE WITH MUSHROOMS

RICE PILAF

RICE PILAF WITH NOODLES

RICE PILAF WITH CRYSTALLIZED
    GINGER

RICE PILAF WITH GRATED RAW
    CARROTS

RICE PILAF WITH BOUQUET GARNI

PINK RICE PILAF

RICE PILAF WITH GREEN AND RED
    PEPPERS

RICE PILAF WITH ORANGE

RICE PILAF WITH PARSLEY

WILD PECAN RICE PILAF

RICE PILAF WITH SAFFRON AND PEAS

FRIED POTATO RIBBONS

SMALL POTATOES IN STOCK AND
    SAFFRON

BAKED POTATOES WITH BASIL BUTTER

BROILED POTATO SLICES

RED-SKIN POTATOES

BROILED GRATED POTATOES

CHEDDAR CHEESE POTATOES

STUFFED BAKED POTATO HALVES

RED PEPPER POTATOES

POTATO PANCAKES WITH SOUR
    CREAM AND CHIVES

WINE-LACED POTATOES

POTATOES SIMMERED IN CHICKEN
    BROTH

FRIED POTATO AND APPLE CAKE

BAKED POTATOES, CHEESE, AND
    SALAMI

BAKED HAM AND CHEESE POTATOES

SHERRIED YAMS WITH NUTS

Rice Pilaf

½ cup butter or other fat
1 medium finely chopped onion
1 cup long-grain rice
2 cups chicken stock, brown
  stock, or water

Salt and fresh pepper to taste
2 tablespoons finely chopped
  fresh parsley

Melt ¼ cup butter or fat in a heavy casserole (one with a tight-fitting lid) and sauté the onion over high heat. When onion is translucent but not brown (about 2 minutes), add the rice. Stir it around to coat the grains with butter. Add stock or water, salt, and pepper. Bring mixture to a full boil over high heat, then cover it tightly and reduce heat to simmer. Cook exactly 23 minutes (use a timer, if possible), and do not lift the lid during this time. Then lift the lid, fluff up the rice with two forks, sprinkle with the remaining ¼ cup butter, which you have melted, and border with chopped parsley.   *Serves 6.*

VARIATION:

Pack rice into buttered timbale molds or custard cups, pack down with back of spoon, and invert. Or pack into a ring mold or charlotte mold.

Rice Pilaf with Noodles

4 tablespoons butter
1 cup fine noodles, uncooked
1 cup rice
2 cups chicken stock

Salt and fresh pepper to taste
½ cup freshly grated Parmesan
  cheese
¼ cup chopped parsley

Melt butter in 2-quart saucepan. Add noodles and rice. Sauté until golden brown. Stir in chicken stock, salt, and pepper. Bring to a boil. Cover. Simmer for about 25 minutes or until rice and noodles are tender and stock is absorbed. Add Parmesan cheese and parsley; toss lightly.   *Serves 4–6.*

Rice Pilaf with Crystallized Ginger

Rice Pilaf (see page 105)
¼ cup finely chopped crystallized
  ginger

Stir crystallized ginger into cooked pilaf and fluff up with two forks. *Serves 6.*

Rice Pilaf with Grated Raw Carrots

½ cup carrots peeled and shredded by hand or in food processor
Rice Pilaf (see page 105)

Stir carrots into cooked pilaf and fluff with two forks. *Serves 6.*

Rice Pilaf with Bouquet Garni

1 celery rib
1 tablespoon parsley sprigs, stems
  removed

Few sprigs of fresh thyme
Bay leaf
Rice Pilaf (see page 105)

Make bouquet garni by laying celery rib on counter. Into its hollow put parsley, thyme, and bay. Fold in half by breaking celery. Tie tightly, leaving string on end for easy removal. Place on rice to cook. Remove before serving. *Serves 6.*

Pink Rice Pilaf

Rice Pilaf (see page 105)
2 medium tomatoes, peeled, seeded and finely chopped

Add tomatoes along with the rice. *Serves 6.*

Rice Pilaf with Green and Red Peppers

Rice Pilaf (see page 105)
4 tablespoons finely chopped red pepper

4 tablespoons finely chopped green pepper

Add peppers with onion.   *Serves 6.*

Rice Pilaf with Orange

Rice Pilaf (see page 105)
½ cup orange juice

1 tablespoon grated orange rind

Substitute ½ cup orange juice for some of stock and add 1 tablespoon grated orange rind.   *Serves 6.*

Rice Pilaf with Parsley

½ cup chopped parsley
Rice Pilaf (see page 105)

Add parsley to pilaf before serving.   *Serves 6.*

Wild Pecan Rice Pilaf

Substitute wild pecan rice for white rice in basic pilaf recipe. Wild pecan rice grows under pecan trees in Louisiana and Mississippi. It takes on the flavor of pecans and is delicious.

Rice Pilaf with Saffron and Peas

2 tablespoons butter
2 tablespoons olive oil
1 medium onion, finely
   chopped
½ teaspoon chopped garlic
1½ cups long-grain rice

½ cup shelled fresh peas
1 teaspoon saffron threads
3 cups chicken stock
   Salt and freshly cracked white
   pepper to taste

Using a heavy casserole that has a tight-fitting lid, heat the butter and oil. Sauté, but do not brown, the onion and garlic (this will take about 3 minutes). Add the rice and peas, stirring around to coat the grains and peas with butter and oil. Dissolve saffron in 1 tablespoon of the stock. Pour remaining stock into the casserole and add the dissolved saffron, salt, and pepper. Bring to a full boil over high heat; immediately cover tightly and reduce heat to simmer. Without lifting lid, cook for 23 minutes. Then remove lid and fluff the rice with two forks. *Serves 6.*

Fried Potato Ribbons

2 or 3 large Idaho potatoes,
   washed but not peeled

Fat for frying
Salt to taste

Place potatoes in a Benriner slicer. Turn the handle and watch the potatoes emerge from the other end in long ribbons. Fill a deep frying pan with fat to a depth of 2 inches. When hot, 375° F., drop ribbons in fat and fry 3–4 minutes. Drain on paper towel. Salt just before serving. *Serves 4–6.*

Note: I purchased the Benriner slicer from a mail order catalog. It's a plastic device with 3 blades; it looks like a large pencil sharpener. If you don't have one, these potatoes can be cut on a mandoline, sliced paper-thin, and then julienned. They are good but not as much fun as the ribbons. A new gadget for doing this job has recently appeared on the market. It is made by Daisy.

Small Potatoes in Stock and Saffron

½–1 teaspoon saffron
1½ cups chicken stock
16–20 small new potatoes,
washed

Salt and fresh pepper to
taste
2 tablespoons butter, melted

Dissolve the saffron in the stock. Place potatoes in a saucepan and pour the stock over. Add salt and pepper. Bring to a boil, cover, and turn to simmer. Cook until potatoes are barely tender, about 8–10 minutes. Pierce each potato with the point of a knife to absorb stock, and continue to cook another 5 minutes. Remove potatoes to a serving dish. Pour melted butter over them. Reduce the saffron stock, if any is left, in the pan and pour over potatoes. *Serves 4–6.*

VARIATION:

Cook the potatoes in water to cover for 10–15 minutes, more or less. Serve warm, adding ¼ cup olive oil and 3 tablespoons finely chopped chives. Toss with salt and fresh pepper to taste. These are unusually good served with Basil Butter (see page 58).

If you prefer, serve baked potatoes with 1 cup yogurt combined with 4 table-spoons chopped chives. Or serve with 1 cup yogurt or cottage cheese combined with ½ cup sliced radishes. Or try a Flavored Butter (see page 169). When I am dieting, I frequently eat a baked potato with nothing on it: I have it as a main course with a salad.

Baked Potatoes with Basil Butter

4–6 Idaho potatoes

Basil Butter (see page 58)

Thoroughly scrub potatoes and place on a rack in a 425° F. preheated oven. Bake 40–55 minutes. Remove, cut a cross on top, and fluff up each potato. Spoon basil sauce over potato. *Serves 4–6.*

Broiled Potato Slices

5 Idaho potatoes   Coarse salt
⅓ cup oil   Freshly cracked pepper

Preheat broiler. Scrub potatoes well. Cut into ¼-inch slices. Place on a baking sheet. Brush potatoes with oil. Broil 6 inches from heat for 7 minutes. Turn and brush with oil. Broil 8 minutes. Drain on paper towels. Sprinkle with coarse salt, and freshly cracked pepper.   *Serves 4–6.*

Red-Skin Potatoes

2–3 red-skin walnut-size potatoes   Salt and fresh pepper to taste
    per person   1–2 tablespoons chives, parsley, or
4 tablespoons butter, melted   dill

Put potatoes in saucepan. Cover with water. Bring to a boil. Boil 10–15 minutes, just until tender. Drain. Return to pan. Add butter, salt, pepper, and herb. Toss.

Serve 2–3 to each person.

Broiled Grated Potatoes

4 medium baking potatoes   2 tablespoons butter, melted
⅔ cup half-and-half cream   Paprika
    Salt and fresh pepper to taste
½ teaspoon finely chopped fresh
    thyme

Peel, dice, and cook potatoes until fork tender. Place in food processor with just quick off-and-on turns to give grated appearance. Or grate by hand. Add cream, salt, pepper, and thyme, stirring potatoes lightly. Use some melted butter to cover bottom of baking dish. Add potato mixture and drizzle on remaining butter. Sprinkle paprika on top. Place under broiler 5–6 inches from top of potatoes to lightly brown—12–15 minutes.

Serves 4–6.

VARIATION:

Bake, instead of broiling, 18–20 minutes at 375° F.

Cheddar Cheese Potatoes

6 tablespoons melted butter
3 large Idaho potatoes, scrubbed and thinly sliced (about 1½ pounds)

Salt and fresh pepper to taste
¾ cup grated Cheddar cheese

Cover bottom of 6-inch skillet with some butter. Layer potatoes in bottom of skillet, overlapping slightly; drizzle with more butter; season with salt and pepper. Repeat layers until all potatoes are used. Place over medium heat until butter is hot and sizzles. Reduce heat to low and cook, covered, about 30 minutes or until potatoes are tender and bottom layer is browned. Sprinkle with cheese; cover and heat a few minutes until cheese melts. Invert onto serving platter.   *Serves 4–6.*

Note: It's not necessary to peel the potatoes.

Stuffed Baked Potato Halves

¾ pound mild or sweet Italian sausage, casing removed
1 large shallot, finely chopped

4 tablespoons butter, melted
4–6 small baking potatoes

Preheat oven to 375° F. Mix sausage and chopped shallot. Melt butter in small sauté pan. Peel potatoes; cut in half lengthwise. Carefully hollow out centers with melon ball cutter, allowing ½-inch-thick edge (potato halves look like a baked potato shell before stuffing). Rinse potatoes in cold water, pat dry with paper towels, roll each potato in melted butter, and place in a small baking dish or pan. Add remainder of melted butter to baking dish. Stuff sausage mix in each potato half. Cover with aluminum foil or wrap each potato in foil and place on small baking sheet. Bake at 375° F. for 30–35 minutes or until fork tender.   *Serves 4–6.*

These potatoes have been a family favorite for years.

Red Pepper Potatoes

6 medium-size potatoes
1 onion, chopped
¾ cup diced sweet red pepper

4 tablespoons butter
Salt and fresh pepper to taste

Peel and cut potatoes into small cubes. Cook in boiling salted water in a medium saucepan until tender, about 15 minutes. Drain. Sauté onion and red peppers in butter in a 10-inch skillet until soft but not brown. Stir in drained potatoes, salt, and pepper. Toss lightly. Sauté, stirring occasionally, for about 5 minutes or until potatoes are golden brown.   *Serves 6–8.*

These pancakes are great served with any of the fruit toppings in this book or with applesauce.

Potato Pancakes with Sour Cream and Chives

2 potatoes, scrubbed, cut into
   pieces (do not peel)
1 small onion, peeled and cut in
   quarters
1 egg, beaten

1–2 tablespoons flour
Salt and fresh pepper to taste
Oil for frying
1 cup sour cream
¼ cup chopped chives

Place the potatoes and onion in blender or food processor, and process until potatoes are finely chopped. Place in a bowl and spoon off any liquid. Add the egg, flour, salt, and pepper and mix well. In an 8-inch frying pan or skillet, place oil to come ¼ inch up sides of pan. When hot, drop the potato mixture in with a tablespoon. Flatten each with the back of the spoon. Fry 4 at a time. Cook 2–3 minutes on one side until brown, turn once, and brown other side, 2–3 minutes. Mix the sour cream and chives together in a bowl and spoon over the pancakes at the table.   *Makes 14–16 three-inch pancakes.*

Wine-Laced Potatoes

1 tablespoon butter
2 tablespoons oil
3 cups potatoes sliced ¼ inch thick

Salt and fresh pepper to taste
½ cup chopped chives
¼ cup white wine

Melt butter with oil in large skillet. Add potatoes, salt, pepper, and chives. Sauté about 15 minutes or until golden brown, turning occasionally. Stir in wine. Cover. Cook 5 minutes.   *Serves 4–6.*

Potatoes Simmered in Chicken Broth

½ cup chopped onion
½ cup chopped celery
½ cup shredded carrots
1 clove garlic, chopped
2 tablespoons butter
1½ cups chicken stock
2 pounds potatoes, peeled and cut in quarters

1 tablespoon chopped fresh basil
Salt and fresh pepper to taste
¼ cup freshly grated Parmesan cheese
¼ cup chopped parsley

Sauté onion, celery, carrots, and garlic in hot butter in a large skillet until tender. Add chicken stock, potatoes, basil, salt, and pepper. Cover. Simmer for 10 minutes. Remove cover. Simmer for 10 minutes or until potatoes are tender and broth is reduced. Sprinkle with Parmesan cheese and parsley.   *Serves 4–6.*

Fried Potato and Apple Cake

As served to me several years ago at the Restaurant D'Olympe in Paris.

1 pound potatoes, cut in chunks
and boiled 10 minutes
1 apple (½ pound), cored and cut
in chunks

Freshly grated nutmeg to taste
6 tablespoons butter

Roughly grate the potatoes in food processor or by hand. Put into a bowl. Grate the apple and combine. Season with nutmeg. Melt 4 tablespoons butter in non-stick 8-inch fry pan. Add apple-potato mixture and press down into a cake. Put on a lid. Cook on medium heat until bottom is brown, about 20 minutes. Keep the cake loose by sliding a spatula underneath. Remove lid and add butter to pan, putting pieces around the edge of the cake to keep it from sticking too much. Continue cooking slowly a few minutes more until brown and crispy on the bottom. To serve, carefully invert potato cake onto a round platter. Cut into pie-shaped wedges to serve.

Serves 4–6.

Note: Season with salt and fresh pepper if you like, but I do not find it necessary.

These can be eaten out of hand or with knife and fork. Place potatoes in paper napkin. No need for butter or salt.

Baked Potatoes, Cheese, and Salami

6 Idaho potatoes
6 strips of salami or ham (4 inches
long by ½ inch wide)
6 strips of Muenster or Cheddar
cheese (4 inches long by ½ inch
wide)

Chopped parsley

Scrub potatoes thoroughly. Bake at 450° F. for 40–45 minutes or until done. Remove from oven. Cut a long vertical gash in each potato. Squeeze potatoes. Insert a strip of salami and cheese into each potato. Sprinkle with parsley.

Serves 4–6.

Baked Ham and Cheese Potatoes

6 medium-sized baking potatoes	Salt and fresh pepper to taste
1 cup diced ham	1½ cups sour cream
¼ cup chopped green pepper	½ cup shredded Swiss cheese
2 tablespoons chopped shallots	

Bake potatoes in a hot oven (450° F.) for 40–45 minutes or until done. Make a cross on top of each potato. Squeeze gently to split open. Combine ham, green pepper, shallots, salt, pepper, and sour cream in a small saucepan. Heat gently; do not boil. Spoon hot sour cream mixture over potatoes. Sprinkle each with shredded Swiss cheese.

Serves 6.

Serve these potatoes out of the shell as mashed sherried yams. The deep orange color of the yams looks attractive on the plate, and the rich moist flavor enhances almost any entrée, especially ham.

Sherried Yams with Nuts

6 medium yams	¼ cup light cream
¼ cup softened butter	⅓ cup coarsely chopped nuts:
¼ cup sherry	peanuts, cashews, pecans, etc.

Preheat oven to 400° F. Bake yams about 40 minutes or until tender. Cut slice off top of potato. Scoop out potato, keeping skin intact. Combine in bowl with butter and sherry; mix well with electric mixer or by hand. Add enough cream to make potatoes light and fluffy. Add nuts; stuff mixture back into shells. If necessary, just before serving heat for 5 minutes.

Serves 4–6.

Recipes in this chapter:

MY MOTHER'S SWEETBREAD AND
  CUCUMBER SALAD

BROILED SALAD WITH THYME

ZUCCHINI AND RED ONION SALAD

SHRIMP AND HONEYDEW SALAD

GRAPEFRUIT SALAD WITH
  WATERCRESS DRESSING

AVOCADO AND RICE SALAD

CREAMY SALAD DRESSING

BIBB LETTUCE WITH TOMATO
  MAYONNAISE

BUTTERMILK DRESSING

CUCUMBER MELON SALAD WITH
  LEMON–PEPPER DRESSING

ORANGE AND RED ONION SALAD

SUMMER FRUIT SALAD

ACCORDION TOMATO AND
  CUCUMBER SALAD

BIBB LETTUCE AND CHERRY TOMATO
  SALAD

BACON, TOMATO, AND RICE SALAD

BLACK WALNUT SALAD DRESSING

AVOCADOS WITH OIL AND VINEGAR

CHEESE AND OLIVE TOSSED SALAD

CREAMY AVOCADO DRESSING

AVOCADO, PINK GRAPEFRUIT, AND
  ORANGE SALAD

DANDELION SALAD

CURRIED POTATO SALAD IN GREEN
  PEPPER SHELLS

PINEAPPLE AND GREEN PEPPER SALAD

CRUNCHY WINTER SALAD

SWEET-AND-SOUR GREENS

GREEN PEA AND SWISS CHEESE SALAD

GORGONZOLA COLE SLAW

TURNIP, RADISH, AND ROMAINE SALAD

COTTAGE CHEESE AND TOMATO
  SALAD ON LETTUCE WEDGES

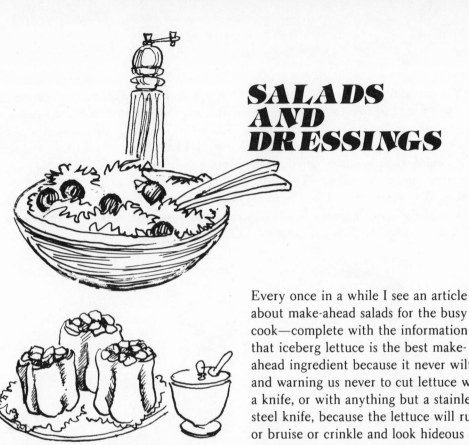

SALADS AND DRESSINGS

Every once in a while I see an article about make-ahead salads for the busy cook—complete with the information that iceberg lettuce is the best make-ahead ingredient because it never wilts, and warning us never to cut lettuce with a knife, or with anything but a stainless steel knife, because the lettuce will rust or bruise or crinkle and look hideous on the salad plate. All nonsense. I've been cutting lettuce with a knife for years. Cutting does not bruise romaine or even the soft buttery lettuces. The cut edges do not rust or wilt in the short time it takes lettuce to go from the knife to the salad bowl.

No salad needs make-ahead preparation—salads are quick and easy, and they give a quick meal a feeling of completeness and elegance. If you are really rushed, it's better to skip the vegetables rather than the salad—the meal will look less bare.

Cabbage is one of the longest-keeping vegetables, and it can be shredded almost instantly to make Gorgonzola coleslaw or crunchy winter salad. Try to keep some on hand for emergencies.

You can vary your salads easily by switching from romaine to Boston to Bibb to curly endive to red leaf lettuce. Vary vinaigrettes by changing to walnut oil or different oils in combination, and use sherry vinegar, or red or white wine vinegar. When good lettuce is difficult to find and you haven't even a head of cabbage, don't use second-best lettuce; serve relishes like radishes, celery hearts, cucumber, or zucchini sticks. In summer I serve big beefsteak tomatoes as a salad, simply sliced, alone or with slices of red onion, plain or drizzled with a bit of good olive oil and a few drops of vinegar. When tomatoes are ripe and fresh and local, they taste much too good to fool with.

This old-fashioned salad is enjoying a revival. It was a company staple in our house, as my mother always served it to very special guests. Now rediscovered, it is making its way onto the menus of elegant "new cuisine" restaurants. Which only goes to show that there's nothing older than even the newest cuisine.

My Mother's Sweetbread and Cucumber Salad

2 pairs large sweetbreads
1 lemon, cut in half
3 small cucumbers, peeled, seeded, and thinly sliced
   Salt and fresh pepper to taste

⅔ cup mayonnaise, preferably homemade
½ cup heavy cream, whipped
   Lettuce leaves
2 tablespoons finely chopped dill

Put sweetbreads into a pan. Cover with cold water and juice of ½ lemon. Bring to a boil. Turn to simmer and cook 15–20 minutes. Drain. Plunge into ice water for 5 minutes to stiffen them. Remove and take off membranes and remove tubes. Cut sweetbreads into cubes. Add the cucumber, juice of ½ lemon, and salt and pepper. Combine the mayonnaise and whipped cream and fold into the sweetbread mixture. Line a bowl with lettuce leaves and fill with salad. Garnish with dill.

Serves 4–6.

Broiled Salad with Thyme

4 Belgian endive
2 fennel bulbs, inside part
8 large mushrooms
1 red onion
   Salt and fresh pepper to taste

2 teaspoons finely chopped fresh
   thyme, or more
4 tablespoons olive oil
   Juice of 1½ lemons

Cut all vegetables into julienne strips. Place on shallow baking pan. Sprinkle over salt and pepper, thyme, and olive oil. Mix well. Set under the broiler 4 inches from unit for about 3 minutes. Toss the vegetables and return to broiler. Cook until vegetables are done, about 5–6 minutes. Remove. Squeeze lemon juice over the vegetables and serve warm.   *Serves 4–6.*

Zucchini and Red Onion Salad

4 small zucchini, sliced (1 pound)
2 medium red onions, sliced
1 large bunch escarole, in bite-size
   pieces

Vinaigrette (see page 176)

Combine all ingredients in bowl. Toss and serve.   *Serves 4–6.*

Shrimp and Honeydew Salad

1½ pounds shrimp, cooked and
   deveined (if long, cut into
   thirds; if small, leave whole)
1 cup thinly sliced celery
   Juice of ½ lemon
1 honeydew melon, cut into
   melon balls

¼ cup homemade mayonnaise
¼ cup sour cream
   Salt and fresh pepper to taste
   Boston lettuce
   Watercress

Combine shrimp, celery, and lemon juice. Refrigerate. Just before serving, drain off liquid. Combine shrimp and melon balls. Add mayonnaise, sour cream, salt, and pepper. (Add enough pepper here, as it points up the melon.) Toss lightly with a fork. Serve in Boston lettuce cups with a few sprigs of watercress on the side.

Serves 4–6.

Grapefruit Salad with Watercress Dressing

3–4 large grapefruit
½ cup olive oil
Juice of 1 lime
1 shallot, finely chopped
Salt and fresh pepper to taste

1 bunch watercress, stems removed and chopped medium coarse
Boston lettuce

Peel and section grapefruit. Chill in refrigerator while making dressing. Whisk olive oil into lime juice, chopped shallot, and seasoning. Add watercress. Chill while arranging grapefruit sections in spokelike design on Boston lettuce. When ready to serve, add a tablespoon of watercress dressing to center of salad.

Serves 4–6.

Avocado and Rice Salad

Rice Pilaf (see page 105)
2 tablespoons lemon juice
2 tablespoons olive oil
8–10 stuffed green olives, sliced

2 tablespoons chopped chervil
3 ripe avocados
Lettuce cups or red curly lettuce if in season

Toss rice with 1 tablespoon lemon juice, olive oil, olives, and chervil. Chill in refrigerator while cutting avocados in half lengthwise. Remove pits. Peel fruit and sprinkle with 1 tablespoon of lemon juice to keep from discoloring. Hollow out a larger hole in center of each avocado half. Fill center with a large mound of the cold rice and serve on your selection of lettuce.

Serves 6.

*Good on cold chicken, fish, meat, or vegetables, aside from salad greens or toma-
to slices.*

Creamy Salad Dressing

4 tablespoons vegetable oil
4 tablespoons heavy cream
3 tablespoons wine vinegar

1 tablespoon Dijon mustard
Salt and fresh pepper to taste

Beat all ingredients in bowl with whisk until thick.   *Makes ¾ cup.*

Bibb Lettuce with Tomato Mayonnaise

1 cup mayonnaise, preferably
   homemade
¼ cup heavy cream
1 tomato, peeled, seeded, and
   finely diced

Bibb lettuce leaves

Thin mayonnaise with heavy cream. Add the diced tomato. Taste for seasoning.
Serve over Bibb lettuce leaves.   *Serves 4–6.*

Serve on raw spinach, cucumber slices, or sliced tomatoes.

Buttermilk Dressing

1 cup buttermilk
1 tablespoon horseradish

1 teaspoon Dijon mustard
Salt and fresh pepper to taste

Combine all ingredients in a bowl and whisk. Or put in a jar and shake.
                Makes 1 cup.

Lemon-pepper dressing is especially good over escarole. Be sure to add all the pepper.

Cucumber Melon Salad with Lemon-Pepper Dressing

2 cucumbers, peeled, seeded, and thinly sliced
1 large cantaloupe, cut in chunks
Lettuce leaves
1 teaspoon Dijon mustard
Salt to taste

1 teaspoon coarsely cracked fresh pepper
Juice of 2 lemons
¾ cup vegetable oil
2 tablespoons finely chopped mint

Mix cucumbers and cantaloupe together. Place on lettuce leaves. Put mustard, salt, and pepper in a small bowl. Add lemon juice. Mix with whisk. Gradually whisk in the oil. Sprinkle mint over top. Spoon dressing over salad.   *Serves 4–6.*

Freshly chopped rosemary is delicious in this salad.

Orange and Red Onion Salad

2 bunches watercress, stems removed
4 oranges, peeled, seeded, and thinly sliced

2 medium-size red onions
Vinaigrette (see page 176)

Arrange watercress on each salad plate. Place the orange slices on the watercress. Thinly slice one onion and finely chop the other one. Sprinkle half the chopped onion on the orange slices; add the other chopped half to the vinaigrette. Arrange the sliced onion over the orange and chopped onion. Spoon dressing over each salad.   *Serves 4–6.*

Summer Fruit Salad

1 cup honey
¼ cup lime juice
1 large honeydew melon

1 medium cantaloupe
1 cup grapes

Combine honey and lime juice to make dressing. Blend well. Chill while preparing fruit. Cut honeydew into 6 wedges; seed and peel. Cut cantaloupe crosswise into slices about 1 inch thick; seed, peel, and cut in half. Place honeydew on chilled salad plate, arch cantaloupe slice over melon and garnish each serving with few grapes. Serve with dressing.   *Serves 4–6.*

Accordion Tomato and Cucumber Salad

1 tomato per person
½ medium unpeeled cucumber
  per person

2 tablespoons freshly chopped chives
Vinaigrette (see page 176)

Peel tomatoes, if you wish. Stand each tomato on stem end. Make seven slits top to bottom, but not all the way through. Slice the cucumber into seven slices and insert them in the slits. Lay each tomato accordion on individual salad plate. Drizzle vinaigrette over each. Sprinkle with chives.

Bibb Lettuce and Cherry Tomato Salad

3–4 heads Bibb lettuce, washed
  and dried
12–16 cherry tomatoes, stemmed

2 tablespoons chopped chives
Vinaigrette (see page 176)
Salt and fresh pepper

Arrange lettuce in salad bowl. Add tomatoes. Sprinkle with chopped chives. Pour enough dressing over to coat greens. Season to taste. Toss.   *Serves 4–6.*

Bacon, Tomato, and Rice Salad

3 cups cooked rice
½ pound bacon, cooked and
  crumbled
2 medium tomatoes, peeled,
  seeded, and chopped

¼ cup chopped green onions
½ cup mayonnaise, preferably
  homemade
Salt and fresh pepper to taste
Salad greens

Combine all ingredients except salad greens; mix well. Pack into 5-cup mold or bowl. To serve, unmold on salad greens. Serve at room temperature.   *Serves 4-6.*

Black Walnut Salad Dressing

1 teaspoon Dijon mustard
  Salt and fresh pepper to taste
¼ cup red wine vinegar

¼ cup walnut oil
¼ cup olive oil
¼ cup chopped black walnuts

Put the mustard, salt, pepper, and vinegar in a small bowl. Whisk to mix. Add the oils gradually while whisking. Fold in walnuts. Pour over salad greens.

Makes about 1 cup.

Avocados with Oil and Vinegar

½ avocado per person
  Cruets of good olive oil and
  vinegar

Salt and fresh pepper to taste

Serve ½ avocado to each person and pass the cruets for each person to help himself. Salt and pepper should also be provided.

Cheese and Olive Tossed Salad

6 cups mixed greens
½ cup chopped green onions
¼ cup chopped red pepper
½ cup pitted ripe olives, sliced

3 tomatoes, quartered
½ cup shredded Cheddar cheese
Creamy Avocado Dressing (following recipe)

Combine greens, green onions, pepper, olives, and tomatoes in large salad bowl. Sprinkle with cheese. Top with avocado dressing. Toss lightly but thoroughly.

Serves 4–6.

Creamy Avocado Dressing

1 large ripe avocado, pitted, peeled, and mashed
Juice of ½ lemon
½ cup sour cream

¼ cup oil
½ teaspoon chili powder
Salt and fresh pepper to taste

Combine all ingredients in a bowl. Mix well.

Serves 4–6.

Avocado, Pink Grapefruit, and Orange Salad

2 ripe avocados, peeled, pitted and cut into eighths
1 large pink grapefruit, peeled and opened into 14 sections
2 oranges, peeled and opened into 16 sections

1 bunch watercress
Fresh mint (optional)
Cruets of oil and vinegar

Arrange the slices of avocado, grapefruit, and orange alternately on individual plates. Tuck watercress leaves on each. Sprinkle with mint if you like. Pass the cruets of oil and vinegar.

Serves 4–6.

Dandelion Salad

2 quarts dandelion greens, washed and dried
½ lb. bacon, diced and cooked crisp
  Bacon fat
2 garlic cloves, peeled and chopped

1 tablespoon sugar
1 tablespoon dry mustard
  Salt and fresh pepper to taste
¼ cup red wine vinegar

Put greens in salad bowl and sprinkle bacon on top. Into the bacon fat in fry pan, put the garlic, sugar, mustard, salt, pepper, and vinegar. Bring to a boil. Pour over salad. Toss quickly and serve. *Serves 4–6.*

VARIATIONS:

Add 1 cup sautéed croutons to salad and/or 1 onion, grated. Use curly endive when dandelion is out of season.

Curried Potato Salad in Green Pepper Shells

6 medium potatoes
¼ cup chopped green pepper
½ cup chopped celery
1 cup mayonnaise, preferably homemade, or ½ cup sour cream and ½ cup mayonnaise

2 teaspoons curry powder
3 tablespoons chopped chives
  Salt and fresh pepper to taste
6 medium green peppers

Cook potatoes in boiling salted water until tender. Drain. Cool slightly. Remove skins and cube. Combine warm potatoes with chopped green pepper and celery in a large bowl. Combine mayonnaise, curry powder, chives, salt, and pepper. Stir into potatoes and toss gently to coat. Cut slices off tops of green peppers. Remove seeds and membrane. Parboil in boiling water for 5 minutes. Drain and plunge into ice water. Pat dry. Spoon potato salad into pepper shells. *Serves 6.*

VARIATION:

Try dressing the potatoes while hot with vinaigrette.

Pineapple and Green Pepper Salad

2 green peppers
1 medium pineapple, cubed
4 tablespoons sherry vinegar

8 tablespoons olive oil
Salt and fresh pepper to taste

Cut peppers in half, remove the seeds and pith, and cut into strips. Add the pineapple, vinegar, oil, salt, and pepper. Toss well before serving. *Serves 4–6.*

Crunchy Winter Salad

1 cup coarsely grated raw turnip
3 cups shredded cabbage
2 cups diced red apples
½ cup chopped peanuts

Juice of ½ lemon
1 cup mayonnaise, preferably homemade, or ½ cup sour cream and ½ cup mayonnaise

Combine turnip, cabbage, apples, and peanuts in a large bowl. Blend together lemon juice and mayonnaise. Add to salad. Toss well. *Serves 4–6.*

Sweet-and-Sour Greens

6 strips bacon
¼ cup cider vinegar
¼ cup water
1 tablespoon sugar

3 cups torn romaine leaves
3 cups torn fresh spinach
4 hard-cooked eggs, sliced
Salt and fresh pepper to taste

Fry bacon in a large skillet until crisp. Remove and drain on paper towels. Pour off drippings except for 2 tablespoons. Add vinegar, water, and sugar to drippings. Bring to boil. Boil 1 minute, stirring constantly. Combine romaine, spinach, and eggs in a large bowl. Pour hot dressing over them. Toss lightly but thoroughly. Add salt and fresh pepper as desired. *Serves 4–6.*

Green Pea and Swiss Cheese Salad

1½ pounds peas in shell
Juice of ½ lemon or lime
¼ cup olive oil
1 clove garlic, chopped
Salt and fresh pepper to taste

1 cup thinly sliced celery
2 cups diced Swiss cheese (½-inch cubes)
1 tablespoon finely chopped dill
Lettuce

Shell peas and place in a saucepan. Add ¼ cup water. Cook 7–10 minutes or until tender. Drain peas and refresh in cold water to set the color. Put into a bowl and add the lemon or lime juice, oil, garlic, salt, and pepper. Mix well. Add the celery, cheese, and dill. Mix again and serve from a lettuce-lined bowl. *Serves 4–6.*

Gorgonzola Cole Slaw

4 cups shredded cabbage
1 cup mayonnaise, preferably homemade
¼ cup milk
1 tablespoon grated onion

1 cup crumbled Gorgonzola cheese
1 cup shredded carrots
½ cup chopped green pepper
Salt and fresh pepper to taste

Crisp shredded cabbage in ice water. Drain. Blend mayonnaise, milk, and onion. Stir in Gorgonzola cheese. Combine cabbage, carrots, and green pepper in large bowl. Add mayonnaise-cheese mixture. Season with salt and pepper. Toss gently but thoroughly until vegetables are well coated. *Serves 4–6.*

Turnip, Radish, and Romaine Salad

½ cup grated raw turnip
½ cup thinly sliced celery
1 cup thinly sliced radishes
4 cups shredded romaine

¼ cup oil
2 tablespoons white vinegar
Salt and fresh pepper to taste

Combine turnips, celery, radishes, and romaine in a large bowl. Blend oil, vinegar, salt, and pepper together. Pour over salad. Toss. *Serves 4–6.*

Cottage Cheese and Tomato Salad on Lettuce Wedges

1½ cups cottage cheese
1½ cups sour cream
   1 cup peeled, seeded, and diced
      cucumber
   1 cup sliced radishes

½ cup chopped green onions
Salt and fresh pepper to taste
Lettuce wedges
Tomato quarters

Combine cottage cheese, sour cream, cucumber, radishes, onions, salt, and pepper; mix well. For each serving, spoon over 4–6 lettuce wedges. Garnish with tomato quarters. *Serves 4–6.*

Recipes in this chapter:

CORN BREAD

MELBA ROUNDS AND FINGERS

BUTTERFINGERS

HOMEMADE BISCUIT MIX

HOT BISCUITS

PANCAKES AND WAFFLES

FRUIT TOPPINGS FOR PANCAKES,
    WAFFLES, CRÊPES, ICE CREAM,
    CAKE

BANANA NUT BREAD

OLD-FASHIONED WHEAT BATTER
    BREAD

GOLDEN POPOVERS

COTTAGE CHEESE PANCAKES

LEMON SCONES

OPEN-FACE CHEESE RADISH
    SANDWICH

CHEDDAR CHEESE PORT WINE SPREAD

BAKED CHEESE FONDUE

CHEESE COOKIES

GRILLED CHEESE AND GREEN PEPPER
    SANDWICH

TOMATO RAREBIT SANDWICH

CHEESE CUSTARDS

STILTON CHEESE WITH CELERY

BAKED BACON AND EGGS

CHICKEN LIVERS AND EGGS

EGGS INDIENNE

STUFFED EGGS SUPREME

MAGGIE AND JIGGS SOUFFLÉ

EGG TIMBALES

BAKED EGGS IN ENGLISH MUFFIN AND
    BACON NESTS

EGG SALAD ROLLED IN LETTUCE
    LEAVES

VERMOUTH-GLAZED EGGS

CHEESE, EGGS, BREADS, AND PANCAKES

You can make bread in one hour—from start to finish, including mixing, kneading, and baking. It will be a slightly heavier loaf than a two- or three-hour bread, because it is a batter bread with no yeast. But it keeps well and it has a wonderful taste right out of the oven. Contrary to whatever else you have heard, fresh bread is at its best hot from the oven. I think that old story about its giving you a stomachache and heartburn was started by nervous mothers who realized they had to tell us something—otherwise there wouldn't be any bread left for dinner. I always eat my bread the minute it comes out of the oven, and I never have had a problem.

Hot breads used to be a staple in Grandmother's day. Though we were always warned about bread, we always had hot biscuits or corn bread on the table. This is another of those old-fashioned ideas that need reviving. Hot biscuits make any meal look like more, and they don't take any time at all. You

131

can even make up your own biscuit mix (see page 134) and whip up a batch in minutes. Look around a dining room in a Southern resort hotel and watch sophisticated people wolfing down hot muffins and good old cornbread. There is something about these American hot breads that brings out the appetite in everybody. It's more than food. It's more than soul food. It's soul-satisfying food.

Waffles and pancakes are the great American breakfast, as American as apple pie, and maybe a little more so. Waffles are so easy and quick—there is nothing simpler than bringing the waffle iron to the table and just cooking as you eat. A portable electric griddle makes pancake preparation simple. I've had my waffle iron twenty years and it's so well seasoned that I don't even have to throw away the first waffle anymore. But for weeks and months I forget all about it. Then some Sunday night when I've been working late and I look up at the clock and finally think: Oh, what's in the house for supper? someone will say, "How about waffles?" I break out the old waffle iron and all the toppings I can think of and have a late-night feast.

It is easy to think of cheese and eggs in combination—they are versatile and can appear in every course from appetizer through the entrée and right on to dessert.

Arguments are still raging in the South as to whether sugar should be added or not. Suit yourself. This corn bread is good when herbs or spices of your choice are added to it. Sage is especially good to serve with fowl.

Corn Bread

1 cup flour	4 teaspoons baking powder
1 cup yellow cornmeal	2 eggs, beaten
½ teaspoon salt	1 cup milk
2 tablespoons sugar (optional)	⅓ cup butter, melted

Mix all dry ingredients in a large mixing bowl. Make a well in the center. Combine eggs, milk, and butter and add to the dry ingredients. Stir until smooth.

Butter an 8-inch-square baking pan. Pour in the batter. Place in a 425° F. oven and bake 25–30 minutes, or until the top is golden brown. Cut into 12–16 squares.

Melba Rounds and Fingers

12 slices thin bread   ½ cup butter, melted

For Rounds

Cut rounds from bread, using a 2-inch cutter. Lay on baking sheet. Brush with butter. Bake at 350° F. for 15–20 minutes or longer.   *Makes 24 rounds.*

For Fingers

Cut off crusts. Cut bread into thirds. Brush with the butter and bake as above.
                                                                    Makes 36 fingers.

Note: Use trimmings remaining from bread for crumbs.

Serve these with soup. They are tasty sprinkled with cinnamon and sugar and served as a snack or with tea in the afternoon.

Butterfingers

1 pound loaf bread, sliced and   ½ pound butter, melted
   crusts removed

There should be 16 slices of bread. Cut each slice in 3 pieces. Dip them, one by one, into the melted butter. Lay on baking sheet and bake at 350° F. until bread is toasted, about 20 minutes.   *Makes 48 pieces.*

Homemade Biscuit Mix

6 cups flour	1 tablespoon salt
3 tablespoons baking powder	1 cup vegetable shortening

Put flour and baking powder into a bowl. Add the salt. Cut in the shortening until mixture resembles cornmeal. Store in a covered container. It is not necessary to refrigerate, but I do. To use this mix:

2½ cups mix	Flour for board
¾ cup milk	1 tablespoon butter

Blend the mix and milk together in a bowl. Knead very lightly for 2 minutes. Roll out on a lightly floured board ½ inch thick. Cut into 1½-inch rounds. Place on greased baking sheet. Bake at 425° F. for 15 minutes.   *Makes 20 biscuits.*

Note: Buttermilk can be substituted for milk, in which case add ½ teaspoon soda.

Biscuits were a staple of family meals in my grandmother's day. The secret to good biscuits is not to overmix.

Hot Biscuits

1 tablespoon butter for greasing baking pan	1 teaspoon salt
2 cups flour	1 teaspoon sugar
2 teaspoons baking powder	4 tablespoons butter
	¾ cup milk

Butter a baking sheet. Put flour, baking powder, salt, and sugar into a bowl. Rub in the 4 tablespoons butter until mixture looks like coarse cornmeal. Add milk. Mix well to make a soft dough. Turn out on lightly floured board. Pat out ¾ inch thick. Cut biscuits into 2-inch rounds or cut into 2-inch squares with a knife. Place on buttered baking pan and bake at 450° F. for 12–15 minutes or until biscuits are golden.   *Makes 12 biscuits.*

VARIATIONS:

Chive Biscuits: Add ¼ cup chopped chives to flour and shortening mixture.

Herb Biscuits: Add your favorite herb—2 tablespoons thyme or 1 tablespoon sage.

Spicy Biscuits: Add your favorite spice—1 tablespoon caraway or poppy seed or 1 teaspoon cinnamon.

Saffron Biscuits: Add ½ teaspoon saffron to milk to dissolve.

Orange Biscuits: Add 2 tablespoons grated orange rind to flour and shortening mixture. Before baking, press a tiny sugar cube dipped in orange juice into top of each biscuit.

Pancakes and Waffles

1¼ cups flour	2 eggs, beaten
2 tablespoons sugar	1 cup milk
2 teaspoons baking powder	3 tablespoons oil
½ teaspoon salt	

Pancakes

In bowl, combine dry ingredients; add remaining ingredients, beating just until smooth. Preheat griddle according to manufacturer's directions; grease lightly. Spoon about ¼ cup batter on griddle for each pancake. Cook until top is bubbly and dry; turn and cook to brown underside.   *Makes about ten 5-inch pancakes.*

VARIATIONS:

Ham and Cheese: Increase to 1¼ cups milk; add ½ cup finely chopped ham and ¼ cup grated Parmesan cheese.

Banana Nut: Add 1 cup mashed ripe bananas and ¼ cup chopped nuts.

Wheat Germ: Decrease flour to 1 cup and add ¼ cup wheat germ with dry ingredients.

Bacon: Substitute bacon drippings for oil and add 8 slices crumbled, cooked bacon.

(continued)

Waffles

In basic recipe, increase to 3 tablespoons sugar and ¼ cup oil. Preheat waffle iron according to manufacturer's directions; grease lightly. Spoon about ¼ cup batter on griddle for each waffle. Cook until steam stops during cooking. Makes 8 waffles.

Variations for pancakes can also be used for waffle batter.

You can omit the starch in the toppings, but then the fruit will be more juicy. Serve the pancakes or waffles with maple butter or honey and brandy mixed together.

FRUIT TOPPINGS

For Pancakes, Waffles, Crêpes, Ice Cream, Cake

½ cup sugar	2 cups sliced strawberries
1 teaspoon cornstarch	1 tablespoon butter
½ cup water	½ teaspoon lemon juice

In saucepan, combine sugar and cornstarch. Blend in water until smooth. Cook over medium heat, stirring constantly, until slightly thickened. Add fruit; simmer *just until* fruit begins to cook. Remove from heat; add butter and lemon juice.

Makes about 2 cups.

VARIATIONS:

Blueberries: Increase cornstarch to 2 teaspoons; substitute blueberries for strawberries.

Black Cherries: Increase cornstarch to 2 teaspoons; substitute cherries for strawberries. Omit lemon juice and add 1 tablespoon cherry liqueur.

Peach: Increase cornstarch to 2 teaspoons; substitute sliced peaches for strawberries.

Banana Nut Bread

½ cup softened butter
1 cup sugar
1 cup mashed bananas
2 eggs, well beaten
1 teaspoon lemon juice

1 teaspoon baking soda
2 tablespoons boiling water
1¾ cups flour
1 cup chopped walnuts

Preheat oven to 350° F. Generously grease 3 loaf pans (5½ by 3 by 2 inches). In bowl, cream together butter and sugar. Add bananas, eggs, and lemon juice. Dissolve baking soda in water. Add with flour to banana mixture, stirring until just blended. Add nuts. Divide batter among prepared pans. Bake 35 minutes or until done. Remove from pans to baking rack to cool.   *Makes 3 loaves.*

This bread is rather heavy, but very tasty. Now there is no excuse not to have homemade bread in under an hour.

Old-Fashioned Wheat Batter Bread

2½ cups flour
2 tablespoons packed brown sugar
2 teaspoons baking powder
1 teaspoon baking soda

½ teaspoon salt
2 tablespoons butter
1 cup whole wheat flour
1½ cups buttermilk

Preheat oven to 375° F. Generously grease a 7-inch round cake pan. In bowl, combine white flour, sugar, baking powder, baking soda, and salt. Cut in butter until like coarse cornmeal. Add whole wheat flour and buttermilk; mix. Knead on lightly floured board 5–6 times. Place in prepared pan. With floured knife, cut cross almost to bottom of batter. Bake 40 minutes. If desired, brush with melted butter. Remove from pan to cool.   *Makes 1 loaf.*

Golden Popovers

Oil for greasing molds
2 eggs
1 cup milk

¼ teaspoon salt, if desired
1 cup flour

Preheat oven to 450° F. Grease 10 iron popover pans or individual custard cups very well. Place pans or cups in oven while it is preheating. Place eggs, milk, and salt in blender. Cover and blend at high speed until bubbly. Add flour and blend at high speed until perfectly smooth. Remove heated popover pans and fill half full. Bake at 450° for 15 minutes. Reduce heat to 350° and bake 15–20 minutes longer.
Makes 10 popovers.

Cottage Cheese Pancakes

1 cup cottage cheese
1 cup sour cream
4 eggs

¾ cup flour
1 tablespoon sugar
¼ teaspoon salt

In bowl, combine cottage cheese, sour cream, and eggs; beat until smooth. Add dry ingredients; mix until well blended. Heat griddle according to manufacturer's directions. Drop batter onto hot griddle (¼ cup batter per pancake makes 14 four-inch pancakes; 2 tablespoons batter makes 28 three-inch pancakes). Cook until bubbles appear around edge; turn and brown on second side.

Serve these hot with jam when your Aunt Gertrude comes to tea.

Lemon Scones

3 cups flour
1 teaspoon baking powder
½ teaspoon baking soda
½ teaspoon salt
2 tablespoons sugar

⅓ cup soft butter
2 tablespoons lemon rind
¼ cup lemon juice
¾ cup buttermilk
1 egg, separated

Preheat oven to 425° F. Grease baking sheet. In bowl, combine dry ingredients. With pastry blender, cut in butter until well blended. Add lemon rind, juice, buttermilk, and egg yolk; mix well. Toss on lightly floured board; knead 30 seconds. Roll to ¼ inch thick; cut with diamond cookie cutters. Place on prepared sheet; brush with egg white and sprinkle with additional sugar. Bake 10–12 minutes.　　　　　　　　　　　　　　　　　　　　　　　**Makes 36 scones.**

Open-Face Cheese Radish Sandwich

2 cups cottage cheese	6 slices rye or pumpernickel toast
¼ cup sour cream	1 cup thinly sliced radishes
¼ cup snipped chives	Watercress

Combine cheese, sour cream, and chives in a small bowl; mix well. Spread mixture on each slice of toast. Sprinkle radishes over cheese surface. Wreath each sandwich with watercress.　　　　　　　　　　　　　　　　　　*Serves 4–6.*

Serve with drinks at cocktail time, spread on crackers, melba toast or pumpernickel bread. Or serve instead of dessert.

Cheddar Cheese Port Wine Spread

½ pound sharp Cheddar cheese, grated	½ cup finely chopped pecans
	¼ cup port wine
3 ounces cream cheese, softened	¼ cup chopped parsley

Combine cheeses, pecans, and wine in a small bowl or food processor. Blend well. Shape into a 4-inch mound. Sprinkle with chopped parsley.　　*Makes 1 generous cup.*

Baked Cheese Fondue

1 tablespoon butter for greasing
   baking dish
5 eggs, separated
1¼ cups scalded milk

2 teaspoons Dijon mustard
   Salt and fresh pepper to taste
2 cups soft bread cubes
½ pound Cheddar cheese, grated

Preheat oven to 325° F. Generously butter a 1-quart casserole. In bowl, combine egg yolks, milk, mustard, salt, and pepper; mix well. Add bread cubes and cheese. Using clean bowl and beater, beat whites until soft peaks form; fold into cheese mixture. Carefully pour into prepared casserole. Set in pan of hot water; bake 30 minutes or until knife inserted near center comes out clean. *Serves 4–6.*

Cheese Cookies

2½ cups shredded sharp Cheddar
   cheese at room temperature
½ cup butter, softened
¼ cup milk
1 tablespoon Dijon mustard

¾ cup cornmeal
¾ cup flour
½ teaspoon salt
   Chopped dill
   or paprika

Preheat oven to 375° F. Grease two baking sheets. In bowl, combine cheese, butter, milk and mustard. Beat well with electric mixer. Add cornmeal, flour, and salt; mix well (will be a stiff dough). Force through cookie press onto prepared baking sheet. Sprinkle with dill or paprika as desired. Bake 10 minutes or until lightly browned around edges. *Makes about 5 dozen cookies.*

Grilled Cheese and Green Pepper Sandwich

½–¾ pound cheese, grated (medi-
   um-sharp Colby melts very
   well)
¼–½ cup finely chopped green
   pepper

1 tablespoon Dijon mustard
   Salt and fresh pepper to
   taste
4–6 slices of bread: white,
   whole wheat or rye

Mix all ingredients except bread in a bowl. Toast one side of bread placed on broiler pan 4–5 inches from heat. Turn toast to other side and pile cheese mixture evenly over bread slices. Broil 4–5 minutes or until melted.　　*Serves 4–6.*

Tomato Rarebit Sandwich

3 tablespoons butter	1 egg, beaten
3 tablespoons flour	6 slices toast
1 clove garlic, chopped	6 slices tomato
1 teaspoon Dijon mustard	6 slices cooked bacon
1½ cups milk	Salt and fresh pepper to taste
2 cups shredded sharp Cheddar cheese	

In saucepan, melt butter; blend in flour, garlic, and mustard. Gradually stir in milk. Cook, stirring constantly, until thickened. Add cheese and stir until it melts. Pour a small amount over egg; blend well. Return to pan and cook about 1 minute. In individual serving dishes, place 1 slice toast; top with 1 slice tomato. Top with about ⅓ cup cheese mixture and 1 slice bacon, cut in half.　　*Serves 6.*

These are especially good served with a fresh tomato sauce and/or sautéed mushrooms.

Cheese Custards

2¼ cups heavy cream	1 cup shredded Swiss cheese
4 eggs	½ cup freshly grated Parmesan cheese
Salt and fresh pepper to taste	
Freshly grated nutmeg to taste	

Preheat oven to 350° F. Grease six 6-ounce custard cups. In small bowl, combine cream, eggs, and seasonings; mix well. Stir in cheeses. Pour into prepared custard cups. Set in pan of hot water. Bake 35–40 minutes or until knife inserted near center comes out clean. Serve at once.　　*Serves 6.*

Serve French bread and butter or water biscuits along with this appetizer.

Stilton Cheese with Celery

1 whole Stilton cheese   Celery hearts

Scrape top from Stilton cheese. Wrap the cheese neatly with a white napkin. Serve the cheese with a silver cheese scoop. Place crisp celery hearts in a tall glass. Eat the celery along with the cheese.

Baked Bacon and Eggs

12 slices bacon, cooked and   12 eggs
   drained   ¾ cup heavy cream
½ pound Gruyère cheese, thinly   Salt and fresh pepper to taste
   sliced

Arrange bacon in a shallow baking dish. Cover with thin slices of cheese. Break eggs over cheese. Drizzle the cream over the whites of the eggs. Put dish in a larger pan with hot water half-way up egg dish. Set into a 350° F. oven and bake 15 minutes until eggs are set. Salt and pepper eggs, if desired.   *Serves 6.*

Chicken Livers and Eggs

2 tablespoons butter   6 eggs
½ pound chicken livers   ¼ cup light cream
2 tablespoons snipped chives   Salt and fresh pepper to taste

Melt butter in large skillet. Add livers. Sauté until livers are lightly browned, about 5 minutes. Sprinkle chives over liver. Beat eggs with cream, salt, and pepper. Stir into skillet. Cook over low heat, stirring occasionally, until eggs are softly set.   *Serves 4–6.*

Eggs Indienne

¼ cup butter
¼ cup minced onion
1 clove garlic, chopped
½ teaspoon grated fresh ginger
¼ cup flour
2 teaspoons curry powder*
1½ cups chicken stock
1½ cups light cream

½ cup seedless raisins
1 medium apple, cored and chopped
8 hard-cooked eggs, chopped
4–6 English muffins, toasted
1 avocado, sliced

In saucepan melt the butter. When hot, add onion, garlic, and ginger and cook for 5 minutes. Blend in flour and curry. Cook, stirring, 1 minute. Remove from heat. Add stock and cream. Cook, stirring, until thickened. Add raisins, apple, and eggs; heat. Serve over English muffins; garnish with slices of avocado.   *Serves 6.*

*Amount of curry may vary, depending on hotness.

Stuffed Eggs Supreme

¼ pound mushrooms, chopped
1 teaspoon chopped tarragon leaves
8 tablespoons butter
3 tablespoons flour
Salt and fresh pepper to taste

2½ cups light cream
1 cup grated Swiss cheese
3 tablespoons grated Parmesan cheese
8 hard-cooked eggs
1 cup soft bread crumbs

Preheat oven to 350° F. In small skillet, cook mushrooms with tarragon in 2 tablespoons butter until all liquid evaporates. Melt 4 tablespoons butter in another saucepan. Blend in flour, salt and pepper. Cook, stirring 1 minute. Add cream; cook, stirring until mixture boils and thickens slightly. Remove from heat. Add Swiss cheese and 2 tablespoons Parmesan; stir until cheese melts. To assemble, cut eggs in half lengthwise. Place yolks in small bowl; mash. Add cooked mushrooms and ¼ cup sauce; mix well. Fill whites with yolk mixture. Pour half the sauce in a shallow 1½-quart casserole (11 by 7 by 2 inches). Arrange eggs in sauce; top with remaining sauce. Combine bread crumbs, remaining 1 tablespoon Parmesan cheese, and 2 tablespoons melted butter; toss well. Sprinkle over casserole. Bake 15–20 minutes or until bubbly.   *Serves 4-6.*

I named this after Maggie and Jiggs in the comic strips because Jiggs is fond of ham and cabbage or corned beef and cabbage.

Maggie and Jiggs Soufflé

1 cup finely chopped ham	¼ teaspoon salt
2 cups finely chopped cabbage	⅛ teaspoon freshly cracked pepper
¼ cup butter	per
¼ cup flour	4 egg yolks, slightly beaten
1 teaspoon Dijon mustard	6 egg whites
1 cup chicken stock	⅛ teaspoon cream of tartar

Preheat oven to 375° F. Butter a 6-cup soufflé dish. In saucepan, cook ham and cabbage in butter until tender. Add flour and mustard and stir with wooden spatula. Add chicken stock, salt, and pepper. Whisk until smooth and thickened. Add a small amount to egg yolks; return mixture to pan. Cook, stirring, for 1 minute. Using clean bowl and beaters, beat egg whites with cream of tartar until stiff peaks form. Mix small amount of egg whites into vegetable mixture. Gently fold in remaining whites. Spoon into soufflé dish. Bake 30 minutes.   *Serves 4–6.*

Egg Timbales

2 tablespoons butter	Few sprigs of fresh thyme
2 tablespoons chopped shallots	¾ cup light cream, scalded
1 tablespoon flour	3 eggs, separated
Salt and fresh pepper to taste	2 tablespoons chopped parsley
Freshly grated nutmeg to taste	Tomato Sauce (see page 177)

Preheat oven to 325° F. Generously butter 8 timbale molds (½–¾ cup). In saucepan melt butter and sauté the shallots. Combine flour, salt, pepper, and nutmeg. Add to butter; cook, stirring a few minutes, to cook flour. Add thyme. Gradually add cream, whisking constantly, until thickened. In large bowl, beat egg yolks until thick and lemon-colored. Gradually add sauce mixture, whisking constantly so eggs will not cook. Add parsley. Using clean bowl and beaters, beat egg whites until stiff peaks form. Fold into yolk mixture. Spoon into prepared molds, filling almost to top (mixture rises like soufflé as it bakes, then falls upon cooling). Place molds in pan of hot water. Bake 25 minutes or until knife inserted near center comes out clean. Let stand 5 minutes before removing from mold. Serve with fresh tomato sauce. (Some people will eat 1, others 2.)   *Serves 4–6.*

Baked Eggs in English Muffin and Bacon Nests

3 English muffins, split
12 slices bacon, partially cooked

6 eggs
2 tablespoons chopped parsley

Place 6 English muffin halves on a baking sheet. Shape two slices of bacon around base of each muffin. Fasten with toothpicks (if bacon slices are long enough to encircle the muffin, one slice is fine). Crack egg onto base of each muffin. Bake at 375° F. for 15 minutes or until egg is set. Sprinkle with parsley. *Serves 4–6.*

These rolls can be eaten out of hand and are excellent for a picnic.

Egg Salad Rolled in Lettuce Leaves

6 hard-cooked eggs, chopped
2 tablespoons chopped scallions
¼ cup sour cream

1 tablespoon chopped dill
Salt and pepper to taste
6 lettuce leaves

In bowl, combine all ingredients except lettuce leaves. Set aside. Blanch lettuce in boiling water; drain well. Place about ⅓ cup egg salad in each leaf; roll. *Serves 6.*

VARIATIONS:

Substitute curry powder for dill. Use as a spread on cucumber slices.

Really quick and easy.

Vermouth-Glazed Eggs

3 tablespoons butter
6 eggs
Salt and fresh pepper to taste

⅓ cup dry vermouth
¼ cup chopped parsley

Melt butter in a large skillet until hot and foamy. Break eggs into hot butter. Add salt and pepper. Cook for 2 minutes until barely set. Pour vermouth over eggs. Cover. Cook about 3 minutes or until eggs are set. Sprinkle with chopped parsley.

Serves 4–6.

Recipes in this chapter:

DESSERTS

Stop.

Before you read any of the recipes in this section, think a minute. You are going to make a meal in one hour. That means you are going to have to spend most of the time on the entrée. Maybe you should think about keeping the dessert fairly simple.

At least check the menus in the back of the book and make sure that you are not combining the most complicated and time-consuming entrée with the most involved dessert and appetizer. You can't have dinner ready in an hour if it consists of three forty-minute dishes.

One of the simplest and one of the very best desserts is fresh fruit. You don't need a recipe for this—just see the dessert ideas on page 164 as a reminder of how varied fresh fruit can be.

Fresh Figs in Curaçao

1 cup sour cream	12 fresh figs, peeled and halved
¼ cup curaçao	1 tablespoon brandy

Combine cream and curaçao. Separately combine figs and brandy. Let stand 15 minutes. Drain figs and gently fold into cream mixture.   *Serves 4–6.*

VARIATION:

The fresh figs can also be served with cream or covered with port wine.

Almond Coffee Cake

1 cup blanched almonds	4 eggs
2¼ cups sugar	4½ cups flour
10 tablespoons butter, softened	1 tablespoon baking powder
2 teaspoons vanilla extract	

Preheat oven to 350°F. In covered blender or food processor blend almonds until ground. In large bowl, cream together sugar, butter, and vanilla. Add 3 eggs; mix well. Stir in almonds. Combine flour and baking powder; gradually add to almond mixture, stirring to make a stiff dough. Turn onto lightly floured board; knead just to blend. (Can be made ahead to this point and refrigerated.) Divide dough in half. Press each half into 10-inch circle on well-greased baking sheet. Beat remaining egg; brush over top of cake. Using tines of fork, make crisscross pattern over top of cake. Bake 20 minutes; serve warm.   *Makes two 10-inch coffee cakes.*

Daiquiri Peaches

½ cup honey	Rum
Juice of 2 limes	Freshly grated nutmeg to
6–8 peaches, halved, stoned, and peeled	taste
	½ cup sour cream

Mix honey and lime juice together. Dip peaches in the mixture. Place the peaches cut side up in a shallow baking pan. Fill the center of each peach with 2 table-spoons rum and sprinkle with nutmeg. Place under broiler for 2 minutes or until light brown. Serve with sour cream.   *Serves 4–6.*

Fried Peaches

4 tablespoons butter	½ cup heavy cream
6–8 peaches, halved, stoned, and peeled	Freshly grated nutmeg to taste
1 cup light brown sugar	

Melt the butter in a skillet. Add the peaches. Sprinkle with the sugar. Let simmer, uncovered, about 20–30 minutes, turning frequently, When just ready to serve, add the cream. Serve hot sprinkled with nutmeg.   *Serves 4–6.*

VARIATION:

Substitute nectarines, apples, or pears.

Glazed Pears

6 ripe Bosc pears	½ cup orange juice
1 teaspoon grated orange rind	¼ cup Cointreau
Freshly grated nutmeg	

Halve, core, and peel pears. Place cut side up in a large, shallow, buttered baking dish. Combine orange rind, nutmeg, orange juice, and Cointreau in a small sauce-pan. Heat to boiling. Pour over pears. Cover with foil. Bake at 350° F. for 30 minutes or until tender, basting 3 times with orange mixture. Serve warm.

Serves 6.

VARIATION:

Substitute peaches for pears and serve with sour or heavy cream.

Very rich, not overly sweet, fudgy type.

Toasted Almond Fudgies

½ cup butter
3 squares unsweetened chocolate
¾ cup sugar
1 teaspoon vanilla extract

2 eggs
½ cup flour
¼ cup slivered toasted almonds

Grease an 8-by-8-by-2-inch baking dish. Melt ½ cup butter and chocolate in saucepan over very low heat. Remove from heat and beat in sugar and vanilla. Beat in eggs. Add flour. Mix well. Add nuts and pour into prepared pan. Bake at 350° F. for 30–40 minutes. Cut into squares.   *Makes about 12–16 squares.*

Broiled Fruits with Sugar Crust

1 tablespoon butter, softened
2 oranges, diced
1 large banana, sliced
3 pears, peeled, cored, and sliced
1 apple, cored and thinly sliced
¾ cup brown sugar

½ cup finely chopped pecans
6 tablespoons melted butter
Juice of ½ lemon
1 teaspoon grated lemon rind, or more

Arrange fruits in a buttered 10-inch baking dish. Combine remaining ingredients. Sprinkle over fruit. Broil about 8 inches from heat for 8–10 minutes or until mixture is melted and bubbly. Cool 10 minutes before serving.   *Serves 4-6.*

Honey-Glazed Peaches

6 large peaches, halved, stoned, and peeled
½ cup honey

2 tablespoons butter
Juice of ½ lemon
1 teaspoon grated lemon rind

Arrange peaches in a shallow greased baking dish, cut side up. Combine honey, 2 tablespoons butter, lemon juice, and rind in a small saucepan. Bring to a boil. Pour over peaches. Cover with foil. Bake at 350° F. for 20 minutes, basting with syrup several times. Serve warm. *Serves 4–6.*

VARIATION:

Substitute pears for peaches and serve with heavy or sour cream.

This dessert separates into a wet cake with creamy sauce underneath. It's scrumptious served with coffee ice cream.

Hot Fudge Baked Pudding

1¼ cups flour
¾ cup sugar
¼ cup cocoa
3 teaspoons baking powder
½ teaspoon salt
¾ cup milk
2 tablespoons butter, melted

1 teaspoon vanilla extract
¾ cup chopped pecans
½ cup brown sugar
3 tablespoons cocoa
1½ cups boiling water
Whipped cream

Combine flour, sugar, cocoa, baking powder, and salt in a bowl. Add milk, butter, and vanilla. Beat well. Stir in pecans. Spread batter in buttered 13-by-9-by-2-inch baking pan. Combine brown sugar and cocoa. Sprinkle over batter. Pour boiling water over mixture. Bake at 350° F. for 40 minutes. Cool 15–20 minutes. Cut in 12 squares. Serve very warm topped with whipped cream. *Serves 12.*

Nectarines in Curaçao

6–8 nectarines, peeled, pitted, and
    sliced

¼ cup curaçao or more
Mint leaves

Arrange nectarine slices in a bowl. Sprinkle over the curaçao. Toss to coat well. Let stand 15 minutes. Garnish each serving with fresh mint leaves. *Serves 4–6.*

This is the only way I will eat rhubarb for dessert.

Stewed Rhubarb, Strawberries, and Bananas

2 pounds rhubarb, trimmed and cut into 1-inch pieces
¾ cup sugar, or less
1 cup strawberries, hulled and sliced

1–2 medium bananas, peeled and sliced
Sour cream (optional)

Put rhubarb and sugar in a saucepan. Simmer slowly until it reaches doneness desired, 10–15 minutes or less. Remove from stove. Add the berries and bananas. Mix well. Serve warm or chill. Put a tablespoon of sour cream on top of each serving if you like.   *Serves 4–6.*

Sangría Grapes

1 lemon, sliced
1 orange, sliced
2 tablespoons sugar
2 cups red wine

¼ cup brandy
3–4 cups seedless grapes, stemmed, rinsed, and dried
4–6 small cinnamon sticks

Place lemon and orange in pitcher. Add sugar, wine, and brandy. Place grapes in 4–6 stemmed glasses. Add wine mixture to each glass. Add a lemon and orange slice to each. Garnish with cinnamon stick. Chill until ready to serve.   *Serves 4–6.*

Cardamom Peaches

1 cup sugar
1 cup water
2 cups white wine
1-inch vanilla bean

1 teaspoon crushed cardamom seeds, or more
6 peaches, halved, stoned, and peeled

Bring sugar, water, wine, vanilla, and cardamom to a boil in a saucepan. Boil 5 minutes. Turn to simmer. Add the peaches, cover, and simmer 10–20 minutes, depending on ripeness of fruit. To test, pierce fruit with tip of small knife.

Serves 4–6.

VARIATION:

Pears may be substituted for peaches.

Fruit Compote

3 navel oranges, peeled and sectioned	1 tablespoon sugar
	Freshly grated nutmeg to taste
1 cup seedless grapes, halved	1 teaspoon grated fresh ginger
1 pint strawberries, sliced	

Combine fruits in bowl. Combine sugar and spices. Toss with fruit. Refrigerate until ready to serve.

Serves 4–6.

VARIATION:

Just before serving, blend in 1 cup plain yogurt.

South Seas Compote

1 pint strawberries, hulled and cut in half	¾ cup fresh orange juice
	¼ cup honey
3 large oranges, peeled and sectioned	2 bananas, sliced
	Freshly grated coconut

Place strawberries and oranges in serving bowl. Combine orange juice and honey; mix well. Pour over fruit. Refrigerate until ready to serve. Add bananas and mix. Serve garnished with coconut.

Serves 4–6.

Spiced Fall Compote

4 large cooking apples
1 cup water
¼ cup sugar
1 stick cinnamon broken in 2–3 pieces
1 tablespoon butter
Salt to taste
3 large oranges, peeled and sectioned

Grated rind of 1 lemon
¼ cup red wine
¼ cup Grand Marnier, curaçao, or Cointreau
½ cup chopped walnuts

Peel, core, and slice apples; reserve skins. In small saucepan, combine skins and water; bring to a boil. Reduce heat and cook over low heat about 10 minutes. Meanwhile, in another saucepan, combine apples, sugar, cinnamon, butter, and salt. Add liquid from skins; bring to a boil. Reduce heat and cook, stirring occasionally, over low heat until apples are *just barely* tender (about 5–8 minutes); remove cinnamon. Combine with remaining ingredients except walnuts in serving bowl; refrigerate until ready to serve. Serve garnished with walnuts.   *Serves 4–6.*

Baked Lemon Soufflé with Rum Sauce

¼ cup butter
¼ cup flour
1 cup milk
¼ cup sugar
5 egg yolks
Grated rind of 1 lemon
¼ cup lemon juice
7 egg whites

Sauce:

2 egg yolks, beaten
3 tablespoons sugar
1 cup milk
2 tablespoons rum
½ cup heavy cream, whipped

Preheat oven to 375° F. Generously butter and lightly sugar a 6-cup soufflé dish; set aside. In saucepan, melt butter; blend in flour. Gradually add milk. Cook, stirring constantly, until mixture comes to boil and thickens. Add sugar, stir, and remove from burner. Beat yolks until thick and lemon-colored. Add to flour mixture with lemon rind and juice. Place mixture in bowl. Set in freezer to chill. Meanwhile, beat egg whites until stiff but not dry. Add a small amount of egg whites to custard mixture; mix well. Gently fold egg whites into custard mixture. Pour into prepared soufflé dish. Bake 30 minutes or until browned on top.

While soufflé is baking, prepare sauce. In saucepan, combine egg yolks and sugar; gradually add milk. Cook, stirring constantly, until mixture thickens slightly and coats metal spoon. Remove from heat; add rum. Chill in freezer. About 5 minutes before soufflé is done, fold chilled custard sauce into whipped cream. Serve over soufflé.

Serves 4–6.

Strawberries Dipped in White Chocolate

¾ pound white chocolate, cut up   30 large strawberries

Put the chocolate in a saucepan and melt slowly while stirring over direct heat. (Or do it over simmering water.) Do not scorch. Remove from stove when melted. Hold berries by stem end and dip the pointed ends into the white chocolate halfway up the berry. Twist the berry to remove excess chocolate. Place on a baking sheet lined with wax paper. Refrigerate 10–15 minutes to set.

Rich Apple Bars

Crust:

¾ cup butter, softened
¼ cup sugar
1 egg, beaten
1 teaspoon vanilla extract
2 cups flour
¼ teaspoon salt

Topping:

½ cup flour
⅓ cup sugar
½ cup butter, softened

Filling:

5 cups peeled and thinly sliced tart cooking apples
Juice of ½ lemon
¼ cup sugar
3 tablespoons flour
2 teaspoons grated lemon rind
About 1 teaspoon freshly grated nutmeg, or less
1½ cups grated sharp Cheddar cheese

Preheat oven to 425° F. Grease jelly-roll pan (15 by 10 by 1 inch). Combine all ingredients for crust; mix well. Press firmly into prepared pan. Combine apples with lemon juice; toss to coat well with remaining filling ingredients. Arrange over crust. Combine flour and sugar for topping; cut in butter until mixture is crumbly. Sprinkle over apples. Bake 25 minutes or until apples are tender and top is brown. Cut into squares.   *Makes fifteen 3-inch squares.*

Fruit Crunch

1 pound plums, pitted and quartered
1 pound nectarines or peaches, pitted, peeled, and sliced
¼ cup packed brown sugar
1 teaspoon ground cinnamon
1 cup plus 1 tablespoon flour

1 cup sugar
1 teaspoon baking powder
½ teaspoon salt
½ teaspoon freshly grated nutmeg
1 egg, well beaten
¼ cup melted butter

Preheat oven to 375° F. Combine fruit, brown sugar, cinnamon, and 1 tablespoon flour in a medium-size baking dish. Combine remaining ingredients except butter; mix until crumbly. Sprinkle over fruit; drizzle with butter. Bake 40 minutes or until top is brown.   *Serves 4–6.*

Grand Marnier Soufflé

4 tablespoons butter
4 tablespoons flour
1 cup milk
2 tablespoons sugar
4 egg yolks

1 teaspoon grated orange rind
¼ cup orange juice
¼ cup Grand Marnier
5 egg whites

Preheat oven to 375° F. In saucepan, melt butter; blend in flour. Gradually add milk. Cook, stirring constantly, until mixture comes to a boil and thickens. Add sugar. Cook 1 minute. Pour into bowl, and add egg yolks one at a time, beating well after each addition. Add orange rind and juice and Grand Marnier. Chill in freezer 10 minutes. Meanwhile, beat egg whites until stiff but not dry. Beat a small amount of whites into custard mixture, then gently fold in remaining egg whites. Spoon the mixture into a 1½-quart soufflé dish. Bake 25–30 minutes. Remove and serve at once.

Serves 4–6.

Sour Cream Cookies

1 cup sugar
2 tablespoons butter, softened
¼ cup sour cream
1 egg
1 teaspoon vanilla extract

1¼ cups flour
¼ teaspoon baking powder
¼ teaspoon baking soda
½ teaspoon salt

In bowl, cream together sugar and butter; add sour cream, egg, and vanilla. Combine remaining ingredients. With wooden spoon (do not use mixer) add to creamed mixture. Drop by level teaspoons, about 2 inches apart, onto well-greased baking sheet. Sprinkle with additional sugar. Bake 6–8 minutes, until lightly browned. Let stand 1 minute before removing to baking rack to cool.

Makes about 4 dozen 2-inch cookies.

Pecan Balls

½ cup butter, at room temperature
2 tablespoons sugar
1 teaspoon vanilla extract

1 cup flour
1 cup chopped pecans
About ½ cup confectioners' sugar

Preheat oven to 350° F. In small mixer bowl, cream together butter, sugar, and vanilla with electric beater. Gradually add flour; mix well. With wooden spoon, stir in nuts (it may be necessary to mix with hands at this point). Shape into ¾-inch balls (about 1 level teaspoon); place on ungreased baking sheet about 1 inch apart. Bake 15 minutes. While still warm, roll in confectioners' sugar; cool on wire rack.

Makes 36–40 cookies.

Marble Cookies

1 square (1 ounce) semisweet chocolate (or use unsweetened chocolate for darker color)	1 egg yolk
	1 teaspoon vanilla extract
	1½ cups flour
½ cup butter, at room temperature	½ teaspoon baking powder
	¼ teaspoon salt
½ cup sugar	3 tablespoons milk

Preheat oven to 350° F. Melt chocolate. Meanwhile, in small mixer bowl, cream together butter, sugar, egg yolk, and vanilla with electric beater until light and fluffy. Combine flour, baking powder, and salt. Add with milk to creamed mixture. With wooden spoon, blend in melted chocolate to make a marbled mixture. Place on waxed paper; form into 1½-inch roll. Wrap tightly and place in freezer about 20 minutes or until firm. Cut into ¼-inch slices; place 2 inches apart on ungreased baking sheet (cookies spread slightly when baked). Bake 10 minutes; cool on cake rack.   *Makes thirty 2-inch cookies.*

Honeydew Melon with Seedless Grapes

1 honeydew melon	¼ cup port wine
2–3 pounds green seedless grapes	½ cup honey

Cut melon in half and remove the seeds. Take out the fruit with a melon baller. Put into a bowl. Remove grapes from stems. Combine with melon. Scrape remaining flesh from melon shell and place in food processor or blender. Add port and honey. Purée and pour over fruit. Serve in stem glasses.   *Serves 4–6.*

Melon Balls with Sparkling Cider

1 medium watermelon or honeydew or Persian melon	1 bottle sparkling cider

Scoop out balls from the melon. Divide among dessert dishes. Just before serving, put ½ cup of iced sparkling cider over each.   *Serves 4–6.*

Crushed Peaches with Vanilla Cream

6–8 ripe peaches, pitted and
    peeled
½ cup confectioners' sugar

1 teaspoon vanilla extract
1 cup heavy cream

Crush or mash peaches in a bowl. Add sugar. Mix. Add vanilla to heavy cream. Add to peaches and chill for 10 minutes. Spoon into dessert dishes.   *Serves 4–6.*

VARIATION:

Substitute 1 quart strawberries, washed, hulled, and mashed, for the peaches.

Broiled Oranges with Brown Sugar

3–4 large California oranges
¼ cup Grand Marnier

½ cup light brown sugar

Peel and slice oranges about ¼ inch thick. Place slices in a flat dish with sides to marinate with the Grand Marnier for 30 minutes or longer. Place orange slices on broiler rack of pan and sieve light brown sugar over them. Broil 4–5 inches from top of fruit to heat. Pour any juice in bottom of broiler pan over each serving on dessert plate.   *Serves 4–6.*

Fresh Fruit Compote for Winter

2–3 grapefruits, sectioned
  4 oranges, sectioned
  ½ pound red grapes, halved and
    seeded

2 tablespoons sugar
2 tablespoons Kirsch

Mix all fruit together in a bowl. Sprinkle sugar and Kirsch over fruit and chill 10–15 minutes. Spoon into dessert dishes.   *Serves 4–6.*

Top-of-the-Stove Blueberry Pudding

Blueberries

2 tablespoons butter
½ cup sugar
1 teaspoon cornstarch
⅛ teaspoon salt
½ teaspoon cinnamon
2 cups hot water
  Juice of ½ lemon
2 cups blueberries

Dumplings

1 cup flour
1½ teaspoons baking powder
½ teaspoon salt
¼ cup sugar
3 tablespoons shortening
⅓ cup milk
1 egg, beaten
  Freshly grated nutmeg
  Cream or milk

Melt butter in deep 10-inch, straight-sided skillet that has a tight-fitting lid. Combine ½ cup sugar, cornstarch, ⅛ teaspoon salt, and cinnamon and stir into butter. Add water and cook until clear, stirring constantly. Add lemon juice and berries. Bring to a boil and top with dumplings.

For dumplings, put flour, baking powder, salt, and sugar into a bowl. Cut in shortening until mixture is crumbly. Add milk to beaten egg; stir into flour mixture until flour is well moistened. Drop by tablespoons on top of boiling berry mixture, or drop dumpling mixture with an ice-cream scoop. Sprinkle top of dumplings with nutmeg. Cover tightly. Reduce heat to low and cook for 20 minutes. Serve warm with cream or milk.   *Makes 8 good-size dumplings; serves 4–6.*

All hard sauce should be cold, served on a hot dessert. Also, hard sauce can be made into rosettes from a pastry tube and stored in freezer.

Quick Sautéed Apples

Apples

4 large Golden Delicious apples or
  baking apples in season
  Juice of ½ lemon
6 tablespoons butter
  Freshly grated nutmeg

Hard Sauce

5 tablespoons butter (softened)
1¼ cups confectioners' sugar
2 tablespoons Calvados (apple
  brandy)

Wash and peel apples, cut in quarters, and core. Cut each quarter in thirds into a bowl with lemon juice. Toss around to keep apples from discoloring. Melt butter in 10-inch sauté pan on high. When butter is foaming, add apple wedges so they all lie flat in bottom of pan. Place lid on pan. When apples steam, turn heat to low. Cook for about 10 minutes, turning apples halfway through the cooking time. Test apples for fork tender (not mushy). While apples are cooking, make hard sauce.

Cream butter until softened, add sugar, and beat until fluffy, adding Calvados a little at a time. For quick chill, place in freezer. Serve hot apples in low fruit dishes with hard sauce.

Serves 4–6.

These easy, pretty babas are light and delicate even though they are made with no yeast.

Rum Babas

Fine bread crumbs	¼ cup lukewarm milk
2 eggs	1 tablespoon orange juice
1¼ cups sugar	Grated rind of 1 orange
½ cup plus 2 tablespoons flour	1 cup water
2 teaspoons baking powder	2 tablespoons rum or brandy
3 tablespoons butter, melted	1 cup heavy cream, whipped

Preheat oven to 375° F. Butter 6 custard cups and dust with fine bread crumbs. Set on a trivet or place in a small shallow oblong pan. Beat eggs until fluffy. Add ¼ cup sugar and continue beating on high speed of mixer until sugar is dissolved. Sift flour and baking powder together and add them. Add melted butter, warm milk, orange juice, and orange rind. Mix vigorously. Pour the same amount into each custard cup. Bake at 375° F. for 25 minutes. Remove from oven and loosen from molds after 2–3 minutes.

Boil 1 cup sugar and water for a few minutes until it forms a thin syrup. Cool slightly. Flavor with rum or brandy. Pour syrup over molds—a tablespoon at a time—so the babas will absorb it. Each will take 3 tablespoons of syrup. When cool, serve with whipped cream.

Serves 6.

Lemon Ladyfingers

4 eggs, separated, at room temperature
⅛ teaspoon salt
¾ cups granulated sugar

Rind of 1 lemon, grated fine
⅔ cup flour (measured lightly)
Confectioners' sugar

Grease and flour ladyfinger pans or a large cookie sheet. In large bowl of electric mixer, at high speed, beat egg whites and salt until soft peaks form. Gradually sprinkle in ¼ cup granulated sugar; continue to beat until sugar is dissolved and egg whites form stiff, glossy peaks. In another mixer bowl with mixer at medium speed and then high, beat egg yolks, lemon rind, and ½ cup granulated sugar. It will be a stiff batter. Fold flour into egg yolks by hand. Fold egg yolk mixture into beaten egg whites. Batter will be light and well mixed. Use level tablespoon of batter spread into each mold. This takes time and batter is thick. If you only have two ladyfinger pans, a repeated baking can be done with no fear of not rising. Or, using a pastry bag with ½-inch tip tube, pipe batter in 3-inch lengths about 1 inch apart on cookie sheet. Sprinkle cakes with confectioners' sugar before placing in the oven. Bake at 350° F. for 15 minutes.   *Makes 40–50 cakes, depending on size.*

Sinfully rich, fairly wet pudding.

Apple Nut Pudding

1½ cups sugar
2 eggs
½ cup oil
1 teaspoon vanilla extract
2 cups flour
1 teaspoon baking powder
1 teaspoon baking soda
1 teaspoon cinnamon
½ teaspoon freshly grated nutmeg
½ teaspoon salt
⅓ cup buttermilk

¾ cup chopped pecans
2 cups thinly sliced cooking apples

Sauce

¾ cup sugar
⅓ cup buttermilk
1 teaspoon vanilla extract
1 tablespoon corn syrup
¼ pound butter
2 tablespoons grated lemon rind

Preheat oven to 350° F. Butter a 2½-quart (13-by-9-by-2-inch) baking dish. In large bowl, mix together 1½ cups sugar, eggs, oil, and 1 teaspoon vanilla. Combine flour, baking powder, baking soda, spices, and salt. Add alternately with buttermilk to creamed mixture. Fold in nuts and apples. Spread in prepared pan. Bake 30 minutes. Meanwhile, combine all ingredients for sauce in saucepan; heat just to a boil. With fork, poke holes over top of cake; top with warm sauce.

Serves 12.

Orange Sour Cream Cake

¾ cup softened butter
1½ cups sugar
1 tablespoon orange rind
2 eggs
2 cups flour
1 teaspoon baking soda

1 cup sour cream
1 cup orange juice
1 cup raisins
¼ cup chopped dates
½ cups chopped nuts
2 tablespoons honey

Preheat oven to 350° F. Generously grease a 1½-quart (12-by-9-by-2-inch) shallow baking pan. Cream together butter and sugar. Add orange rind and eggs, one at a time, beating well after each addition. Combine flour and baking soda. Add alternately to creamed mixture with sour cream and ½ cup orange juice. Fold in raisins, dates, and nuts. Spoon into prepared pan. Bake 35 minutes. Combine remaining ½ cup orange juice and honey. Pour over cake; return to oven for 5 minutes.

Serves 12.

Baked Apples with Bourbon

4–6 medium Winesap apples,
McIntosh, Roman Beauty, or
any baking apples in season
Juice of ½ lemon
1 cup light brown sugar, packed

4 tablespoons butter, melted
4–6 tablespoons bourbon
Cream, whipped cream, or
sour cream

Preheat oven to 375° F. Core each apple and peel around top about one-third of the way down from stem. Dip tops in lemon juice. Place in shallow baking dish or pan. Mix sugar and melted butter. Pour 1 tablespoon bourbon into each apple cavity. Bake at 375° F. for 45–50 minutes. Halfway through baking, spoon glaze over apples. Test apples with fork for tenderness in 45–50 minutes. Serve apples in low dessert dishes with cream, whipped cream, or sour cream.

Serves 4–6.

Peaches in Honey

6–8 peaches, pitted and sliced thin   ¼ cup honey

Slice peaches into a bowl and add the honey. Mix well. Chill before serving in stem glasses.   *Serves 4–6.*

Pears and Raspberries

4–6 pears, peeled, cored, and   1 pint raspberries
   sliced across in circles   4–6 tablespoons sour cream

Arrange pear circles on dessert plates. Mound a few of the berries in the center of each pear. Spoon sour cream over each serving.   *Serves 4–6.*

Other Dessert Ideas

Apples, Cheese, and Nuts

Apples, polished, in a bowl, served along with Roquefort cheese, softened, and walnuts in the shell.

Grapes

A bowl of grapes, bunches of different types: red, purple, green.

Cheeses

Present three kinds of cheese on a marble slab—one hard, one semisoft, and one soft. Serve French bread, butter in a crock, and unsalted crackers.

Melons

Slice into chunks, or balls if there is time, a selection of various melons in season: cantaloupe, honeydew, watermelon, Persian, cranshaw.

Fresh Fruits

Fill a bowl with fresh fruit to be eaten out of hand: apples, oranges, plums, apricots, cherries, bananas, pears, grapes, and figs.

Cut-up Fresh Fruits

- Add lemon or orange juice to mixed cut-up fresh fruit.
- Sprinkle cut-up fresh fruit with white or brown sugar to taste, or add honey.
- For fresh fruit combinations, mix and match what is in season, such as oranges, grapefruit, strawberries, blueberries, blackberries, pineapple, apples, pears, nectarines, peaches, bananas, kiwis.
- Serve cut-up fruit or berries with sour cream, whipped cream, or yogurt.
- Select exotic fruits when they are in season—mangoes, persimmons, kiwis, and papaya—and serve with wedges of lime.
- Sprinkle fresh fruits with chopped fresh mint or ginger.
- Douse cut-up fruits with rum or brandy or a fruit liqueur such as curaçao.

Recipes in this chapter:

FLAVORED BUTTERS
FENNEL BUTTER
MAPLE BUTTER
SUGARED PECANS
CHOCOLATE SYRUP FOR DRINKS
DEPRESSION CANDY
HOMEMADE HORSERADISH
DUCK STOCK
DILLED MUSHROOMS AND CARROTS
PICKLED GARDEN RELISH
HORSERADISH CREAM
CUCUMBER SAUCE
CRÊPES
CRANBERRIES WITH SHERRY
LEMON SAUCE
VINEGAR MINT SAUCE
BRANDIED HONEY
VINAIGRETTE
BÉARNAISE SAUCE
TOMATO SAUCE
CHICKEN STOCK
BOUQUET GARNI
FISH STOCK
DEVILED WALNUTS
POLONAISE SAUCE
COURT BOUILLON
TARTAR SAUCE
CUSTARD SAUCE
MAYONNAISE AND VARIATIONS
ALMOND MAYONNAISE
BLENDER MAYONNAISE
HOLLANDAISE SAUCE
BLENDER HOLLANDAISE

MISCELLANY

Gifts from the Kitchen

What can you give the host or hostess who has everything? Easy. A jar of homemade mayonnaise. Or herb butter made with home-grown herbs and packed into a crock. Homemade horseradish, basil sauce, and tartar sauce will delight and astonish friends who have tried only commercial versions. Pickled garden relishes, depression candy, deviled walnuts, and sugared pecans are all quick, easy to make, and genuinely personal gifts. If your hosts have small children, be sure to bring along a jar of homemade chocolate syrup. There is nothing like it on the market anymore.

Picnics

For years I've been telling myself that I loved picnics, but then one morning I took a long look in the mirror and decided to admit the truth to myself and

167

everyone else. Sometimes picnics are fun. And sometimes picnics are a pain in the basket.

Picnics are fun when they're grown-up picnics and you can bring real food. Things like mini meat loaf, hot soup in a thermos, and cold fruit soup in another thermos. Fried duck, ham, egg salad rolled up in lettuce leaves, and ginger-glazed chicken are grown-up dishes that pack well in a picnic basket and will get you lots of compliments.

Picnics are also fun when they are kid picnics, and you bring simple sandwiches and plain old American standbys like potato salad and watermelon. Kid food doesn't have to be junk food. But when you try to mix the two, picnics are a pain. You unpack a basket of grown-up delights, you pass them around, and the kids mope and sigh over their plates because it tastes just like company dinner. So remember, one kid makes it a kids' picnic, and all the adults will have to sneak their fried duck and fruit soup on the sly.

Covered dish parties don't have to be picnics, but they are a lot of fun—if you organize things so that everybody doesn't bring the same favorite recipe for chili, with lots and lots of beans. I keep hoping we'll all discover covered dish parties and make them popular again. They began to disappear around the time when the ladies discovered that tuna fish casserole was even cheaper than chili and beans. I remember going to covered dish dinners with my mother when I was very young. I used to look under every cover very carefully, and

then nine out of ten times refuse to eat anything but what we brought from home. My mother said I was impolite, but even then I knew better than to trust to luck in a crowd of cooks. Know your dish makers when you throw your covered dish party, and never judge a covered dish by its cover.

Cocktails

Have a little pity on your guests at cocktail parties. They are going to be carrying a glass in one hand almost constantly, and since they are going to empty that glass one or three times, hand-eye coordination will suffer slightly. Not so much that you will have to take their keys away and refuse to let them drive home—as we are all advised in those safety ads put out by insurance companies. But enough so that balancing a plate full of juicy food, or manipulating little sticks of vegetables from loose and clotty dips to the mouth, is an invitation to minor personal tragedy. Some hosts never seem to give thought to the fact that they are, in one short afternoon, responsible for hundreds and hundreds of dollars in cleaning bills.

I like to serve almonds and olives at cocktail time. You can use one kind of olive, mix and match green and black, Italian, Greek, and Spanish. Buy freshly roasted almonds from a nut store, or put them on a baking sheet with a bit of oil and toast them in a slow oven for a few minutes, salting them just before serving.

If a cocktail party is late in the afternoon, or going to last more than a couple of hours, you may want more substantial food. This book is filled with ideas easy to prepare and more or less safe to eat.

Flavored Butters

12 tablespoons butter, softened

Place butter in food processor or bowl.

FOR HERB BUTTER:
Add 2 tablespoons chopped rosemary
add 2 tablespoons chopped basil
add 2 tablespoons chopped chervil
add 2 tablespoons chopped tarragon
add 2 tablespoons chopped parsley
add 2 tablespoons chopped dill
add 2 tablespoons finely chopped mint

FOR SHALLOT BUTTER:
Add 2 tablespoons chopped shallots

FOR GARLIC BUTTER:
Add 1 tablespoon chopped garlic

FOR LEMON BUTTER:
Add 1 tablespoon lemon juice
and 1 teaspoon grated lemon rind

FOR CAPER BUTTER:
Add 1–2 tablespoons capers, drained

FOR MAÎTRE D'HÔTEL BUTTER:
Add 2 tablespoons chopped parsley,
and 2 tablespoons lemon juice

Fennel Butter

8 tablespoons butter, softened	1 tablespoon freshly chopped
2–3 tablespoons finely chopped	parsley
fresh fennel leaves	

Place butter in a bowl. Add fennel and parsley. Beat until well mixed. Serve on broiled fish or in fish baked in parchment.

Makes ½ cup.

Great on pancakes and French toast

Maple Butter

12 tablespoons butter   1 cup maple syrup

Place butter in food processor or mixer bowl and cream until very light. Add syrup in a thin stream and continue beating until fluffy and pale.

Makes about 2 cups.

This recipe is an adaptation of one used by a cousin in the family. She would never give the exact recipe, as she sold these nuts commercially to support herself and her father, whom she kept in a pint of whiskey a day.

Sugared Pecans

2¼ cups sugar	2 teaspoons vanilla extract
1 cup sour cream	5 cups pecans
Salt to taste	

Brush a baking sheet with melted butter and set aside. In a saucepan, mix together the sugar, sour cream, and salt. Bring slowly to a boil and stir until soft ball stage is reached, 236° F. on a candy thermometer. Remove from burner and add vanilla. With a wooden spatula, beat until the mixture loses its gloss. It should begin to thicken at this point. Add the pecans. Stir to coat well. Place on baking sheet and separate the nuts, using two forks.   *Makes 1½ pounds or more.*

Chocolate Syrup for Drinks

   2 cups cocoa
1½ cups sugar
   2 cups hot water

1 cup corn syrup
1 tablespoon vanilla extract

In a saucepan mix together cocoa, sugar, and hot water. Add corn syrup. Boil 3 minutes, stirring. Add vanilla. Cool. Store in jar in refrigerator.   *Makes 1 quart.*

Note: For hot chocolate, stir 1–2 tablespoons chocolate syrup into 1 cup hot milk. For chocolate milk, add 1–2 tablespoons chocolate syrup to 1 cup cold milk. Use also for chocolate sodas and milkshakes.

We used to make this when I was a small girl. I had to crack the walnuts and remember the stains they left on my small fingers. The sugar was always melted in a black iron skillet.

Depression Candy

   Butter
2 cups sugar

1½ cups black walnuts or other nuts

Heavily butter a baking sheet. Put sugar in heavy fry pan and cook while stirring over medium flame until sugar melts and turns an amber color. This will take about 15 minutes. Strew the nuts over the baking sheet and carefully pour the sugar evenly over nuts. Let stand in a cool place until hard. Break into pieces and eat!   *Makes a little over 1 pound.*

Wear goggles when making this or you surely will cry.

Homemade Horseradish

½ pound fresh horseradish,
   peeled and cut into chunks
3 tablespoons heavy cream

3 tablespoons vinegar
1 tablespoon Dijon mustard
Salt and fresh pepper to taste

Drop the horseradish through feed tube of food processor and chop, using the steel blade. Remove horseradish to a bowl. Combine cream, vinegar, and mustard. Add the cream mixture to the horseradish. Add salt and pepper, if desired.

Makes about 1 cup.

Duck Stock

Trimmings and giblets from
   ducks, backs hacked into pieces
1 small carrot, cut into chunks
1 onion, quartered

1 celery rib, chopped
Salt and fresh pepper to taste
Few sprigs of thyme
Few sprigs of parsley

Put all ingredients into saucepan. Cover with water. Bring to a boil, half cover, and turn to medium heat. Boil 30 minutes or longer. Strain. Reduce to half.

Makes 1 cup or less.

Note: This stock is great to add to rice or soup or to moisten vegetables.
   For duck soup, add this stock to 5–6 cups chicken stock. Add 1 cup julienned vegetables if desired. Cook 3–5 minutes.

Serves 4–6.

Dilled Mushrooms and Carrots

3 pounds small mushrooms
1 pound carrots, cut in ½-inch
   pieces
2 cups water
2 cups white vinegar

½ cup sugar
¼ cup salt
¼ cup chopped fresh dill
2 teaspoons whole peppercorns
6–12 cloves garlic

Place enough water in water bath to cover 6 pint jars or 12 half-pint jars by 1–2 inches; cover and bring to boil. Combine mushrooms and carrots in boiling water; simmer 5 minutes. Drain well. Meanwhile, combine water, vinegar, sugar, salt, dill, and peppercorns; bring to boil. Pack sterilized jars with carrots and mushrooms; top with clove of garlic (if using half-pint jars, use 12 cloves garlic). Pour vinegar mixture over vegetables to cover. Wipe jars clean; seal. Process 20 minutes; cool.   *Makes 6 pints or 12 half-pints.*

Pickled Garden Relish

1 small cauliflower, broken in tiny flowerets
4 carrots, peeled, cut in 2-inch strips or julienned
4 large long ribs of celery, in 1-inch pieces
2 green peppers, cut in 2-inch strips
2 small white onions, thinly sliced

½ cup wine vinegar
½ cup salad oil
¼ cup sugar
Salt and fresh pepper to taste
1 tablespoon chopped oregano leaves
½ cup water

In large kettle, combine all ingredients. Bring vegetables to a boil, stirring occasionally. Reduce heat to simmer. Cover pan and cook for 5 minutes. Cool. Store in refrigerator.   *Makes 5 pints.*

Serve this over fish.

Horseradish Cream

2 cups heavy cream   ¼ cup freshly grated horseradish

Reduce 2 cups heavy cream to 1 cup over medium heat. Add the horseradish. Stir and serve hot or cold.   *Makes 1 cup.*

Use this as a sauce for fish.

Cucumber Sauce

1 cup sour cream
1 cup mayonnaise, preferably
   homemade
1 tablespoon Dijon mustard

2 medium cucumbers, peeled,
   seeded, and chopped
2 tablespoons finely chopped dill
Salt and fresh pepper to taste

Put the sour cream, mayonnaise, and mustard in a bowl. Add the cucumbers, dill, salt, and pepper and fold together gently.
Makes about 3 cups.

Crêpes

½ cup flour
2 eggs
2 egg yolks
¼ cup vegetable oil or melted

butter
½ cup milk
Oil for crêpe pan

Put all ingredients except oil into a blender or food processor. Blend well. Or put all ingredients into a bowl and whisk. Strain if lumpy. Batter should be the consistency of heavy cream. Film a seasoned crêpe pan with a bit of oil. Add 2–3 tablespoons batter and swirl pan in all directions. Fry one side until edges are brown, about 1 minute. Turn over and fry second side about 30 seconds.
Makes 5–6 twelve-inch crêpes or 8–10 seven-inch crêpes.

Cranberries with Sherry

1 cup sugar
1 cup dry sherry

2–3 cups fresh cranberries
½ cup roughly chopped walnuts

Dissolve sugar and sherry in pan over medium heat. Add the cranberries and cook, while stirring, about 5–8 minutes or until the berries pop. Cool 10 minutes and add the walnuts. Store in refrigerator.
Makes 3–4 cups.

Serve this with fish or vegetables.

Lemon Sauce

2 eggs
2 egg yolks
  Juice of 1 lemon
  Salt and fresh pepper to taste
1 cup milk

2 tablespoons finely chopped parsley, chives, or dill, or 2–3 tablespoons capers, rinsed and
drained

Put the eggs, egg yolks, lemon juice, salt and pepper, in a small heavy pan.
Whisk, off the heat, until well blended. Add milk and place on low heat. Whisk
constantly until mixture thickens, about 5 minutes. When thick, remove from
heat and add desired herb or capers. Check seasoning.   *Makes 1½ cups.*

Excellent with broiled lamb chops.

Vinegar Mint Sauce

¾ cup vinegar
 2 tablespoons sugar

2 tablespoons water
½ cup chopped mint leaves

Combine all ingredients in a pan. Bring to a boil; boil for 1–2 minutes. Let stand
10–15 minutes.   *Makes about ¾ cup.*

Serve on pancakes or waffles.

Brandied Honey

1 cup honey

2 tablespoons brandy

Combine honey and brandy in a bowl. Serve warm or cold.   *Makes 1 cup.*

Vinaigrette

1 teaspoon salt	2 tablespoons vinegar or lemon
½ teaspoon freshly cracked black pepper	juice
	6 tablespoons oil

Whisk all ingredients together in a bowl. Pour over salad just before serving.

Makes ½ cup.

This makes enough dressing for any one of the following: 3–4 Belgian endives; 3–4 Bibb lettuces; 1 Romaine lettuce; 2–3 bunches of watercress; or 10 ounces spinach.

Béarnaise is recommended for use with steak, poached salmon and chicken supremes. I also like it with lamb. Make certain that the sauce is served on hot *food.*

Béarnaise Sauce

1 tablespoon chopped shallots	½ cup melted butter, very hot but not browned
½ cup tarragon vinegar	
3 tablespoons finely chopped fresh tarragon	Salt and fresh pepper to taste
3 egg yolks	2 tablespoons chopped fresh parsley (optional)

In a small heavy pan, over moderately high heat, put shallots, vinegar, and tarragon. Cook, stirring with a wooden spatula, for about 5 minutes or until almost all the liquid evaporates. (Be careful not to let it burn.)

Remove pan from heat. Add the egg yolks and 2 tablespoons of cold water; whisk together until well blended. Return pan to heat and, raising and lowering the pan to keep mixture from becoming hot, whisk until mixture is the consistency of heavy cream.

Remove pan from heat and whisk in 4 tablespoons of the hot melted butter, 1 tablespoon at a time. Again returning the pan to the heat, keep whisking as you add the remaining hot melted butter in a thin stream. Whisk until the mixture is thick. Season with salt and pepper. If you want to stir in the parsley, you might want to strain the béarnaise sauce first.

Makes ¾–1 cup.

Tomato Sauce

4 pounds plum tomatoes
2 tablespoons butter
2 tablespoons oil
1 onion, finely chopped
2 large cloves garlic, or more or less, according to your taste
Tiny pinch of sugar (not much, but do use more sugar than salt here)

Salt and freshly cracked black pepper to taste
4–6 fresh basil leaves, finely chopped
¼ cup chicken stock

Slice off the tips of the tomatoes. Drop them into boiling water for 10 seconds, then plunge into cold water with ice cubes. Squeeze each tomato in your hand and skin will slip off in one piece. Finely chop the tomatoes. Heat the butter and oil in a noncorrosive pan. Sauté onion and garlic together for 5 minutes—do not brown. Add tomatoes, sugar, salt, pepper, basil, and stock. Simmer 25 minutes or until sauce gives up liquid. *Makes 5–6 cups.*

Chicken Stock

4 pounds chicken backs, wings, necks, or a 4-pound whole chicken
1 cup sliced carrots
1 cup sliced celery, with leaves
4 medium onions, peeled
4 whole cloves
1 cup dry white wine

1 clove garlic, mashed
1½ teaspoons chopped thyme
1 bay leaf
3 sprigs parsley
2 tablespoons tomato paste
1 tablespoon salt
Freshly cracked black pepper

Place all ingredients and 4 quarts of cold water in a deep kettle or stock pot. Slowly bring to a boil. Skim; reduce heat and half-cover the kettle. Simmer gently for 1½ hours. Remove the chicken and strip the meat from the bones (use it in any recipe that calls for cooked chicken). Return bones to the kettle and simmer for another 2½ hours. Wring out a cheesecloth of double thickness in cold water, and use it as a lining for a sieve. Strain the stock through this. Stock can be stored in refrigerator for up to a week, if boiled every day, or in the freezer for up to 2 months. If a recipe calls for extra-strong stock, boil, uncovered, over moderately high heat, to reduce by one-third. *Makes 2–3 quarts.*

Bouquet garni is indispensable for flavoring soups, rice, stews, and ragouts.

Bouquet Garni

1 rib celery
1 bay leaf

3–4 sprigs of parsley
Few sprigs of fresh thyme

Make a sandwich of the celery; lay herbs on half the rib, fold the other half over, and tie with a string. Leave one end of the string long enough to tie to the handle of the pot or casserole so it will be easy to remove.

Fish Stock

1 cup sliced onion
½ cup sliced celery
½ cup sliced carrot
2 pounds fish bones and trim-mings, all from lean fish

1 cup dry white wine
Bouquet garni
Salt and freshly cracked white pepper to taste

Put all ingredients and 1 quart of cold water into a kettle or stock pot and bring to a boil. Skim. Reduce heat, half-cover the pot, and simmer 30 minutes. Strain through a fine sieve.

Makes 3–4 cups.

Deviled Walnuts

2 tablespoons butter
½ teaspoon dry mustard
½ teaspoon chili powder
½ teaspoon Worcestershire

⅛ teaspoon salt
2 cups walnut halves or pieces
2 tablespoons grated Parmesan cheese

Preheat oven to 300° F. In saucepan, combine butter and seasonings; heat to melt butter. Add walnuts, toss to coat evenly. Spread nuts on baking sheet. Bake 15 minutes or until toasted; remove from oven. While still warm, sprinkle with cheese.

Makes 2 cups.

Polonaise Sauce

½ cup butter
½ cup soft bread crumbs

2 hard-boiled eggs, finely
chopped

Melt the butter in a small skillet. Add the crumbs and toss until lightly browned.
Add the chopped egg. Stir and serve over hot asparagus, cauliflower, or broccoli.

Enough for 4–6 servings.

Court Bouillon

2 cups dry vermouth or other dry
white wine, or 1 cup cider vinegar
½ cup chopped onion
½ cup chopped carrot
½ cup chopped celery

2 teaspoons salt
8 peppercorns
3 sprigs of parsley
1 bay leaf
1 clove
½ teaspoon dried thyme

Put all ingredients and 2 quarts cold water into a large saucepan or kettle. Bring to
a boil and boil rapidly for 30 minutes. Strain and cool.   *Makes 9–10 cups.*

Serve this with fish, crab cakes, and soft-shell crabs.

Tartar Sauce

1 cup homemade mayonnaise
1 small white onion, peeled and
grated
1 tablespoon chopped parsley
1 tablespoon chopped tarragon or
chervil

2 tablespoons chopped dill pickle
1 tablespoon chopped olives
2 teaspoons horseradish
1 tablespoon capers
Salt and fresh pepper to taste

Mix all ingredients together in bowl.   *Makes 1 generous cup.*

Use this sauce on berries, fruits, stale cake, babas, and fruit soufflés.

Custard Sauce

2 cups light cream
4 egg yolks
½ cup sugar
2–3 tablespoons liqueur (Grand Marnier or other), or 2 tablespoons rum or cognac, or ¼ cup orange or lemon juice plus 1 tablespoon grated rind,

or 1 tablespoon vanilla extract, or for spicy sauce, add cinnamon, ginger, or nutmeg to taste.

Scald the cream. Beat egg yolks with sugar until thick. Add hot cream slowly, stirring. Cook until mixture coats the back of a spoon. Flavor as desired.

Makes 2½ cups.

Mayonnaise and Variations

Salt and fresh pepper to taste
3 egg yolks
1 teaspoon mustard, Dijon style or dry

1½ cups oil (any kind you select)
1–2 tablespoons vinegar or lemon juice

In a bowl, mix the salt, pepper, egg yolks, and mustard. Whisk well. Begin adding the oil a teaspoonful at a time. Continue to whisk until the mixture emulsifies (thickens). Add the oil, a little more rapidly, in a thin stream, as you whisk. Finish with 1–2 tablespoons vinegar or lemon juice, depending on consistency desired.

Makes 1½ cups.

VARIATIONS:

Add to basic mayonnaise any of the following puréed vegetables: the white part of cooked leeks; a carrot, peeled and cooked; a little cooked fresh spinach or sorrel (this is quite good with fish).

For fruit salad, add 1 tablespoon chopped mint.

For shrimp or fish, add 1 teaspoon saffron.

For fish or shrimp, add 1 tablespoon dill.

For fish, add 1 or more tablespoons capers.

Serve almond mayonnaise as a dip for artichokes.

Almond Mayonnaise

Mayonnaise (preceding recipe) made with juice of ½ lemon   **½ cup chopped toasted almonds**

Fold almonds into mayonnaise just before serving.   *Makes about 2 cups.*

Blender Mayonnaise

Using ingredients listed for mayonnaise on page 180, blend salt, pepper, egg yolks, mustard, and vinegar or lemon juice with 2 tablespoons of the oil for a few seconds to mix. With blender on high speed, add the remaining oil in a thin stream. Stop blender as soon as mayonnaise thickens.

Hollandaise Sauce

½ **cup butter**
3 **egg yolks**
2 **tablespoons lemon juice**
  Salt and fresh pepper to taste

Melt the butter, but be careful not to brown it. In a small heavy pan that is not aluminum, place the egg yolks and 3 tablespoons of cold water. Over high heat, raising and lowering the pan constantly so as not to let it overheat, whisk together the yolks and water. If the outside of the pan gets too hot, the sauce will curdle. If necessary, remove the pan from the heat entirely—but don't stop whisking. Do this for about 10 minutes or until the mixture begins to mound. It should have the consistency of heavy cream.

Remove the pan from the heat and whisk in ¼ cup of the hot melted butter, a tablespoon at a time (4 tablespoons in all). Return the pan to high heat, keep whisking, and add the remaining hot melted butter in a thin stream. Whisk until the mixture is thick and creamy—this should take about 5 minutes—and continue to move the pan on and off the heat.

Add lemon juice, salt, and pepper. If necessary to wait a while before serving, place the pan over a pan of warm water and whisk now and then. If the sauce seems too thin, return it to the stove—still moving pan to keep it from overheating—and whisk until it thickens. *Makes ¾–1 cup.*

Note: If the sauce should curdle, you can rectify it by whisking in 1 tablespoon of cold water or 1 tablespoon of boiling water. Another method is to whisk an egg yolk in a bowl, then whisk the sauce into it very slowly.

VARIATIONS:

Add 1 tablespoon chopped mint for serving with lamb; add 1 teaspoon saffron for fish or shrimp; add 1 tablespoon dill for fish or shrimp.

Blender Hollandaise

Using the same ingredients, same measures, as preceding hollandaise sauce, blend the egg yolks, lemon juice, salt, and pepper for 1 minute. Turn blender to high speed and pour in the very hot melted butter in a thin stream. The sauce will thicken and it will hold over warm water until serving time—but whisk it now and then.

MENUS

The part I like best about writing cookbooks is designing menus—imagining, experimenting, and testing to decide what goes with what is the most fascinating and the most fun of any of the work that goes into my books.

For this book, for the first time, I have divided the recipes into kinds of food, and left the menus for last. I thought long and hard before I did it—and finally decided that presenting recipes in menu form can be limiting. Some readers think they can't serve roast lamb because they don't have fresh peas to go with it. Other readers never notice a recipe for kohlrabi because it may be listed on a menu with chicken and they don't like chicken.

So I changed the form of the book, just slightly. The work that went into this section was still the most exciting and satisfying of all. And I emphasize again, as I always have before, that these menus are merely suggestions, not orders. If you find good fresh spinach instead of peas, please make the spinach instead. As long as you are using fresh ingredients, you will never go far wrong in taste combinations.

When I began putting this section together I tried grouping meals by time: hour meals, half-hour meals, and fifteen-minute meals. But that eventually got silly. There are, no matter what anybody says, no fifteen-minute meals. You can cook a Chinese stir-fry in seconds, but it still takes time cutting and slicing all those ingredients, with or without a food processor. It takes fifteen minutes to merely wash the vegetables. For some cooks all these recipes will be half-hour or forty-five-minute recipes; for others an hour, or even more. That shouldn't matter. All these menus can be prepared quickly and easily—more so than any other kind of cooking you do. So you don't have to rush. If you are slow, practice will make you faster. If your practice doesn't make you faster, well, nobody ever starved in five or ten minutes. My mother told me that just as your mother told you that. And it's a little bit of wisdom we should pass along, whenever we have the chance, to our own families and friends. A little consideration for the cook, please.

Breakfast, Brunch, and Lunch

"What's lunch?" my daughter says. "Unless you mean the meal I eat every weekday on my lunch hour, I don't ever have lunch. And breakfast is the quickest and craziest meal of the day; the one I most often skip."

For many of us, breakfast, brunch, and lunch are weekend or vacation meals. But that doesn't mean that they are unimportant. For those long lazy mornings when there's no work to worry about, a breakfast slides comfortably into brunch and can be one of the most delightful meals of the week. Don't spend too much time and effort on these meals—the food is important, but it tastes better if you have the feeling that you've loafed through the preparation as well as the eating.

My favorite drink for brunch is a mimosa, a combination of champagne and orange juice. Use a decent champagne and take time to squeeze fresh orange juice. Mimosas are such good drinks that you can suddenly discover you're sitting around the house in your night clothes with only half the Sunday paper read, too giddy on champagne to do anything but go back to bed. Not always a bad idea on a lazy day, but be forewarned: it's easier to arrange your schedule around mimosas than it is to arrange mimosas around your schedule.

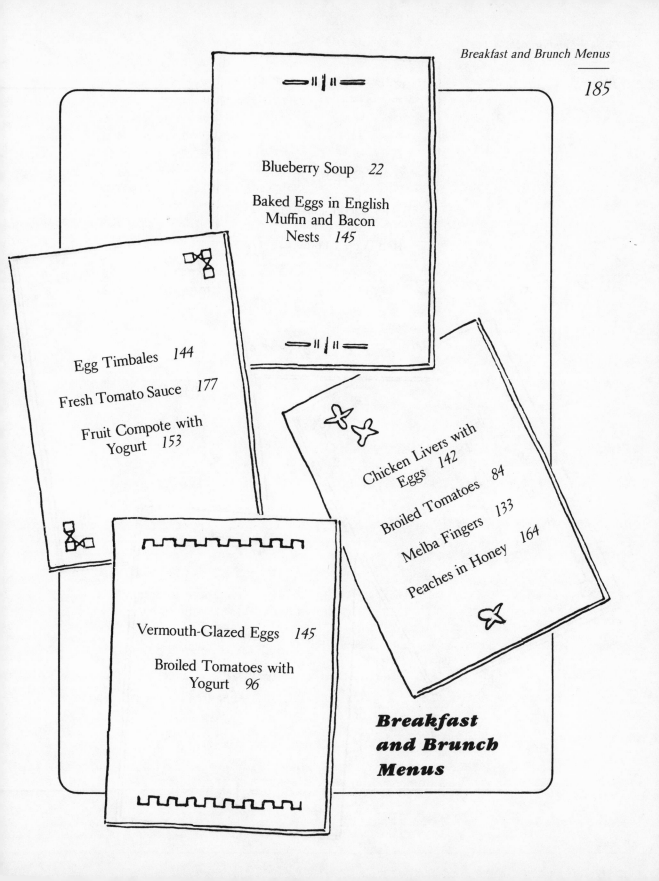

Blueberry Soup *22*

Baked Eggs in English
Muffin and Bacon
Nests *145*

Egg Timbales *144*

Fresh Tomato Sauce *177*

Fruit Compote with
Yogurt *153*

Chicken Livers with
Eggs *142*

Broiled Tomatoes *84*

Melba Fingers *133*

Peaches in Honey *164*

Vermouth-Glazed Eggs *145*

Broiled Tomatoes with
Yogurt *96*

**Breakfast
and Brunch
Menus**

Grapes   *164*

Baked Bacon and Eggs   *142*

Red Pepper Potatoes   *112*

Bacon Pancakes   *135*

Maple Butter   *170*

Chicken Livers with Pears   *41*

Sautéed Mushrooms   *83*

Wheat Batter Bread   *137*

Butter Crock and Jam

Baked Cheese Fondue   *140*

Butterfingers   *133*

Fresh Fruit   *165*

Broiled Canadian
Bacon   *28*

Banana Nut Bread   *137*

Fresh Fruit   *165*

Broiled Philadelphia
Scrapple   *30*

Quick Sautéed Apples   *160*

Broiled Potato Slices   *110*

Chicken Livers on
Skewers   *40*

Toasted English
Muffins

Broiled Sliced Oranges
with Grand Marnier   *146*

Glazed Pears   *149*

Pork Patties with Sage
and Orange   *38*

Golden Popovers   *138*

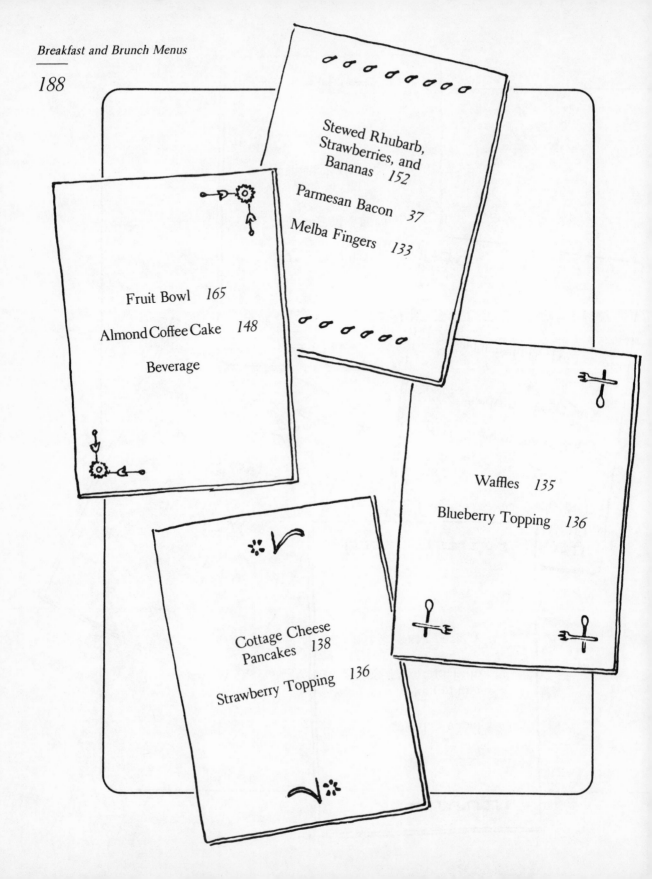

Stewed Rhubarb,
Strawberries, and
Bananas   *152*

Parmesan Bacon   *37*

Melba Fingers   *133*

Fruit Bowl   *165*

Almond Coffee Cake   *148*

Beverage

Waffles   *135*

Blueberry Topping   *136*

Cottage Cheese
Pancakes   *138*

Strawberry Topping   *136*

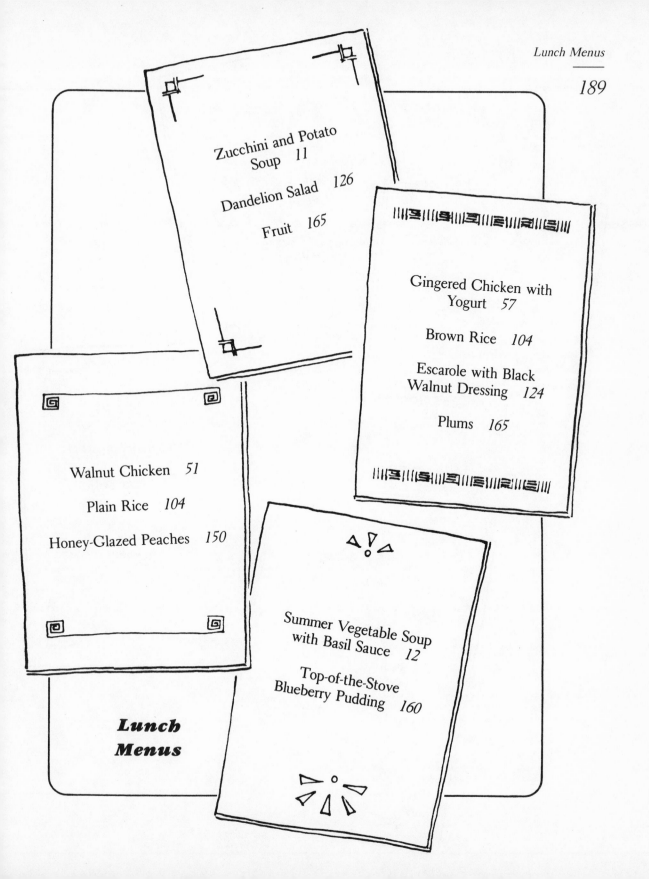

Zucchini and Potato
Soup   *11*

Dandelion Salad   *126*

Fruit   *165*

Gingered Chicken with
Yogurt   *57*

Brown Rice   *104*

Escarole with Black
Walnut Dressing   *124*

Plums   *165*

Walnut Chicken   *51*

Plain Rice   *104*

Honey-Glazed Peaches   *150*

Summer Vegetable Soup
with Basil Sauce   *12*

Top-of-the-Stove
Blueberry Pudding   *160*

**Lunch
Menus**

Crêpes Bombay *72*

Sliced Tomatoes,
Vinaigrette *176*

Sliced Oranges with
Grand Marnier *165*

Stuffed Eggs
Supreme *143*

Crunchy Winter Salad *127*

Polished Apples and
Roquefort Cheese *164*

Eggs Indienne *143*

Rice Pilaf with
Crystallized Ginger *106*

Melon Balls with
Sparkling Cider *158*

Egg Drop Soup *15*

Shrimp Tempura,
Dipping Sauce *78*

Fresh Fruit in Season *165*

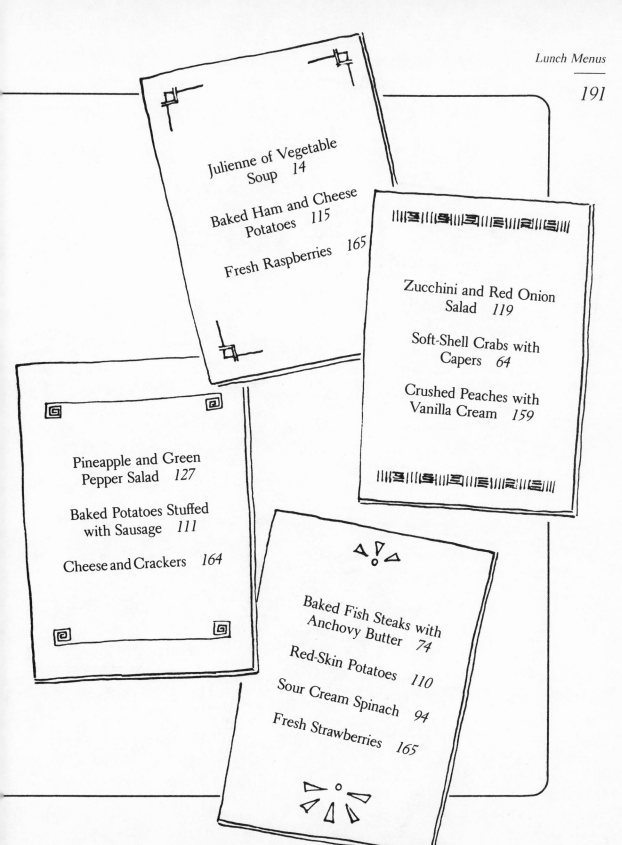

Julienne of Vegetable
Soup *14*

Baked Ham and Cheese
Potatoes *115*

Fresh Raspberries *165*

Zucchini and Red Onion
Salad *119*

Soft-Shell Crabs with
Capers *64*

Crushed Peaches with
Vanilla Cream *159*

Pineapple and Green
Pepper Salad *127*

Baked Potatoes Stuffed
with Sausage *111*

Cheese and Crackers *164*

Baked Fish Steaks with
Anchovy Butter *74*

Red-Skin Potatoes *110*

Sour Cream Spinach *94*

Fresh Strawberries *165*

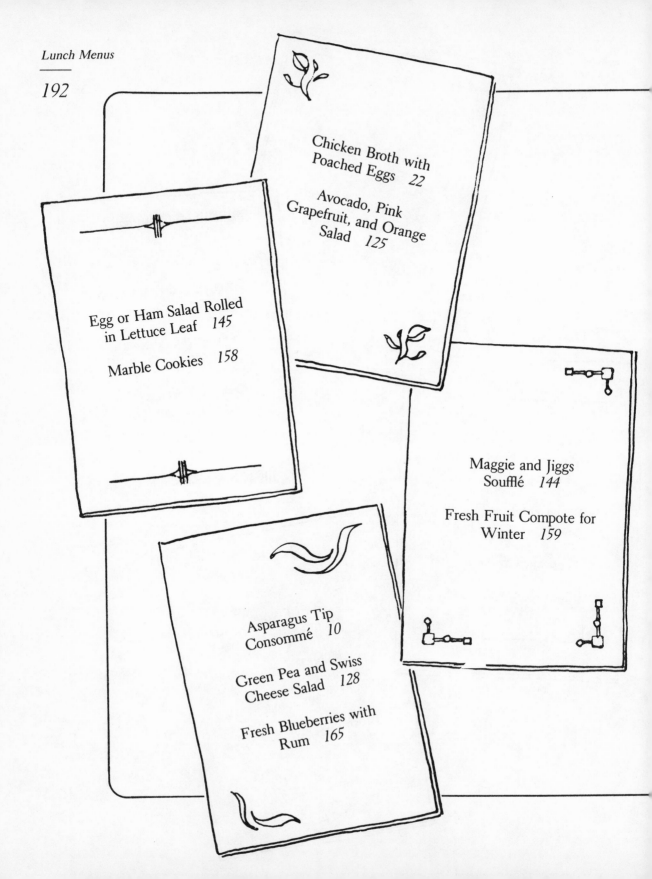

Chicken Broth with
Poached Eggs *22*

Avocado, Pink
Grapefruit, and Orange
Salad *125*

Egg or Ham Salad Rolled
in Lettuce Leaf *145*

Marble Cookies *158*

Maggie and Jiggs
Soufflé *144*

Fresh Fruit Compote for
Winter *159*

Asparagus Tip
Consommé *10*

Green Pea and Swiss
Cheese Salad *128*

Fresh Blueberries with
Rum *165*

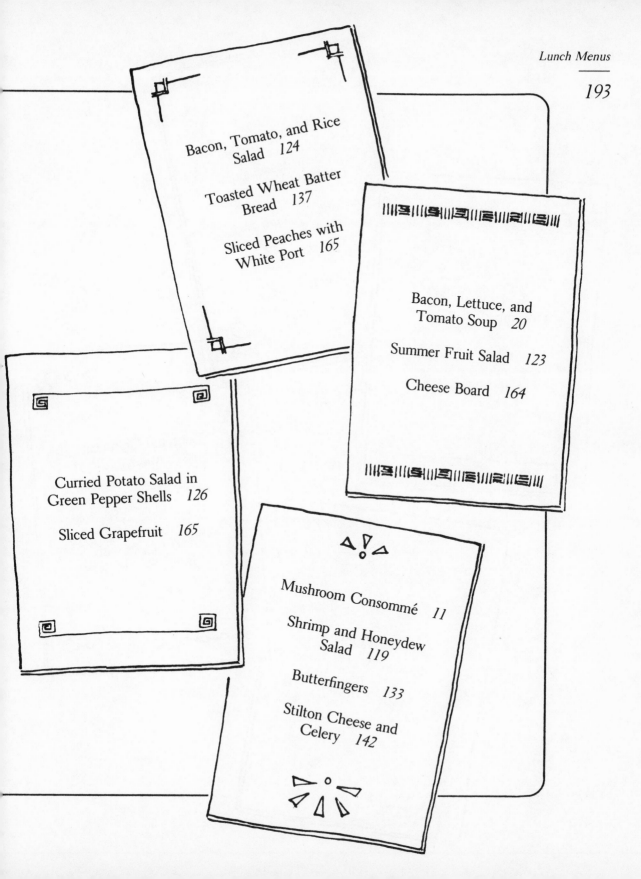

Bacon, Tomato, and Rice
Salad *124*

Toasted Wheat Batter
Bread *137*

Sliced Peaches with
White Port *165*

Bacon, Lettuce, and
Tomato Soup *20*

Summer Fruit Salad *123*

Cheese Board *164*

Curried Potato Salad in
Green Pepper Shells *126*

Sliced Grapefruit *165*

Mushroom Consommé *11*

Shrimp and Honeydew
Salad *119*

Butterfingers *133*

Stilton Cheese and
Celery *142*

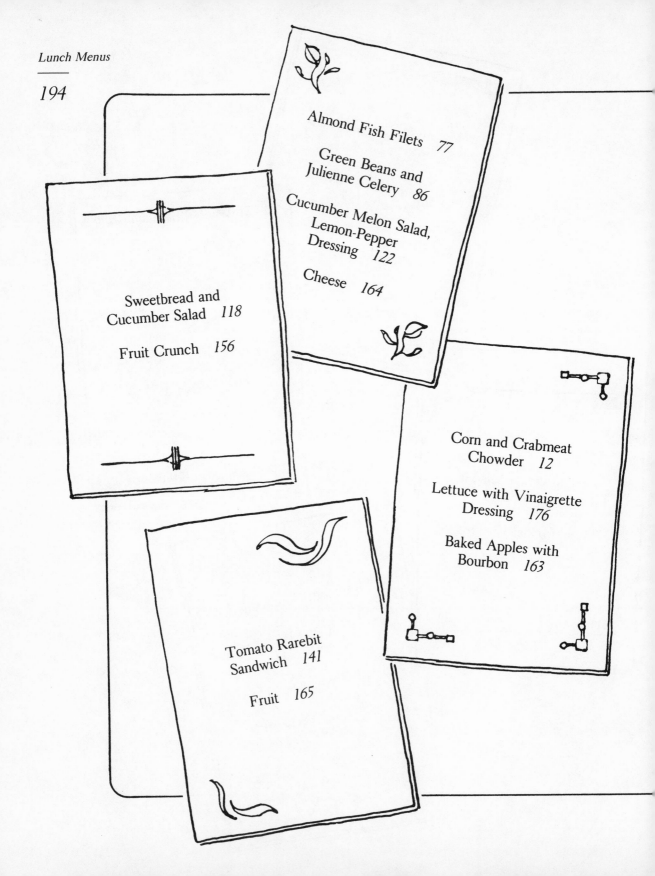

Almond Fish Filets *77*

Green Beans and
Julienne Celery *86*

Cucumber Melon Salad,
Lemon-Pepper
Dressing *122*

Cheese *164*

Sweetbread and
Cucumber Salad *118*

Fruit Crunch *156*

Corn and Crabmeat
Chowder *12*

Lettuce with Vinaigrette
Dressing *176*

Baked Apples with
Bourbon *163*

Tomato Rarebit
Sandwich *141*

Fruit *165*

Cream of Cauliflower
Soup   15

Melba Rounds   133

Sangría Grapes   152

Cheese Custards   141

Fresh Tomato Sauce   177

Lettuce Leaves,
Vinaigrette Dressing   176

Sautéed Apples   36

Open-Face Cheese
Radish Sandwich or
Grilled Cheese and
Green Pepper
Sandwich   139–40

Bunch of Grapes   164

Dinners

Only a few short years ago, cookbooks and food columnists were worrying that the family dinner was becoming a thing of the past—a victim of television and busy schedules.

But for the working couple, dinner has become much more than a meal. It is the time that they have to spend together, comparing their working days, enjoying each other, and rewarding themselves for getting through one more day of career-building.

Families with teen-agers do have a special problem with dinner. If there are two teen-agers in the family, one always seems to be out of the house when the other one is home. If both are by some strange coincidence home at the same time, one is always asleep when the other is awake. One is always hungry while the other is on a crash diet to lose one pound, or in training and unable to eat anything except raw eggs in milk. The best way to deal with teen-age taste in food, and teen-age eccentricities about food, is to lure them to the table. No matter how severe the diet, no matter how rigorous the training schedule, your teen-ager makes one or two stops at the local fast-food emporium a week. If you haven't seen them at the table for a while, announce casually that tomorrow night is crispy chicken wing night or promise them baked hot fudge pudding for dessert. Promise them good food. Your only competition is mass-produced hamburgers and freeze-dried potato shreds masquerading as French fries. You can beat the fast-food shop on the corner, once a week at least, by giving the kids what they want. Almost any teen-ager will find time to eat good home cooking.

Sautéed Sauerkraut with
Bacon *97*

Red-Skin Potatoes *110*

Sour Cream Cookies *157*

Fresh Fruit *165*

Baked Shoulder Lamb
Chops, Zingy Sauce *46*

Summer Squash
Sauté *101*

Lettuce with Buttermilk
Dressing *121*

Fresh Pears *165*

Stuffed Veal Chops *43*

Puréed Butternut
Squash *92*

Sautéed Apples with
Hard Sauce *160*

Loin Lamb Chops with
Parsley and Garlic *42*

Carrots with Pistachios *100*

Lettuce with Creamy
Dressing *121*

Cheese and Crackers *164*

**Dinner
Menus**

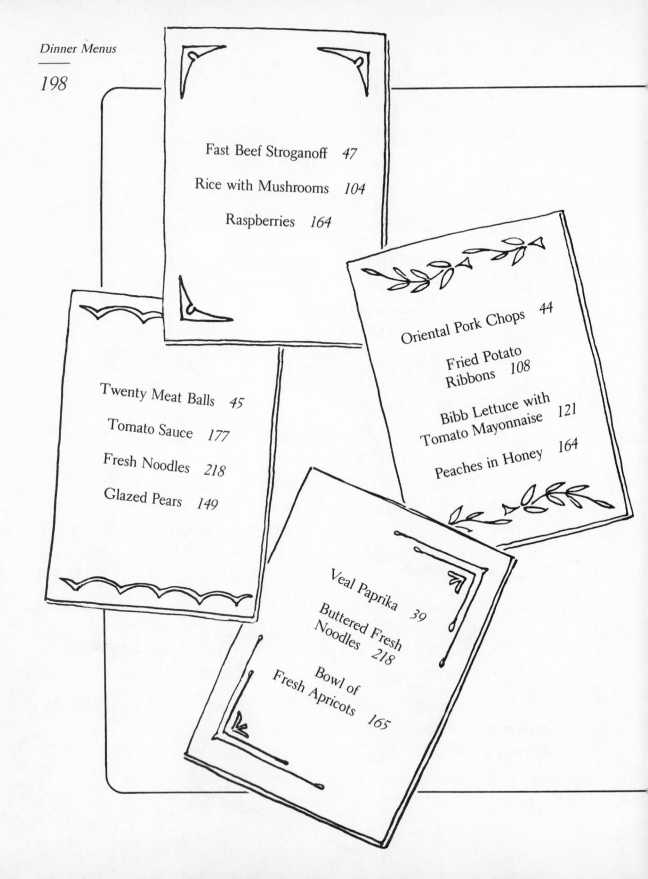

Fast Beef Stroganoff   *47*

Rice with Mushrooms   *104*

Raspberries   *164*

Oriental Pork Chops   *44*

Fried Potato
Ribbons   *108*

Bibb Lettuce with
Tomato Mayonnaise   *121*

Peaches in Honey   *164*

Twenty Meat Balls   *45*

Tomato Sauce   *177*

Fresh Noodles   *218*

Glazed Pears   *149*

Veal Paprika   *39*

Buttered Fresh
Noodles   *218*

Bowl of
Fresh Apricots   *165*

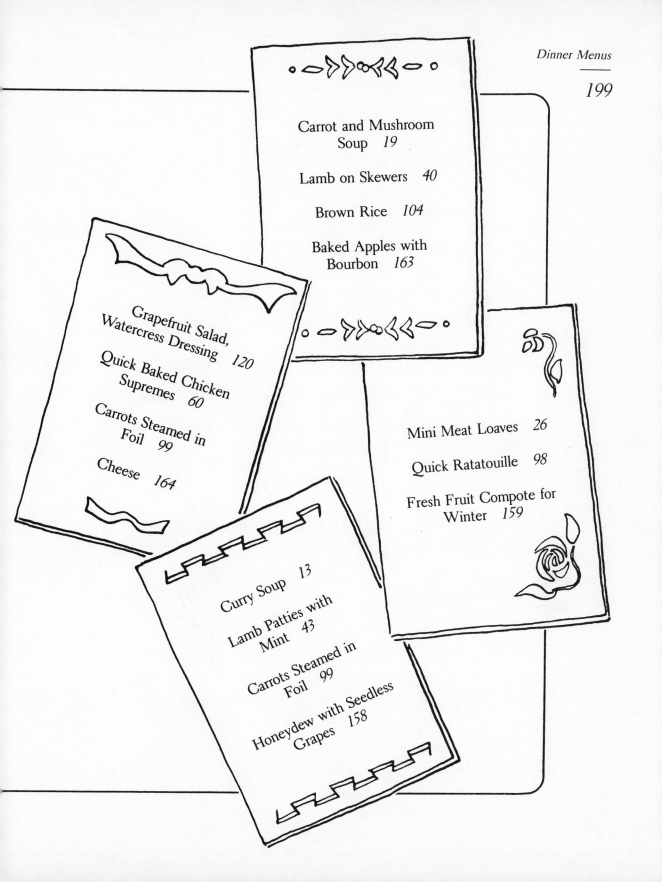

Carrot and Mushroom
Soup *19*

Lamb on Skewers *40*

Brown Rice *104*

Baked Apples with
Bourbon *163*

Grapefruit Salad,
Watercress Dressing *120*

Quick Baked Chicken
Supremes *60*

Carrots Steamed in
Foil *99*

Cheese *164*

Mini Meat Loaves *26*

Quick Ratatouille *98*

Fresh Fruit Compote for
Winter *159*

Curry Soup *13*

Lamb Patties with
Mint *43*

Carrots Steamed in
Foil *99*

Honeydew with Seedless
Grapes *158*

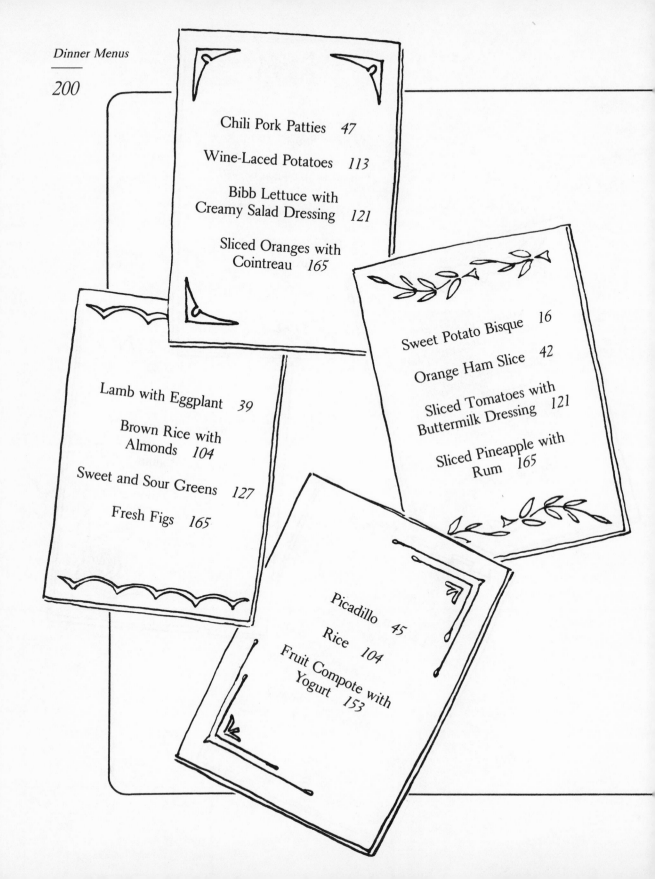

Chili Pork Patties   *47*

Wine-Laced Potatoes   *113*

Bibb Lettuce with
Creamy Salad Dressing   *121*

Sliced Oranges with
Cointreau   *165*

Sweet Potato Bisque   *16*

Orange Ham Slice   *42*

Sliced Tomatoes with
Buttermilk Dressing   *121*

Sliced Pineapple with
Rum   *165*

Lamb with Eggplant   *39*

Brown Rice with
Almonds   *104*

Sweet and Sour Greens   *127*

Fresh Figs   *165*

Picadillo   *45*

Rice   *104*

Fruit Compote with
Yogurt   *153*

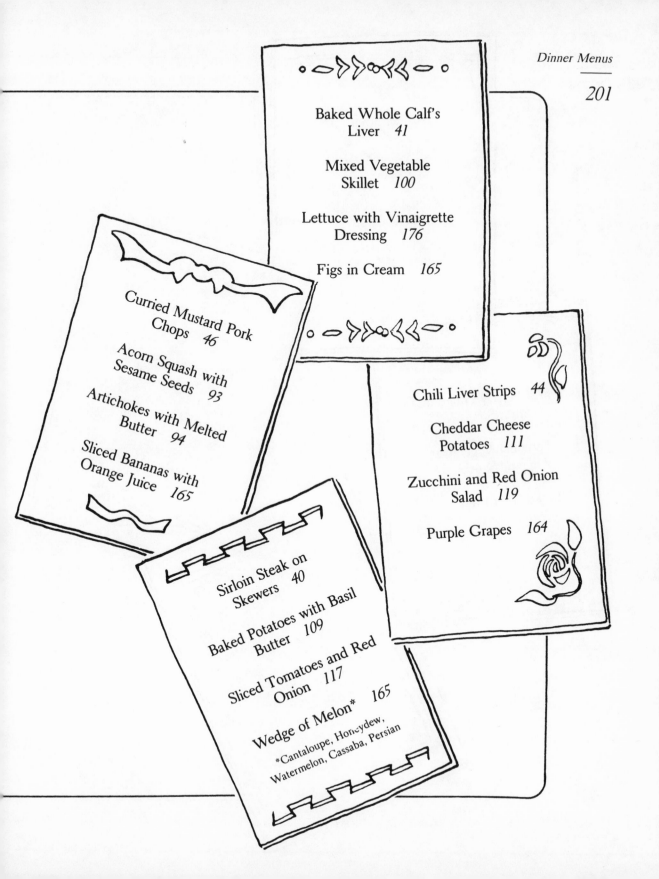

Baked Whole Calf's
Liver *41*

Mixed Vegetable
Skillet *100*

Lettuce with Vinaigrette
Dressing *176*

Figs in Cream *165*

Curried Mustard Pork
Chops *46*

Acorn Squash with
Sesame Seeds *93*

Artichokes with Melted
Butter *94*

Sliced Bananas with
Orange Juice *165*

Chili Liver Strips *44*

Cheddar Cheese
Potatoes *111*

Zucchini and Red Onion
Salad *119*

Purple Grapes *164*

Sirloin Steak on
Skewers *40*

Baked Potatoes with Basil
Butter *109*

Sliced Tomatoes and Red
Onion *117*

Wedge of Melon* *165*

*Cantaloupe, Honeydew,
Watermelon, Cassaba, Persian

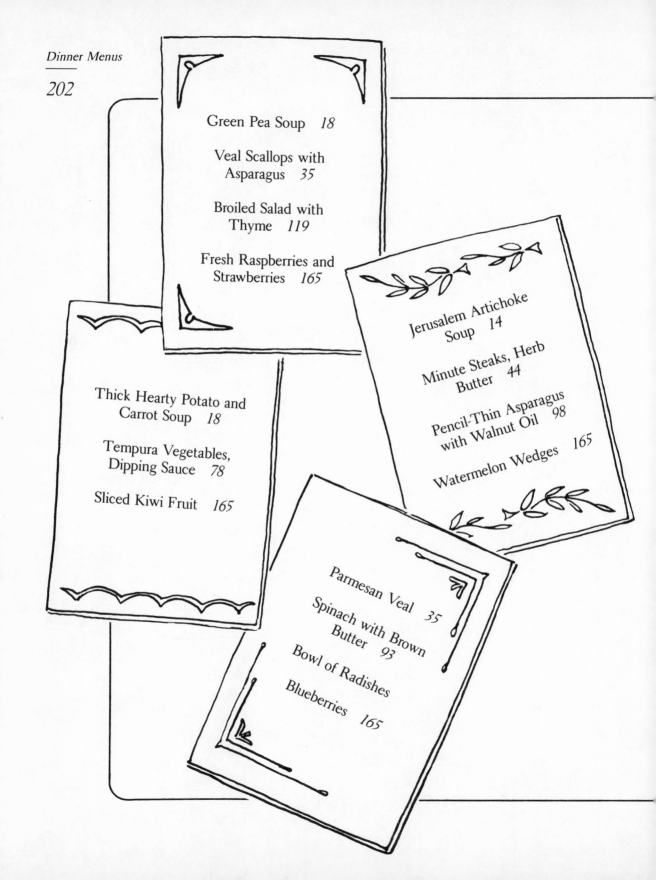

Green Pea Soup   *18*

Veal Scallops with
Asparagus   *35*

Broiled Salad with
Thyme   *119*

Fresh Raspberries and
Strawberries   *165*

Jerusalem Artichoke
Soup   *14*

Minute Steaks, Herb
Butter   *44*

Pencil-Thin Asparagus
with Walnut Oil   *98*

Watermelon Wedges   *165*

Thick Hearty Potato and
Carrot Soup   *18*

Tempura Vegetables,
Dipping Sauce   *78*

Sliced Kiwi Fruit   *165*

Parmesan Veal   *35*

Spinach with Brown
Butter   *93*

Bowl of Radishes

Blueberries   *165*

Slivers of Liver with
Orange *42*

Rice Pilaf *105*

Bibb Lettuce and Cherry
Tomato Salad *123*

Cheese and Crackers *164*

Boiled Artichoke,
Hollandaise Sauce *94*

Veal Scaloppine
Marsala *34*

Carrots and Zucchini *85*

Cantaloupe with Port
Wine *164*

Medallions of Pork *34*

Shredded Red Cabbage
with Wine *87*

Bowl of Watercress

Nectarines *165*

Butterflied Leg of
Lamb *36*

Fried Potato and Apple
Cake *114*

Iced Celery Hearts

Bowl of Cherries *165*

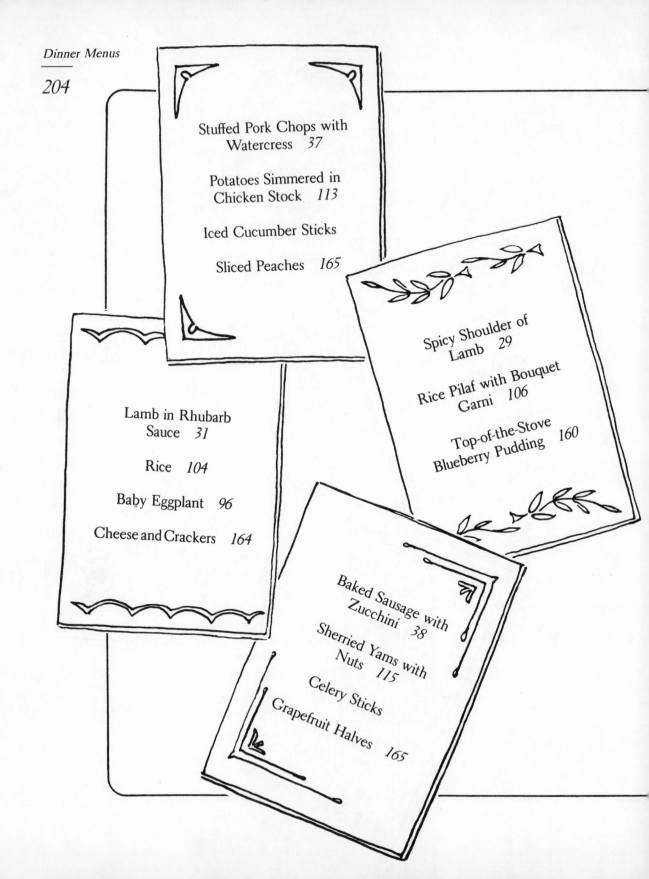

Stuffed Pork Chops with
Watercress *37*

Potatoes Simmered in
Chicken Stock *113*

Iced Cucumber Sticks

Sliced Peaches *165*

Spicy Shoulder of
Lamb *29*

Rice Pilaf with Bouquet
Garni *106*

Top-of-the-Stove
Blueberry Pudding *160*

Lamb in Rhubarb
Sauce *31*

Rice *104*

Baby Eggplant *96*

Cheese and Crackers *164*

Baked Sausage with
Zucchini *38*

Sherried Yams with
Nuts *115*

Celery Sticks

Grapefruit Halves *165*

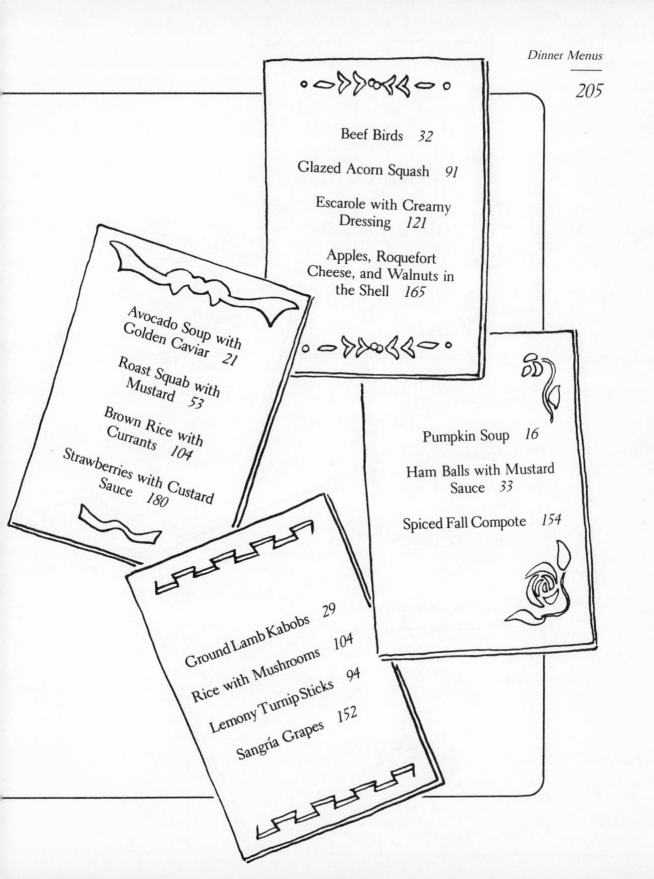

Beef Birds *32*

Glazed Acorn Squash *91*

Escarole with Creamy
Dressing *121*

Apples, Roquefort
Cheese, and Walnuts in
the Shell *165*

Avocado Soup with
Golden Caviar *21*

Roast Squab with
Mustard *53*

Brown Rice with
Currants *104*

Strawberries with Custard
Sauce *180*

Pumpkin Soup *16*

Ham Balls with Mustard
Sauce *33*

Spiced Fall Compote *154*

Ground Lamb Kabobs *29*

Rice with Mushrooms *104*

Lemony Turnip Sticks *94*

Sangría Grapes *152*

Chicken with
Mushrooms *56*

Wax Beans with Lemon
and Oil *99*

Sliced Peaches with
Cinnamon Custard *180*

Chicken Thighs with
Rosemary *51*

Potato Pancakes with
Sour Cream and
Chives *112*

Leaf Lettuce
Vinaigrette *176*

Melon Chunks *165*

Broiled Duck *52*

Rice Pilaf with Green
and Red Peppers *107*

Parsnips with Parsley *96*

Cranberries with
Sherry *174*

Vegetable Fritters *86*

Mulligatawny Soup *17*

Baked Lemon Soufflé,
Rum Sauce *154*

Chicken in Saffron
Cream *56*

Buttered Noodles *218*

Lettuce with Vinaigrette
Dressing *176*

Blueberries *165*

Roast Tarragon
Chicken *54*

Mushrooms in Cream *82*

Baked Zucchini and
Tomatoes *84*

Crushed Strawberries in
Vanilla Cream *159*

Wild Rice Soup *21*

Fried Duck *55*

Bowl of Relishes

Baked Apples with
Bourbon *163*

Ginger-Glazed Chicken
52

Brown Rice with
Almonds *104*

Stuffed Onions *92*

Raspberries with
Whipped Cream *165*

Chicken with Apple
Cream *54*

Cabbage Timbales *88*

Zucchini and Red Onion
Salad *119*

Tangerines *165*

Chicken Breasts with
Béarnaise or Basil
Butter *59*

Braised Sliced Celery *91*

Rice Pilaf with Parsley *107*

Grand Marnier Soufflé *156*

Chicken Thighs with
Vermouth *51*

Green Beans with Lemon
and Oil *99*

Pink Rice Pilaf *106*

Sliced Oranges and
Grapefruit with Rum *165*

Mint Julep Chicken *59*

Rice Pilaf with Grated
Carrots *106*

Orange and Onion
Salad *122*

Cheese *165*

Greek Lemon Soup *15*

Chicken Breasts with
Ham and Cheese *59*

Buttered Noodles *218*

Honeydew Slices with
Mint *165*

Cream of Broccoli
Soup *15*

Quick Chicken Supremes,
Baked *60*

Rice Pilaf with Orange *107*

Fresh Figs *165*

Shreveport Crab Soup *19*

Easy Broiled Chicken *53*

Okra and Tomatoes *85*

Cardamom Peaches *152*

Crispy Chicken
Wings *58*

Easy Summer Squash *95*

Wild Pecan Rice *106*

Fresh Fruit with Spiced
Custard Sauce *180*

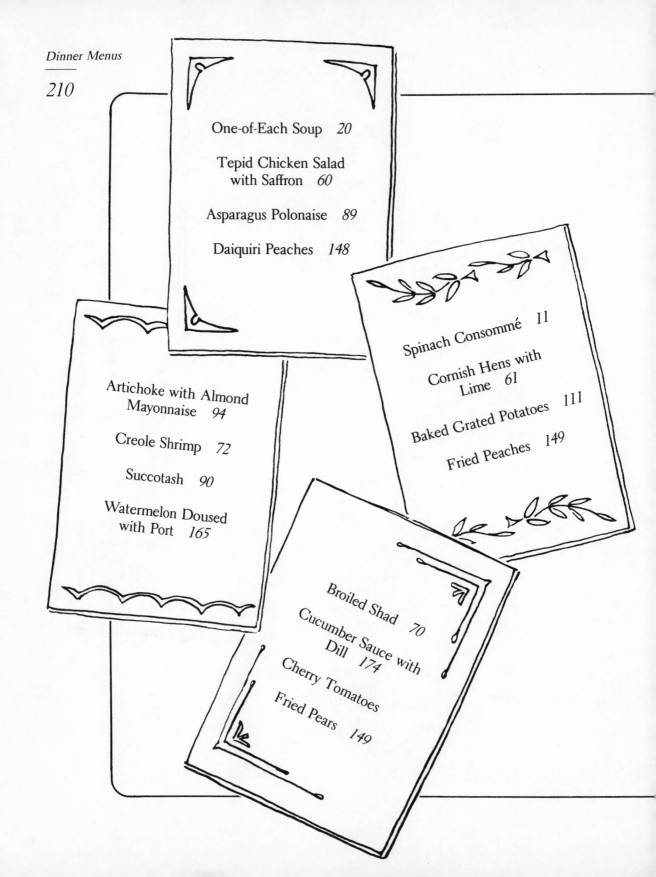

One-of-Each Soup   *20*

Tepid Chicken Salad
with Saffron   *60*

Asparagus Polonaise   *89*

Daiquiri Peaches   *148*

Spinach Consommé   *11*

Cornish Hens with
Lime   *61*

Baked Grated Potatoes   *111*

Fried Peaches   *149*

Artichoke with Almond
Mayonnaise   *94*

Creole Shrimp   *72*

Succotash   *90*

Watermelon Doused
with Port   *165*

Broiled Shad   *70*

Cucumber Sauce with
Dill   *174*

Cherry Tomatoes

Fried Pears   *149*

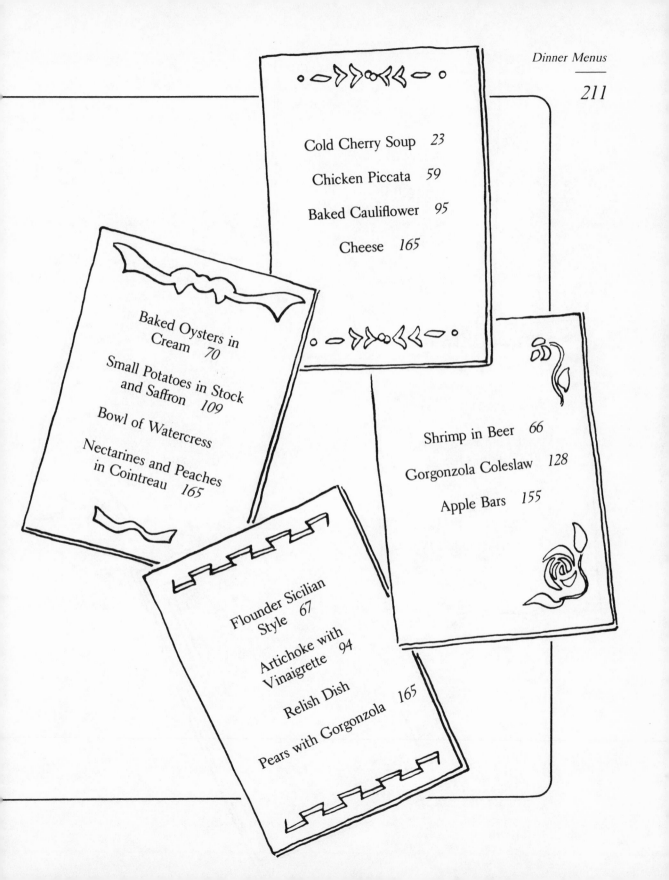

Cold Cherry Soup   *23*

Chicken Piccata   *59*

Baked Cauliflower   *95*

Cheese   *165*

Baked Oysters in Cream   *70*

Small Potatoes in Stock and Saffron   *109*

Bowl of Watercress

Nectarines and Peaches in Cointreau   *165*

Shrimp in Beer   *66*

Gorgonzola Coleslaw   *128*

Apple Bars   *155*

Flounder Sicilian Style   *67*

Artichoke with Vinaigrette   *94*

Relish Dish

Pears with Gorgonzola   *165*

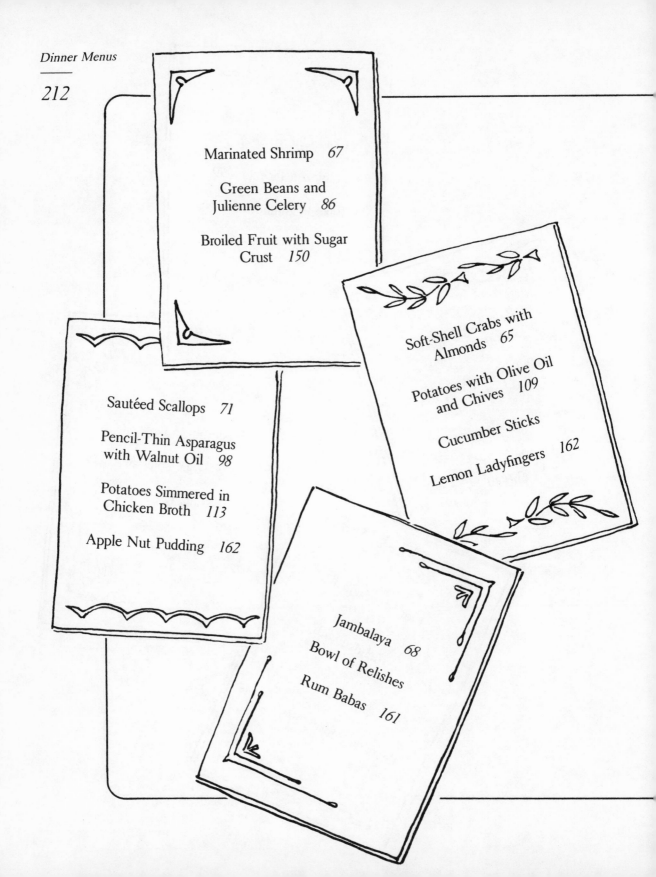

Marinated Shrimp *67*

Green Beans and
Julienne Celery *86*

Broiled Fruit with Sugar
Crust *150*

Soft-Shell Crabs with
Almonds *65*

Potatoes with Olive Oil
and Chives *109*

Cucumber Sticks

Lemon Ladyfingers *162*

Sautéed Scallops *71*

Pencil-Thin Asparagus
with Walnut Oil *98*

Potatoes Simmered in
Chicken Broth *113*

Apple Nut Pudding *162*

Jambalaya *68*

Bowl of Relishes

Rum Babas *161*

Poached Salmon Steaks,
Lemon Sauce *68*

Asparagus Loaf *88*

Boiled Red Skin
Potatoes *110*

Cardamom Peaches *152*

Accordion Tomato and
Cucumber Salad *123*

Baked Flounder Filets
with Herbs *73*

French Peas *87*

Strawberries Dipped in
White Chocolate *155*

Oven Baked Scallops
with Spinach *75*

Rice Pilaf with Saffron
and Peas *108*

Fresh Fruit *165*

Fried Catfish *77*

Green Tomato Sauté *90*

Baked Onions *84*

Crushed Peaches in
Vanilla Cream *159*

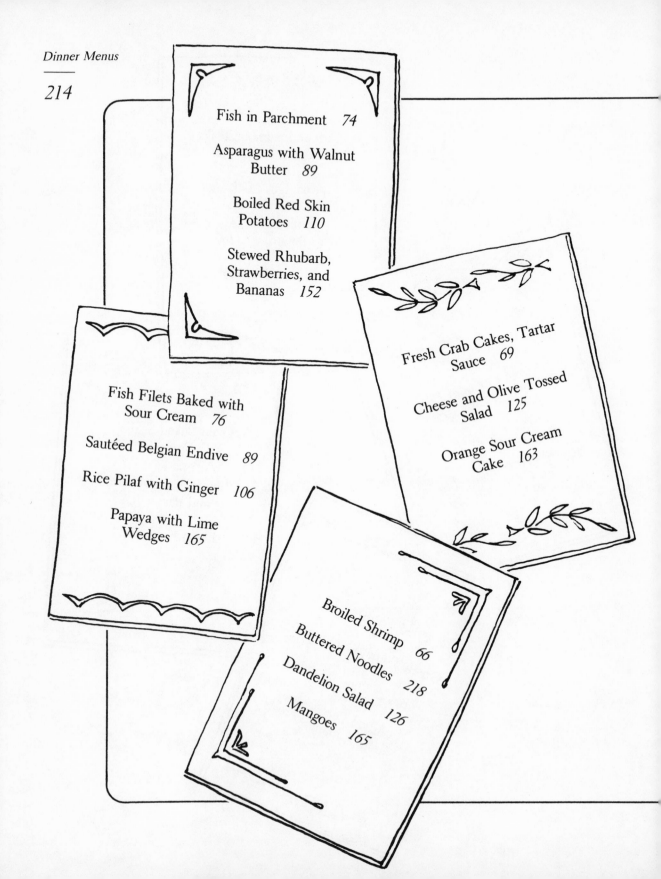

Fish in Parchment   74

Asparagus with Walnut
Butter   89

Boiled Red Skin
Potatoes   110

Stewed Rhubarb,
Strawberries, and
Bananas   152

Fresh Crab Cakes, Tartar
Sauce   69

Cheese and Olive Tossed
Salad   125

Orange Sour Cream
Cake   163

Fish Filets Baked with
Sour Cream   76

Sautéed Belgian Endive   89

Rice Pilaf with Ginger   106

Papaya with Lime
Wedges   165

Broiled Shrimp   66

Buttered Noodles   218

Dandelion Salad   126

Mangoes   165

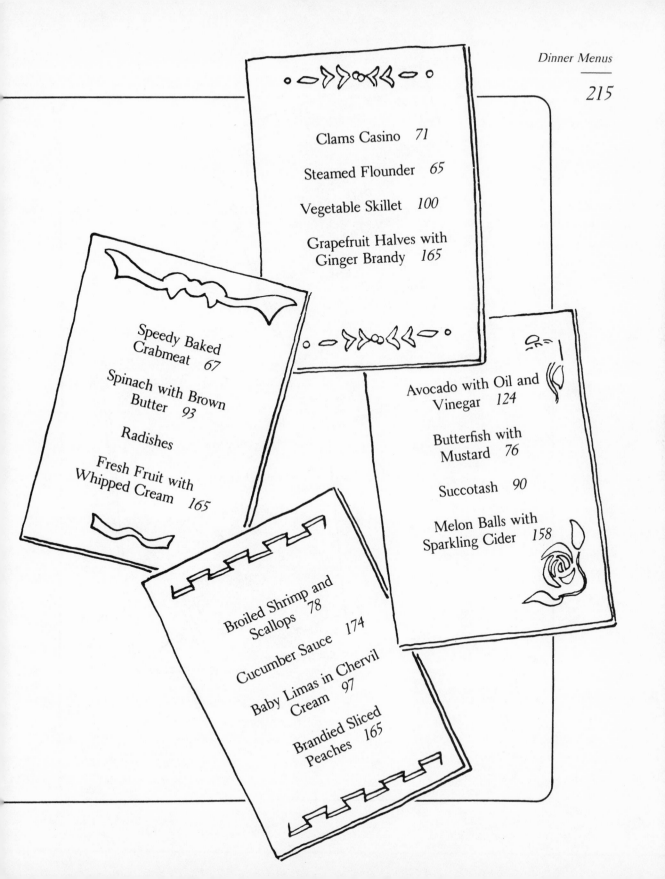

Clams Casino   *71*

Steamed Flounder   *65*

Vegetable Skillet   *100*

Grapefruit Halves with
Ginger Brandy   *165*

Speedy Baked
Crabmeat   *67*

Spinach with Brown
Butter   *93*

Radishes

Fresh Fruit with
Whipped Cream   *165*

Avocado with Oil and
Vinegar   *124*

Butterfish with
Mustard   *76*

Succotash   *90*

Melon Balls with
Sparkling Cider   *158*

Broiled Shrimp and
Scallops   *78*
Cucumber Sauce   *174*

Baby Limas in Chervil
Cream   *97*

Brandied Sliced
Peaches   *165*

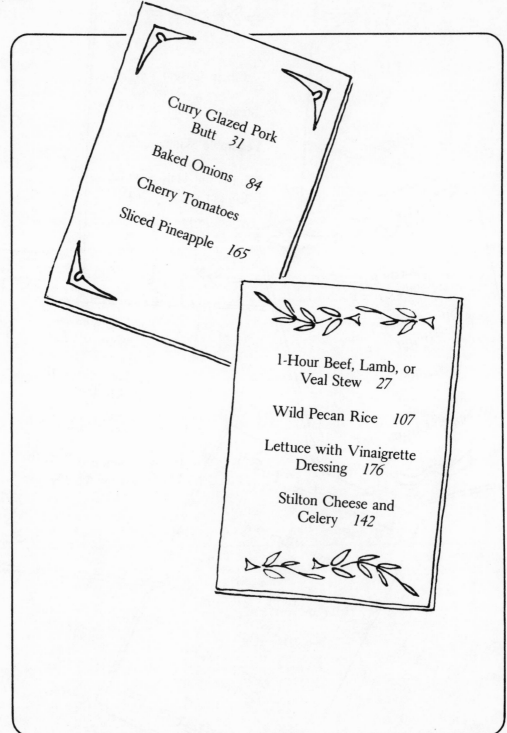

Curry Glazed Pork
Butt *31*

Baked Onions *84*

Cherry Tomatoes

Sliced Pineapple *165*

1-Hour Beef, Lamb, or
Veal Stew *27*

Wild Pecan Rice *107*

Lettuce with Vinaigrette
Dressing *176*

Stilton Cheese and
Celery *142*

QUICK TIPS

You bought this book because your schedule demands that you not spend too much time cooking—and because you like good food. So try a few tips to make food easier to fit into your schedule.

Whenever you are hard-boiling eggs, boil a few extra. Mark them with an x and put them in the refrigerator. You can always make a quick first course by deviling or stuffing them, or following the recipes on pages 142–145.

Whenever you roast a chicken, roast two. Cold roast chicken makes a delicious summer meal served with salad and a fresh vegetable. Or make the chicken salad on page 60.

When you make mini meat loaves (page 26), make enough to put some away in the fridge. Cold meat loaf is quite the same as pâté; it will do for a first course or snack and for a delicious sandwich.

Take the time to cut or have your butcher cut meat into finger-size pieces or very small pieces—the meat will cook faster, stay tender, and develop good flavor. See the basic one-hour stew on page 27.

Learn to use the julienne disk on your food processor. Or practice on a mandoline until you get fast. Buy one of those julienne contraptions made by

Mouli—they work fine, too. If nothing else, grate vegetables on your hand grater and they will cook faster.

If you are cooking in an hour and have only one oven, don't worry if you're faced with two different foods that call for two different temperatures. If you don't have the time to cook things separately, just average things out, and set the oven to 350°F. That's a good round number which will not really hurt anything (soufflés excepted). This simple tip has saved many students many long and anxious moments in the kitchen.

In a very big hurry? Wash the vegetables carefully and forget about peeling them. I mash potatoes and turnips now with the skins on. It doesn't look as elegant, but it does taste delicious. Somewhere in America there are cooks who still string celery, but I stopped that long ago. Your family and guests will never notice.

If you are trying to cool something quickly, place it over a bowl of ice and stir until cold. This is quicker than the freezer and anyway if you put it in the freezer there is a law that says you will always spill bright red sour cherry soup on the box of vanilla ice cream in the freezer and some of it will leak through.

Plan ahead and have plenty of ice on hand—there is another law that says if you try to use the same ice for the guests' drinks, you'll discover that the soup spilled on the ice, too. After you've filled the glass.

If you have time to cook an entrée and nothing else, you can fool yourself and your dinner companions into thinking it's a full-course meal. Smoked salmon, served alone or with dill mayonnaise, is a no-work first course that can be eaten while you are waiting for the rest of the dinner to be cooked. Prosciutto, served with melon, pears, figs, or pineapple, is a ready-made appetizer, garnished with a wedge of lime.

Fresh noodles—either homemade or bought from a specialty store that makes fresh pasta daily—fill up the plate and can be tossed with the pan juices of the entrée or with butter and cheese, fresh basil, or fresh tomato sauce.

Herb butters, always a great idea to keep on hand, can be added to steak, fish, or chicken—anything broiled, poached, or sautéed will look better and taste better with a little medallion of herb butter on top. And it even seems more elegant.

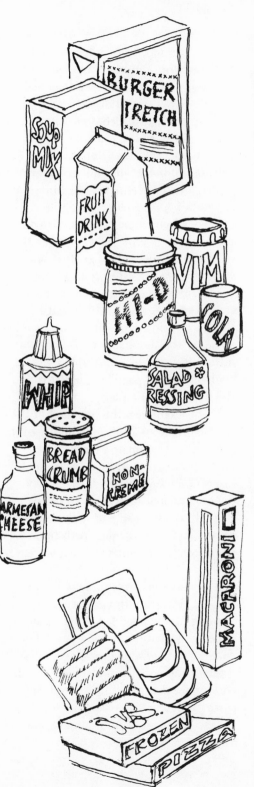

WHAT HAS HAPPENED TO AMERICAN FOOD?

For years I rubbed a well-known brand of cooking oil on ring molds to keep cakes from sticking. I started demonstrating this trick in class one day and—the cake stuck. I thought that someone must have scoured the ring with steel wool or Brillo, which will sometimes take off the cure if it's done long and persistently enough. So I gave the ring mold another coat of oil and tried again. Still stuck. I had to go on with the class, but when I went home later, for my own peace of mind I tried the same recipe with another ring mold. Stuck. Oiled it and tried again. Tried all my ring molds. Cakes stuck to every one of them. Finally my family came home and asked me, "What's for dinner?"

"Nothing much," I said, "unless you're hungry for a lot of broken cakes. Something's wrong with all my ring molds."

But I was soon to find out. It wasn't the molds. It was the oil. During the oil crisis and the rapid inflation of food prices, many cooking oils went so high that manufacturers simply changed their formulas. They put in more or less cotton or peanut or linseed oil—without bothering to mention the fact, and without caring that it made the oil a little less usable. I was blaming my ring pans when I had merely stumbled on one more example of the deterioration of American food.

Sometimes I think too much is made of that deterioration. Some people seem to have eaten their last decent meal when they were five or six years old. And I suspect that's because they wouldn't have it any other way—they seem to enjoy the fact that everything is lousier, enjoy it so much that it's hard to believe they're not exaggerating just a little bit.

But I spend a lot of time cooking for my classes, and some food has definitely changed, for the worse. Cream cheese, which I used to love straight from the supermarket package, is now so heavily loaded with stabilizers and emulsifiers that it has the consistency of bubble gum. I get my cream cheese from a cheese shop now, the kind that comes with a label saying "All Natural, No Additives." It tastes like cream cheese and, oddly enough, it doesn't cost any more than emulsified cheese. Actually, I suppose, it should cost less. It costs money to put additives in, not leave them out.

Unsalted butter, which I used to buy in the supermarket, also has to come from a specialty store now. It costs a little more, but at least it hasn't been frozen. Frozen butter picks up ice crystals and the water stays in the butter after it thaws. Put a lump of frozen butter in the pan and it starts to sizzle as the water boils out—and goes on sizzling and sizzling. Eventually you can get the water out if you cook it long enough, but you can't do that if you're cutting the butter into flour to make pastry. I had a few pastry disasters until I switched to specialty store butter.

My cream comes from a nearby dairy, a tiny independent one that still sells cream in glass bottles. It is not stabilized, so it won't keep for months in the refrigerator—and it doesn't taste stabilized. It is also so thick that I have trouble pouring it out of the bottle—it is so heavy that I actually have to add a little water to whip it. And it costs $2 a quart instead of the 89¢ a pint that stabilized cream costs.

Mushrooms used to get dark if they were exposed to light. Now, unless you buy them at a farmer's market, they've been treated with sodium bicarbonate and wrapped in plastic. So they stay bone white and turn slimy. That is, they stay white until you wipe them off with a damp cloth, when they turn pink! One more item on the specialty shopping lists.

No wonder supermarkets are in trouble. The only things you can buy there with any confidence are tissue paper and plastic garbage bags. Cheese comes shrink-wrapped in plastic; it's waxy, cardboardy, and tasteless; and it costs more than real cheese in a cheese store. Whatever they've done to cottage cheese has made it both gummy *and* full of runny white liquid—plus increased the calories.

I never buy meat except at a butcher store nowadays—even the pork in those big open refrigerated trays has a weird reddish or pinkish cast to it. Some meat packer decided to soak everything in blood to make it look "appetizing" (though there's nothing appetizing to me in a pork roast the color of a raw beet). And all the blood in those meats—which we pay for, since it adds weight—makes roasts so wet that they don't roast at all. They just boil in the oven. They taste tough and they simply will not brown properly. If you get a roast like this, tell the butcher it's his fault; and if he can't get you better meat, find a butcher who will.

Packaged yeast has changed. A few years ago, it just got weaker. I don't know how the manufacturer managed that; but I do know that you have to let the yeast work a little longer in warm water now, to make sure it grows up to the old strength.

I check the labels on all the imported products I buy. German beers, French mustards, Italian pasta, olive oil, and vinegar—the only thing imported about many of those things is the name. And as soon as I find out that they're made in America, I switch brands. Something happens to food mass produced in this country. Emulsifiers happen. The formula is changed so that it can be more easily turned out by a machine, or something is added to make sure that it will have a shelf life of five or six years. You're much better off

getting fresh pasta from one of those specialty stores where it is made fresh daily than you are buying "imported" spaghetti packed in Brooklyn.

The last ham I ever bought from a major packing house was three years ago. I sliced the leftovers to make myself a sandwich for lunch and sat down eating at the typewriter, working on a recipe. It was two bites before I realized: All I'm tasting is the whole wheat bread. Why spend money on something without any real taste? I buy country hams now, or locally produced hams from my butcher. They cost a lot more. But at least I'm paying for ham, not water; and I don't have to use white bread to know what kind of meat is in the sandwich.

Packaged bacon must be stretched on a rack before it's wrapped up in all that plastic—it feels like rubber when it's raw, and when it cooks it shrivels up to nothing. I buy slab bacon instead, have the butcher cut it half an inch thick, and cook it by starting in a cold iron skillet, on low flame, so it cooks slowly and gets crisp and crunchy all the way through.

Sausages have turned a horrible flesh color, so that they look pinkish gray raw, and they won't brown no matter how they're cooked.

Sometimes it seems as if nobody cares about food in America.

And sometimes it seems as if everybody cares about food. Though mass-produced food is getting worse and worse, there is more good food available in specialty stores than there ever was before. Pistachios are now grown in California—better than any of the pistachios we used to get from Iran. When I first started teaching my classes, I could never find greens like arugula or roquette; now they're available every summer. After years of nothing but big potatoey Delicious apples, I find tiny tart Granny Smith and McIntosh everywhere now. In my area there is a farm that produces fresh herbs year around—in a greenhouse in winter. There are other farms that raise pheasant and duck and partridge in big open-air cages hundreds of yards long filled with the bushes and greens that give those birds their natural taste. My butcher is able to get meat that is every bit as good as meat used to be years ago—and sometimes even better. My daughter and her friends have turned their backyards into gardens—they club together, spade up one plot at a time, and raise their own fresh fruit and vegetables.

We seem to be separating into two entirely different food cultures: one all natural, one all artificial. And strangely enough, the stores that stock the artificial preserved food, the stuff designed so that they can keep it on the shelves forever and never throw anything away, are having the most trouble. Another chain of supermarkets has just gone broke in my home town— and the little stores that supply the home-grown spices and carefully raised poultry have never been busier.

Maybe that's the secret. The rapid rise in food prices has made it possible for little local producers and small stores to compete with the big chains. Compete—and beat their prices. So maybe what's happening to American food is something good. Maybe we're discovering that food that can't go bad can never be very good. And that locally produced food is often the very best we can eat—especially if you buy it fast, and cook it while it's fresh.

INDEX

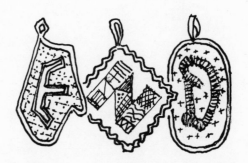